Better Late Than Never

Also by Kimberla Lawson Roby

THE REVEREND CURTIS BLACK SERIES

Sin of a Woman
A Sinful Calling
The Ultimate Betrayal
The Prodigal Son
A House Divided
The Reverend's Wife
Love, Honor, and Betray
Be Careful What You Pray For
The Best of Everything
Sin No More
Love & Lies
The Best-Kept Secret
Too Much of a Good Thing
Casting the First Stone

STANDALONE TITLES

Copycat
Best Friends Forever
A Christmas Prayer
The Perfect Marriage
Secret Obsession
A Deep Dark Secret
One in a Million
Changing Faces
A Taste of Reality
It's a Thin Line
Here and Now
Behind Closed Doors

Better Late Than Never

KIMBERLA LAWSON ROBY

GRAND CENTRAL
PUBLISHING

NEW YORK   BOSTON

Grand Central Publishing
Hachette Book Group
1290 Avenue of the Americas, New York, NY 10104
grandcentralpublishing.com
twitter.com/grandcentralpub

First Edition: July 2018

Grand Central Publishing is a division of Hachette Book Group, Inc. The Grand Central Publishing name and logo is a trademark of Hachette Book Group, Inc.

The publisher is not responsible for websites (or their content) that are not owned by the publisher.

The Hachette Speakers Bureau provides a wide range of authors for speaking events. To find out more, go to www.hachettespeakersbureau.com or call (866) 376-6591.

Library of Congress Cataloging-in-Publication Data
Names: Roby, Kimberla Lawson, author.
Title: Better late than never / Kimberla Lawson Roby.
Description: First edition. | New York ; Boston : Grand Central Publishing, 2018. | Series: Curtis Black ; 15
Identifiers: LCCN 2018003846| ISBN 9781455569762 (hardcover) | ISBN 9781538713709 (large print) | ISBN 9781478967514 (audio download) | ISBN 9781455569755 (ebook)
Subjects: | BISAC: FICTION / Family Life. | FICTION / Coming of Age. | FICTION / African American / Christian.
Classification: LCC PS3568.O3189 B48 2018 | DDC 813/.54—dc23
LC record available at https://lccn.loc.gov/2018003846

ISBNs: 978-1-4555-6976-2 (hardcover), 978-1-4555-6975-5 (ebook), 978-1-5387-1370-9 (large print)

Printed in the United States of America

LSC-C

10 9 8 7 6 5 4 3 2 1

For my husband and love of my life,
Will, for suggesting that I write
the first book in this series
and for loving and supporting
me year after year.

For the best mother ever,
Arletha Tennin Stapleton.
Thank you for everything, Mom.
I will love and miss
you always.

For my cousin,
Darlene Tennin Baldwin,
for always supporting me. I love
you, and you will forever
be missed.
October 23, 1958 – July 2, 2017

And for all my wonderful readers
who have read
every...single...title
in the series, I am eternally
grateful to each of you.

A Message for My Readers

Dear Readers:

As much as I always knew that this particular day would come, it still doesn't seem real. But nonetheless, the fifteenth and final book in my Reverend Curtis Black series is now complete, and you, my wonderful readers, are preparing to read it.

It is also pretty hard to believe that, as of this very month, January 2018, the Reverend Curtis Black series has been in existence for nineteen years. For nearly two decades, I have been writing about this fictional family who I grew to love and care about on so many levels, and I have to say I'm so glad I did, as each of these Reverend Curtis Black characters will hold a very special place in my heart forever.

This sentiment alone makes me think about one of my most-asked questions relating to the series, which is, "Who is your all-time favorite character?" For years,

A Message for My Readers

I have been asked this question, but even today, my answer remains the same: My all-time favorite character in the series is Curtis's youngest son, Matthew. I used to wonder why that was, but early on I realized that, of all the family members, Matthew was the one person who genuinely tried his best to do the right thing—not just every now and then, but all the time. He certainly wasn't perfect, the same as none of us is, but even when he did make mistakes, he always felt great remorse and never fell into a habit of repeating them. He also cared about everyone, his family and others, and he treated people the way he wanted to be treated.

Another reason, I love Matthew is because no matter how many times his parents hurt or embarrassed him—thanks to their infidelity issues and other public scandals—Matthew never stopped loving them, and he never used his pain or dysfunctional family drama as an excuse to act badly. Instead, he continued being the amazing child whom any parent would be proud to have.

The other most-asked question I receive is the following: "Is your Reverend Curtis Black series based on a real-life pastor?" Of course, the answer is no; however, I will say this: I have been in church my entire life, and I have seen and heard a lot. So much so that the younger Reverend Curtis Black would be considered meek and mild compared to many real-life pastors I know. Not to mention the great number of ministers nationwide who my readers have shared stories about for years. Yes, I knew about some of what was happening in my home state of Illinois, but it wasn't until I wrote the first book in the series and traveled around on tour that I learned there was at least one "Reverend Curtis Black" residing in every single city in the country.

At first, I was stunned, but it wasn't long before I realized that corruption in the church wasn't new. What I discovered was that ministers had been involving themselves in scandals well before I or the generation before me were born. The only difference was that, back then, it wasn't talked about openly. There is no doubt that, behind closed doors, people shared with each other what they knew, but for the most part, problems in the church were discussed in a hush-hush fashion, and many folks pretended that they didn't exist at all.

And to be honest, had my husband, Will, not suggested that I write about the problems that occur in some churches, I'm not sure I ever would have. Especially since there are, in fact, so many wonderful men of God—honorable pastors with great integrity— ministering everywhere. However, because I had decided from the start that I would always write about real-life issues, even in a fictional format, I had shared with Will how, for my third book, I wanted to write something that everyone would either know about or, at least, have heard of. It was then that he recommended this particular topic, and from there, Reverend Curtis Black was created.

Still, when *Casting the First Stone* was released, it was never my intention to write a sequel or create a series. But after writing my fourth and fifth novels, which had nothing to do with Reverend Curtis Black, readers began asking me when I was going to write another story about him. I was shocked to hear that people wanted to read another book centering on a wayward pastor who saw nothing wrong with committing one sin after another on a daily basis. But, sadly, readers everywhere knew him in real life and could relate to the storyline.

So as it turned out—after my literary agent, the late Elaine Koster, encouraged me to give my readers what they were asking for—I wrote the second book in the series, *Too Much of a Good Thing*, and then the third, *The Best-Kept Secret*. My plan was to call my series a trilogy and then move on to other characters for good. But as fate would have it, I went on to write a new title in the series almost every single year until December 2017, the month I finished writing *Better Late Than Never*. This is also the book I believe has the most different storyline of the entire series.

In the past, Curtis has subtly mentioned how terrible his childhood was…how once he'd left for college, he'd never looked back…how he'd pretended that he didn't even have a biological family…how he'd remained estranged from his mom and sister until his mother's passing…and how he hadn't seen his sister ever since. That is, until now, in *Better Late Than Never*. So, of course, it is Curtis's reconnection with his sister that forces him to relive all the trauma and abuse that he endured as a child, and readers will finally witness very disturbing scenes through Curtis's own painful, vivid memories.

It has always been my desire to tell this aspect of Curtis's story, but the reason I waited to do so until the end of the series was because I first wanted to bring Curtis full circle. I wanted him to grow spiritually, mentally, and emotionally, and become a true man of God. I wanted him to become a loyal and faithful husband to Charlotte and become an even better father than he already was to his children. I wanted to show that anyone, no matter how deceptive, cruel, or sinful they might be, can turn their lives around for the better. My goal was to prove that even the worst person can change if he or she wants to, and Curtis most certainly has. Which is the reason it was finally time to reveal how awful his childhood truly was, and how it definitely helped shape him into the not-so-likable man he became. By no means does Curtis's disturbing childhood justify all of the many sins he committed, but it does explain one very important thing: Whatever happens in your childhood, good or bad, will affect you for the rest of your life. It shows how crucial loving and caring for a child really is and that when that child doesn't receive either, life for him or her as an adult doesn't always turn out so well.

Then, as far as my feelings about the series as a whole, very few plot twists surprised me—maybe because many of the characters had no problem saying or doing the unthinkable. But the one thing that did shock me with *Better Late Than Never* was the fact that, as I was writing certain scenes about Curtis's childhood and those relating to his sister's illness, tears streamed down my face. Partly because of what my characters were having to suffer through, and partly because Curtis and his family members have become very real to me. They became very real to me a long, long time ago, and I have truly cared about their well-being. I wanted them all to become better people and be happy. I wanted each of them, not just Matthew, to begin treating others the way they wanted to be treated. Most of all, I wanted them to adopt and maintain strong Christian values and high moral standards—to love, honor, and respect God, no matter what. I wanted for them what I want for myself and all of humanity: to simply be the best people we can be.

There is yet another question, though, that I'm sure I'll begin receiving soon and that is, "What will you miss most about the series?" And the answer is this: I will so miss reading email messages and social media comments from all of you, asking when the next Reverend Curtis Black book is going to be released! I will also miss reading your awesome feedback about the characters, the individual storylines, and how you could relate your own lives to the series. But more than anything—and yes, I am in tears as I write this sentence—I will miss the way you have loved and encouraged me as a writer for so many years. Your love for the Reverend Curtis Black series quickly turned my writing career into the kind of success I wasn't expecting, and I am eternally grateful to all of you. Your support has meant everything, and while I will certainly continue doing what I love—writing and speaking around the country—I won't ever forget my Reverend Curtis Black series experience or your kindness.

Just as I mentioned above in terms of the way I feel about my characters, you, too, will remain in my heart forever—the only difference is that you will remain there in a much deeper and profound fashion. I will, of course, never be able to thank you enough, but please know that I sincerely thank God for you and that I love all of you so very much.

With much appreciation and many blessings to you always,

Kimberla Lawson Roby

Chapter 1

After all these years, Curtis still thought about many of the terrible things he'd done to so many people. But thank God—more than a decade ago, he'd finally changed for the better. It had been hard, walking the straight and narrow, but today, this second Sunday in March, he was still a true man of God, a faithful husband, a loving father, and the best grandfather on this side of heaven.

In addition to that, there was the church he'd founded nearly twenty years ago, Deliverance Outreach. Even now, as he sat inside his massive first-floor study, reviewing the sermon he would deliver in a couple of hours, he smiled with gratitude. They'd finally moved into the newly constructed building, which seated five thousand people, but already the congregation filled it near capacity every Sunday. Originally the membership had consisted of only five thousand parishioners, with four thousand attending regularly. But after Curtis's eldest son Dillon's church had burned to the ground, more than half of that congregation had joined Deliverance Outreach. So, because of this, Curtis had seen no other choice except to begin holding two services again, the same as they'd done at the smaller building. He wasn't complaining, though, not when he was very glad to see so many people wanting to belong to a church, and most important, wanting to hear and learn God's Word.

Curtis read through more of his sermon, which was entitled Keeping God First, No Matter What, and for some reason he thought about Raven, his former daughter-in-law. Like any Christian should, he had forgiven her, but there was no way he would ever forget the trouble she'd recently tried to cause him; not to mention the other time she'd betrayed him. Years before, she'd worked as his chief financial officer and had stolen six figures from the church, and then last year, she'd publicly lied to her online following, as well as to the members of her church, about being sexually assaulted. She'd claimed that a well-known pastor had raped her, purposely leaving many folks nationwide to assume that she was referring to Curtis. She hadn't mentioned his name, but rumors had quickly begun circulating, and had Dillon not gone to great measures to stop his ex-wife, Curtis wasn't sure how things might have turned out. At the very least, his reputation as a pastor would have been tainted and possibly ruined for good, not to mention his family would've had to endure yet another horrific scandal. But Dillon had stepped up and protected his father and made sure Raven was arrested and sent to prison.

Curtis leaned back in his chair, thinking about his own sordid past again. At first he wasn't sure why, but then he realized it was likely because he couldn't help taking at least some responsibility for the way Raven and Dillon had turned out. They were both adults, but Curtis knew he hadn't been the best example for any young minister. He knew he hadn't lived up to the true calling God had placed on his life, and that it was he who both his son and former daughter-in-law had learned their deceptive ways from. He'd indirectly shown them how to become the kind of clergyman—or in Raven's case, clergywoman—who only cared about three things: making lots of money, gaining extreme notoriety, and becoming as powerful as possible. From leading women on and sleeping with as many of them as he wanted, to fooling innocent members of his congregation out of their hard-earned income, to denying his own son Dillon for too many years to count, to having two children with other women while he was married to someone else, to blackmailing folks who wouldn't do what he asked...Curtis had done it all.

He certainly wasn't worthy of his Heavenly Father's forgiveness, not with the way he'd hurt his family, his parishioners at three different churches, and even strangers. But God had delivered him from every ounce of the life he'd once led, and he couldn't be more content. He and Charlotte were truly happy, and he was finally on great terms with all four of his children, all at the same time: Dillon, Alicia, Matthew, and Curtina. Then, if that wasn't enough, the four of them were very close. This hadn't always been the case, particularly when it came to Dillon and the rocky relationship he'd had with all three of his siblings, but God had worked everything out and they loved each other the way brothers and sisters should.

Curtis smiled and picked up the sterling-silver-framed photo of his handsome seven-year-old grandson, MJ. He was nearly the same age that Matthew had been when Curtis had met him for the first time, and MJ was the most important family member to everyone. His dad, stepmom, aunts, uncle, grandmother—and of course, Curtis, too—spoiled him as often as they could, and Curtis loved his little grandson with every part of his being. So yes, life was good, and Curtis couldn't help shedding a few tears of joy.

After a few more minutes passed, his cell phone rang. He didn't recognize the incoming number, but since he rarely received calls from anyone this early on a Sunday morning, he wondered if one of his parishioners was calling with an emergency.

"Hello?"

"Curtis?" said the man on the other end.

"Yes. Who's calling?"

"Jason. Your brother-in-law."

"Jason. What a pleasant surprise. How are you?"

"Well, I've been better, but we're hanging in there."

Curtis's heart sank. The last time he'd seen or spoken to his sister was the day their mom had been funeralized, and all he could hope was that Trina was okay. "I'm almost afraid to ask what's wrong."

"I'm sure. And to be honest, there's no easy way to say this except to just tell you. Trina has been diagnosed with stage four cancer. Endometrial adenocarcinoma."

"Oh dear God. No."

Jason sighed. "I know, and I'm sorry to have to call you with such painful news."

Tears filled Curtis's eyes. "I am so sorry. I'm really, really sorry."

"Needless to say, this has been a tough pill for all of us to swallow. For Trina, me, and the children."

"How long has she been dealing with this?"

"About a year."

Curtis's stomach tied in knots. "A whole year?"

"Yes, and I wanted to call you then. But, as you can imagine, Trina insisted that I didn't. And she doesn't know that I'm calling you now, either."

"Well, I'm glad you did, because if nothing else, I can at least begin praying for her. And I can ask my congregation to pray for her, too."

"Exactly."

"This is just too much," Curtis said, trying to control his tears. "I mean, have her doctors given her a specific prognosis? Is she taking treatments right now?"

"That's actually part of the reason I wanted to contact you. She's had two surgeries and chemo…but it didn't help."

"What about experimental drugs? New studies at the top medical facilities?"

"She's already tried one experimental drug, but if anything, that made her worse. But even if there was something else, she's already made it very clear that she's done with everything. The side effects were dreadful, and she's decided that she just wants to live out the rest of her life without any added problems."

Curtis was heartbroken. Distraught. Numb. "This is awful."

"Yeah, it is, but I really think it's time you come see her."

"Are you sure? Because even after Mom died, I tried to call her a few times and she never answered. She never called me back, and we haven't spoken in almost twenty years."

"At this point, I don't think any of that matters. I mean, I haven't mentioned your name to her lately, but I still think you should come."

"What about this afternoon? Is that too soon?""

"No, the sooner the better."

"Then I'll just go ahead and preach the early service as planned and ask one of my assistant pastors to do the second. I should be on my way no later than ten thirty and there by noon."

"Sounds good, and Curtis, thank you for agreeing to come. Trina probably doesn't know it, but she needs her big brother right now. More than she ever has."

Curtis felt his eyes welling up again and swallowed more tears. "Thank you for calling to let me know what's going on. I really appreciate it."

"You're welcome, and we'll see you this afternoon."

Curtis set his phone down, swiveled his high-backed chair around, and stared out of the large picture window. Many thoughts circulated in his mind, both good and bad, but what he thought about most was how selfish he'd been.

How he'd cut off his mom and sister right after leaving home for college. *What in the world was I thinking?*

Now Curtis covered his wet face with both hands, sobbing like a child. Just as he hadn't spent any time with his mom before she'd passed, he'd done the same thing with his sister—his only biological sibling. And he couldn't be sorrier. He was filled with deep regret, and if he could turn back time he would. It was true that Trina was still alive, but now she had stage four cancer, and she might only have so much time left to live. Of course, there was one thing that Curtis still knew: God had the final say. So, from this point on, he would be praying and trusting God for his sister's total healing. He would trust Him completely and cherish every single moment he had with her.

Chapter 2

Charlotte slipped on her fuchsia satin robe, tied the belt, and left her bedroom. She'd just finished showering for church, and now she was headed to Curtina's room to make sure she was up and getting ready.

She stopped in front of Curtina's door and knocked three times. But there was no response. So she tried opening it—only to discover it was locked. She knocked again much harder. But there was still no answer, and Charlotte was through being cordial. "Curtina, open up this door! And I mean open it now!"

Finally, Curtina opened it, but the moment their eyes locked, Curtina raised her eyebrows, turned away, and went back over to her bed. She plopped down on it, picked up her phone, and started typing.

Charlotte walked into the room and folded her arms. "Didn't we tell you to stop locking that door?"

Curtina gazed up at her mother but then continued typing.

"And why aren't you getting dressed for church?"

Curtina still kept typing, likely some pointless text message to one of her little girlfriends, but said, "I will in a minute."

"Put your phone away. Now. And get in the shower."

Curtina never missed a beat. Her fingers kept moving, as though Charlotte weren't even in the room.

But Charlotte was done playing with her. "Give me that phone," she yelled, storming closer to the bed and snatching it from her. "And you've got five seconds to get your behind up and into that bathroom."

"Give me my phone back," Curtina yelled, reaching for it.

Charlotte moved away from her and looked at the screen. She read the words twice, each time feeling stunned...and hurt: Any min she'll be bargin in2 my room like sum madwoman tellin me 2 get ready. She n my dad make me sick.

"Mom, please give me my phone."

Charlotte shook her head and squinted her eyes at her daughter. "Wow...just wow. So, this is what you think of your father and me? After all we do for you?"

"No."

"Then why are you talking badly about us to Taylor? Why are you being so disrespectful? Maybe what *we* need to do is take this little phone of yours for good."

Curtina sighed with disgust, rolled her eyes toward the ceiling, stomped into the bathroom, and slammed the door.

Charlotte took a few deep breaths, because what she wanted more than anything was to burst in there behind Curtina and do what her own mom would have done to her, had she mouthed off that way when she was twelve years old. But for as long as Charlotte had officially been Curtina's mother, ever since she was two, Charlotte had never as much as spanked her, let alone slapped her or yanked her back to her senses. But God help her, today she truly wanted to, and it was taking everything in her to govern her temper. Curtina was spiraling further and further out of control, and this smartphone of hers was the sole cause of it. She was on it all the time, either texting her two best friends, Taylor and Lauren, both of whom were too grown for their own good, or browsing, commenting, or uploading photos to Instagram and Snapchat. Charlotte didn't know what she and Curtis were going to do with her, because over the last few months, she'd begun isolating herself more and more. She went to school and church—by force—but when she was home, she spent all but mealtimes in her room. And sometimes she talked back to Curtis and Charlotte as though they were children. Interestingly enough, she did this more to Charlotte than she did to her father, because as much as Curtis loved his baby daughter, he never allowed her to get away with as much as Charlotte sometimes did.

But while Charlotte stood there, debating whether she should summon Curtina back into the bedroom, she just didn't feel like fighting with her like she was a thirty-year-old woman. So instead, Charlotte left and went back to her own room. Once there, she closed the door and sat on the edge of her bed.

For the last month, she hadn't been sure why alcohol had suddenly begun crossing her mind again on a regular basis. Especially since she and Curtis were happy. To be honest, they'd never been happier. But she knew the problems that they were starting to have with Curtina had something to do with it. And none of it made much sense, because as little as one year ago, Curtina had still been the kind of daughter any parent would have been proud to have. She'd done what she was told with very few objections, she'd gotten straight A's in school, and she'd held the highest respect for not only her parents but also other adults. As of late, however, she'd become a difficult girl who Charlotte and Curtis didn't know, and it was making Charlotte want to drink.

Although, Charlotte did have to admit that Curtina wasn't the only problem she was battling, as she was also tired of being first lady of the largest church in Mitchell. The reason: It was all way too much for her to deal with . . . every . . . single . . . day . . . of . . . every . . . single . . . week.

Charlotte shook her head, wishing she could crawl back under the covers. But as her mind wandered from one thing to the next, she thought about her other children and her sweet little grandson and smiled. They were all doing well, and Matthew and Stacey had just celebrated their second anniversary. Charlotte loved Stacey a lot more than she had Matthew's first wife, Racquel, and what she admired most about Stacey was that she loved and treated MJ as though he were her own. Shockingly, Racquel had seemed fine with the idea of Matthew getting remarried, and she also didn't seem to have a problem with Matthew keeping full custody of their son. She'd been released from the mental institution for a while now and certainly could have petitioned the court for joint custody, but Charlotte could tell she truly wanted what was best for MJ.

Charlotte also had a much better relationship with her stepson, Dillon, someone she once hadn't been able to stand, and of course, Alicia was still more like a younger sister and close friend to Charlotte than she was a stepdaughter. So Charlotte was sure that, to the outside world and even to those close to her, her life seemed perfect.

But it wasn't. She certainly wanted it to be. However, being first lady to nearly seven thousand members was more than a notion. Worse, she was tired of smiling every Sunday morning whether she wanted to or not. She was tired of pretending to be the happiest woman on earth even on the days when she didn't feel well, or she simply wanted to stay home, resting…just because. And sometimes, she desperately wanted to spend the day out, enjoying herself. Because for the life of her, she didn't understand what was so wrong with that. She did love God with all her heart and she knew the importance of worshiping and fellowshiping with other believers, but sometimes she just wanted to be free. She wanted to snatch away the mask she sometimes wore only to satisfy Curtis, her family, and the congregation. Once upon a time, she'd loved dressing to the hilt and purchasing the best clothing money could buy—and being one of the most well-known first ladies in the country. But now she was tired of worrying about what everyone would think, particularly church people—those at Deliverance Outreach, those at local churches, and those in every other city nationwide. Because truth was, she was churched out. She was tired of living her life in a vacuum. Tired of doing only the kind of things that holier-than-thou Christians expected a first lady of a church *to* do. The kinds of things that some of those *same* holier-than-thou church folks weren't even doing themselves. Not to mention the fact that many of them were doing wrong every chance they got.

But to be clear, it wasn't that Charlotte wanted to return to a life of sin, because she didn't. No, what she wanted was to live a life that didn't involve public scrutiny, judgment, and unrealistic expectations. She wanted to focus on connecting with women who genuinely cared about her and not spend her time smiling and making cordial conversation with those who didn't. Those who talked about her behind her back. Those who wanted her husband and didn't try to hide it. Thankfully, Curtis never paid them any mind, and if they approached him in the wrong way, he always set them straight. And more important, Charlotte knew how much Curtis loved her and how dedicated he was to their marriage. Still, it bothered her to know that some wannabe mistresses would always find their way to the church. Women who had no moral values, let alone any God in them. Women who were willing to stoop as low as Charlotte once had herself a few years ago. Foul women who wanted to take her place.

So she just wanted out. She wanted to take a break from Sunday morning services, weekly Bible study, all women's ministry activities, and everything relating to organized religion. She needed some time off. A much-needed, self-ordered sabbatical, if you will. Because if she didn't get it soon, she was going to do a lot more than just think about alcohol. She was going to consume it, enjoy it, and not feel guilty about it. She wouldn't drink to get drunk the way she had in the past, but she would at least have a glass of wine. She would do it to settle her nerves, and so she wouldn't have to think about Curtina and her awful attitude. She would do it so she could forget about everything *church* for a while and be normal.

She would do it because if she didn't, she might lose her mind.

Chapter 3

Charlotte and Curtis had dropped Curtina off at her big sister Alicia's house, and now they'd just exited I-90 east, heading toward the south suburbs of Chicago. At first they'd considered taking Curtina with them to see her aunt Trina, but Curtis had decided that it might be best if he and Charlotte went alone. Curtina, of course, hadn't seemed to care one way or the other, but had still found the audacity to ask if she could stay home while they were gone—all by herself, that is. Needless to say, her request had been denied, as she was proving more and more just how little she could be trusted. Not to mention, Curtis and Charlotte didn't believe a twelve-year-old should be home alone for such a long period of time anyway. Maybe for an hour here and there, whenever it couldn't be helped, but that was it.

"For the life of me," Curtis said, "I don't know what's gotten into that girl."

"Neither do I, but her attitude is really starting to get on my nerves. She's so ornery and disrespectful, and I'm tired of it."

"We're going to have to have a serious talk with her."

"That sounds all good and well, but I don't know if *talking* is going to change anything," Charlotte said, and then filled Curtis in on all that had transpired this morning—including the cruel message Curtina had texted her friend about them.

Curtis glanced over at Charlotte and frowned. "She said what?"

"You heard me. That we make her sick."

"This is crazy. And what's sad and so unfortunate is that I'm hearing this from a number of other people, too. Those who have daughters between the ages of ten and thirteen. They're acting as though they're twenty-one in some cases."

"I've heard the same thing, and it's scary. Very disheartening. I mean, these young girls are so ungrateful. So unruly."

"Well, like I said, we're going to have to have a serious talk with her. And if that doesn't do anything, we'll just start taking away privileges. Beginning with that phone of hers."

"I agree. I don't know if that'll change her attitude, but we have to do something. Before she slips further out of hand."

For the next few minutes, Curtis and Charlotte conversed more about Curtina, but when one of Curtis's favorite gospel songs played on SiriusXM's channel 64, their discussion ceased and it wasn't long before Charlotte thought about the sabbatical she so desperately needed to take. And at this very moment, she wanted to tell Curtis how she felt. Ask him to understand her desire to do this. Make him see what it was like to be first lady through her eyes versus his. But she also didn't want to burden him right now, not when he'd just learned such devastating news about his sister. So she

decided against it. Still, she couldn't help thinking about
how miserable she'd been in service today. For most of the
ninety minutes, she'd barely been able to stand being there,
and she'd also spent much of her time gazing at her watch
and thinking about all the other things she'd rather be doing. She was sorry for tuning out her own husband while he
delivered his morning message, but she just couldn't help
herself. It was the reason that when church had finally been
dismissed, she'd felt totally relieved.

It was sad to admit, but she was now at the point where
she had to make herself go to church on Sunday mornings,
and then once she arrived, she basically counted down the
minutes until service was over. Which was also the reason
she was going to have to find a way to tell Curtis the truth:
She needed a break, and she was going to have to take one,
starting at the beginning of next month—or before then.
That would be three weeks from now, and all she could hope
was that he would be on board with her decision. She knew
he wouldn't be happy, because for one, members of the
congregation would have tons of questions, and two, folks
would begin making assumptions about their marriage. Over
the years, they'd been through a lot and had caused many
family- and church-related scandals, so quite naturally, people would think the worst about her absence. But Charlotte
couldn't worry about any of that. What she needed to do
now was worry about herself, both emotionally and mentally.
Her decision would cause at least some harm to Curtis as
a pastor, but he would just have to support her on this. He
would have to be there for her, no matter what.

When the song ended, Curtis sighed. "I just can't believe my sister has stage four cancer."

Right after service, Curtis had quickly given Charlotte the basic details about Trina's illness and told her that he wanted to go see his sister today, but that had been it.

"So, when you talked to Jason what else did he say? I mean, are her doctors preparing a treatment plan?"

"She's already had surgery and chemo and tried an experimental drug."

Charlotte looked at Curtis. "So, this has been going on for a while, then?"

"A year, and I just wish I'd known before now. I wish I'd spent more time with Trina, and I'll always regret the fact that I didn't."

"But you did try to make things right. After your mom died, you tried on more than one occasion."

"It's still my fault, though. I'm the one who left for college and never looked back. I erased Mom and Trina from all my thoughts. As much as I could, anyway. Then I pretended that Larry was my biological brother, even though I didn't meet him for the first time until I arrived at school. Then I pretended that his mom and dad were my real parents. I created a whole new life for myself, just so I wouldn't have to think about my childhood. I lived a total lie. For years."

"Well, the good news is that Trina is still here now, and you're headed to see her."

"Yeah, but as much as I'm going to keep trusting God to heal her, she's already decided to live out the rest of her life without further treatment."

Charlotte looked out the passenger window with sadness. For Trina, Jason, their children, and Curtis. Whenever anyone became ill before the age of eighty, it always seemed so unfair to Charlotte. She knew we all had to leave our earthly lives at some point, but hearing how sick Trina was in her middle fifties was heartbreaking.

Charlotte searched for the right words to say to Curtis, something that might ease his pain. But she knew she couldn't. Not when he'd learned just a few hours ago that his only immediate family member from childhood was terminally ill, and that there was likely very little time for him to make proper amends to her. Charlotte hated that this was happening to her husband, but the one thing she would do was be there for him. She would support him until the very end. It was true that she was struggling with her own issues, but she would support Curtis as much as she could. Because if there was ever a time when he needed her, it was now.

Chapter 4

Curtis was a nervous wreck. He and Charlotte had just parked in his sister's driveway, gotten out of his SUV, and walked up to the beautiful brick home. Charlotte grabbed Curtis's hand, squeezing it tighter than usual, and Curtis rang the doorbell. During the drive there, he'd said a number of silent prayers, trying to calm his thinking and uneasiness, but now his heart beat faster and faster, and he took a couple of deep breaths, trying to regain his composure.

Charlotte looked up at him. "Everything is going to be fine. You did the right thing by coming here."

Curtis continued holding Charlotte's hand, still attempting to calm his nerves, and finally his brother-in-law, Jason, opened the door.

He smiled. "I'm so glad you made it. Please come in."

Curtis hugged Jason, as did Charlotte, but then he saw a young man in his midtwenties walking toward them. He knew it was his nephew, Eric.

"It's good to see you, Uncle Curtis."

"It's good to see you, too, son."

Curtis hadn't known how either of Trina's children was going to react when they saw him—especially when they'd known for years that their mom had wanted nothing to do with Curtis—but here Eric had even called him *uncle*.

Curtis looked at Jason. "So, does she still not know about me coming?"

"This morning I told her that she was going to have a surprise visitor this afternoon, but that was it."

"Well, I just hope that seeing me doesn't upset her too much. Because we all know how she feels."

"I know," Jason said, "but things are different now. And she's different...because of what she's going through."

Curtis nodded, and then he, Charlotte, and Eric followed Jason down a long, shiny wooden corridor and around a corner. They stopped in front of a door that Jason lightly knocked on and eased open. A beautiful lady in her early thirties stood up from a recliner, and just as Curtis had known right away who Eric was, he knew this was his niece, Amber. She was the spitting image of her mother, and Curtis had to stop himself from crying.

"Is she awake, sweetie?" Jason asked his daughter, and then he looked over at his wife, lying in the king-size bed, propped against two pillows.

Amber walked closer to where all of them were standing. "She is."

"How are you?" Curtis asked her.

"I'm okay, Uncle Curtis," she said, with sad eyes, hugging him. "I'm so glad you came."

"Me too," he said, and once Amber hugged Charlotte, Curtis moved closer to the side of the bed and saw Trina watching him. Her skin was a bit pale, dark circles outlined her eyes, and although her hair appeared soft and curly, it wasn't longer than half an inch. Curtis guessed that as a result of her chemo treatments, she had likely cut it. Because from the time she'd been a child, she'd had gorgeous thick, wavy hair.

Curtis half smiled at his sister, still not knowing what to expect. "I hope you don't mind our coming to visit."

To his surprise, Trina smiled back. "I don't, and it's good to see you, Curtis. I mean really, really good to see you."

Curtis had never felt more relieved about anything than he did currently. He'd been so prepared for his sister to turn away and ask him to leave, yet she'd done just the opposite.

Curtis leaned down and hugged her, and she held him, too. Then she and Charlotte embraced.

"Thank you for coming, Charlotte," Trina told her. "I really appreciate it."

Charlotte smiled. "Of course."

Curtis wasn't sure what to say next, and apparently no one else did, either, because the room fell silent.

But finally, Jason spoke. "Why don't you both have a seat? And can we get either of you something to drink?"

"No, I'm fine, but thank you," Curtis said.

"I'll take some iced tea, if you have it," Charlotte added.

Amber smiled. "Well, hopefully my baby brother hasn't drunk all of it. Because that's what he usually does."

"Whatever, girl," Eric said, laughing. "You just made a

huge pitcher of it this morning, so who could drink all of that, anyway?"

"You," she said, and everyone laughed.

"Well, for your information, there's plenty left."

Amber playfully punched her brother on his shoulder and then looked at Charlotte. "I'll pour you a glass now."

"Why don't I come with you?" Charlotte said, already following Amber. "That way Curtis and Trina can spend some time together."

"I think that's a great idea," Jason added, and he and Eric followed the two women out of the room.

Curtis continued standing, just wanting to look at his sister. She stared back at him, but since neither of them seemed to know what to say, Curtis asked her a question. "Do you mind if I pray for you?"

"No, not at all."

Curtis held Trina's left hand with his right one. "Dear Heavenly Father, I come before you right now, first thanking You for another day, and most of all, thanking You for allowing me the opportunity to reunite with my sister. Thank You for answering my prayers. Then, Lord, I now ask that You would please remove all pain and discomfort that my sister is experiencing and that You would heal her body completely. Lord, please make her whole again. Please allow her illness to only serve as a test that will ultimately become her great testimony. And if there is anything that we can do here on earth to help her, Lord, please speak to our hearts, our minds, and our souls. Please give us the wisdom we need, along with total direction. Because while we know that the prognosis Trina has been given doesn't look good to us as human beings, we also know that only You have the final say. So, Lord, I am asking You to heal Your child. I am asking You to perform one of Your awesome miracles on my dear, sweet sister. Lord, we ask this and all other blessings in Your Son Jesus's name. Amen. Amen. Amen."

"Amen," Trina said, opening her tear-filled eyes and holding her brother's hand a bit more securely than before. "Thank you for praying for me, and..." Her voice trailed off, as she took a deep breath and swallowed tears. "Well...I just want you to know how sorry I am. How truly sorry I am for everything."

Curtis was confused. "Sorry for what? You haven't done anything, and I'm the one who will be sorry from now on."

Trina gently slid her hand away from Curtis and patted the side of her bed. "Please sit."

Curtis did what she'd told him.

"It's time for me to forgive you, and it's time you forgave yourself," she said. "And the reason I'm sorry is because I didn't forgive you before now. But it was just that I was so hurt. When you left for college and never called or came back home, it hurt me to my core. It felt like you had died."

"I know, and if I could turn back all those years, I would. If I could talk to that same eighteen-year-old boy and tell him what a huge mistake he was making, I would."

"I loved you and looked up to you, Curtis, and I needed my big brother. But while I won't ever fully understand how you were able to walk away so easily, I have thought about your motives. I've had these last few months to rethink things and to try to see them through your eyes versus mine. And you know what?"

"What?"

"I didn't like what I saw. I mean, Thomas Black was the cruelest, most uncaring man I've ever known, and he made life miserable for all of us. But what I've now come to realize is that our father's evilness must have been a whole lot worse for you than it was for me. Verbal abuse and spankings are one thing, but violent physical abuse is something different...and sadly, Curtis, I know you were the victim of all three things."

Curtis stared at his sister for a few seconds, and then they chatted for a while longer until she began drifting off to sleep. But sadly, he was still replaying everything Trina had said about their father. Words that had taken him back to a very dark place he didn't want to remember.

Thomas stormed into his son's tiny bedroom, as drunk as always. "Didn't...I...tell you...to take that garbage out of here? Didn't I?"

Curtis dropped his Bible onto the floor, the one his aunt Samantha had given him earlier this year for his thirteenth birthday. "I...am...I had to finish my homework. I'll do it now, Dad."

"*You'll do it now, Dad,*" his father said, mocking him, balling up his fist and striking Curtis across his face.

Curtis fell to the floor but quickly scurried across it on his hands and knees to the closest corner he could find. "Dad, I'm sorry. I'll do it right now."

Thomas staggered closer to where his son was cowering in fear, and Curtis took cover with both his hands. But it didn't help.

"I hate the day you were born," Thomas said, kicking Curtis in the stomach, seemingly with all his might, over and over, and Curtis winced and cried out. "You're the reason I never got to move to California, and I'll always hate you for that," he yelled, swinging his leg back as far as he could and kicking Curtis again. "And I don't know what you're readin' that Bible for. Your crazy mama started you doin' that mess when you were a small boy. Don't you know there ain't no God?" he exclaimed, kicking him again. And again. And again. He kicked Curtis so many times, his body went numb. But as Curtis lay there, crying uncontrollably, not a single person came to see about him. Not his mom or his sister. His father had always been a stern, angry, uncompassionate man who had spanked Curtis and Trina just a little too hard when they were small children and then whipped them with belts and tree switches when they'd gotten a little older. But now that Curtis had turned thirteen, something was different. His father's abuse had escalated and turned for the worse, and for some reason, he only inflicted this new level of abuse on Curtis. He still yelled at his timid and seemingly terrified wife as though she were less than a dog on the street, he ruled over her like she was a five-year-old child, and he spent all his money on women and liquor—leaving Curtis's mom to fend for their children all on her own. But Thomas never put his hands on her. He also never did much more than grab Trina by her collar, push her from time to time, or call her awful names. Curtis didn't understand that, although, the more he thought about it, he had heard his father say to his mom, many times, "You'd better be glad I don't believe in hitting women. I never have. Otherwise, you'd be a dead woman."

Curtis's father had always hated him, Trina, and their mom, but now he acted as though Curtis was his sole enemy. Still, no matter how much his father beat him and put him down verbally, he wouldn't let his father win. He also didn't care what his father said about there being no God, because Curtis knew God was real. He didn't understand why the God he kept reading about wasn't protecting him from his father, but at some point, He would—and Curtis wouldn't stop believing and trusting in Him. Not when God was all he had. Not when no one else seemed to care about him, one way or the other.

Curtis lay on the floor, crying all over again, and then heard his father leave the house and slam the front door behind him. Curtis was glad he was gone, but more than anything, he wished he would never come back. He wished his father would just die—and claim the special place in hell that Satan had waiting for him.

Curtis looked at his sister and realized how soaking wet his face was. So he wiped it with both hands. Trina was still asleep, but he was just happy to sit there alone with her in silence. He didn't like that his visiting her was stirring up old wounds, but he was glad to be there nonetheless. And he would come back to see her again tomorrow. He would do so as often as he could, because she was now his priority.

Chapter 5

Today was Monday, and since Curtis and Charlotte's longtime housekeeper, Agnes, had the day off, Charlotte was preparing breakfast. This was also Curtis's only weekday off from the church, and Charlotte enjoyed the time they spent together on Monday mornings.

Charlotte turned off the oatmeal and the scrambled eggs with shredded cheddar cheese, and removed the chicken sausage links that were slow-cooking in a nonstick saucepan. She'd already removed four pieces of seven-grain bread from the toaster, so now she pulled a large glass pitcher of apple juice from the refrigerator and set it on the granite island. Next, she placed four black cast-iron trivets near the apple juice and set the food on them.

Good Morning America was playing in the background, and Curtis was sitting and reading his newspaper. So much of what he read each morning had already been reported on the *Mitchell Tribune*'s web site or Facebook page, but Curtis still loved having his morning paper delivered. Reading the news articles, obituary pages, and sports section was a daily ritual for him, and Charlotte couldn't imagine him not do-ing it.

"Wow," he said. "For the first time in a long time, the obit-uary column hit home for me."

Charlotte pulled three glasses from the cupboard. "I'm sure. And understandably so."

"I mean, she's only fifty-seven. Just two years younger than me."

"I know. I was thinking that same thing yesterday when we were driving to Chicago."

"From the day we're born, our time to leave this earth is already set. Regardless of how old we are. But it's still hard to accept losing my sister at such a young age. I mean, don't get me wrong. I'm not giving up on my faith in God, because I know God's will has to be done—whatever that will is go-ing to be. But I'm also going to continue believing Him for a miraculous turnaround."

Charlotte sat down next to Curtis. "Exactly. We have to keep our faith strong. For Trina, Jason, their children, and us."

"And hey," he said, turning toward Charlotte, "I hope you don't mind my driving back over this morning to see her. I know we usually spend every Monday together, but for a while, I just want to spend as much time as I can with Trina."

"Of course. I'm glad you're going, and I have to say, it felt so good seeing how happy the two of you were yesterday. It's such a blessing."

"Yes, it is."

Charlotte saw the bittersweet look on Curtis's face, and

while she'd sort of made up her mind a couple of hours ago to tell him about her church sabbatical, now she couldn't. He was so focused on his sister's illness, and it just wouldn't be good to give him something else to worry about. There was also the chance that he might consider her decision to be a selfish one, something that would certainly cause problems in their marriage. And she didn't want that. They were in a great place, and she wanted them to stay there, so it was best to keep her feelings about being a first lady to herself. At least for now.

Curtis glanced at his watch. "Have you even seen Curtina this morning? She knows we like her to be down here when we say grace."

"Before I came down to start breakfast, I went in her room to make sure she was getting ready for school. And as usual, she was already texting someone on that phone of hers."

Curtis looked toward the back staircase, the one leading upstairs from the family room. "Curtina!"

Their home wasn't small, not by anyone's definition, yet with the volume and tone of voice Curtis had just used, Charlotte knew Curtina had heard him. Still, she didn't respond.

But instead of yelling out to her again, Curtis picked up his phone and texted her, and Charlotte shook her head.

"What did you tell her?"

"That she had two minutes to get down here or else."

Interestingly enough, almost exactly two minutes later, Curtina walked into the kitchen, texting and ignoring them.

31

Even as she sat down in one of the three seats across from them, she still didn't look up from her phone.

Curtis leaned back, folded his arms, and squinted his eyes. "Put it down. Now. And leave it down until I tell you to pick it back up."

Curtina blew a loud sigh and dropped her phone on the island in a huff. Then she slumped back in her chair and folded her arms the same as Curtis had, except instead of looking at either of her parents, she gazed at Robin Roberts, George Stephanopoulos, Michael Strahan, and the rest of the *GMA* anchors. She completely ignored Charlotte and Curtis, and Charlotte was glad this wasn't her week to carpool Curtina and her two friends. Actually, since Charlotte took turns with Taylor's mom, Jackie, and Lauren's mom, Alice, transporting the girls for two weeks at a time, both to and from school, it gave all three mothers the much-needed break they enjoyed. And right now, with Curtina acting out the way she was, Charlotte was glad to know that it would be another four weeks before it was her turn again. She'd just finished her two-week stint on Friday, and she couldn't be happier.

Curtis picked up the remote control and clicked off the television.

"Dang!" Curtina exclaimed.

"Dang, nothing," Curtis said. "And what have I told you about using that word?"

"I don't see what the big deal is. It's not a cuss word."

"Girl, I don't care what it is. I'm telling you not to use it again. Do I make myself clear?"

"Yeah," she mumbled.

"What? I didn't hear you."

"Yes," she said, still looking at the television.

"And I'll tell you something else," he said. "From now on, when we have meals together, I want you present. No phone and no pretending like we're not sitting right here in the room with you."

For the next few minutes, Curtis and Charlotte ate their food and conversed about one thing or another, but Curtina still sat with her arms folded.

Finally, Curtis couldn't take it anymore. "What's wrong with you?"

"Nothing."

"Then why are you so upset and rebellious all the time? And walking around with such an ugly attitude?"

"Because you and Mom treat me like a baby. You're always trying to control me."

"That's because technically you are a baby," he said matter-of-factly.

"I'm not. I'm twelve, remember? Or have you somehow forgotten that?"

Curtis scrunched his eyebrows. "Excuse me?"

Charlotte saw the look of regret on her daughter's face right away, but it was too late for her to take back her smart comment.

Curtis set his fork down. "Look, I don't know who you think you are or what's going on with you. But I'll tell you this: You'd better fix whatever it is."

Curtina looked down at her lap, still sitting with her arms folded.

"And eat your breakfast."

"I'm not hungry."

"Fine. Starve if you want. That's on you," Curtis said, and then saw her eyeing her lit-up smartphone. She had an incoming text message, so Curtis reached across the island and picked it up. He typed in her four-digit code, but the phone wouldn't open. So he typed it again. Still, nothing happened. "Didn't I tell you not to change that passcode again? Did I or did I not tell you that your mom and I are to have access to your phone at all times?"

"It was an accident."

"What was an accident?"

"Changing my passcode. I didn't mean to."

"You must think we're stupid. Now, what is it?"

"What's what?"

"What's the passcode, Curtina?"

She frowned and hesitated, but then told him. "Nine three two zero."

Curtis typed it in and he and Charlotte saw a message from Taylor asking Curtina why she wasn't responding.

But when Curtis tried to scroll up to read previous messages, he frowned again. "Why is this the only text on your phone when we clearly saw you typing when you walked in here?"

"I always delete my messages."

"Why? Because you're texting about things you shouldn't?"

"No."

"Then why?"

"No reason. I just do."

"Yeah, well if we keep having problems with you and you don't start back bringing A's in here, we're taking this phone away. And then you really will feel like we make you *sick*," he said, letting her know that he knew about that "Mom and Dad make me sick" comment Charlotte had told him about yesterday.

"What?" she said, finally unfolding her arms and casting a dirty look at Charlotte. Then she looked back at her father. "Why?"

"Because you have a nasty attitude, and using your phone is a privilege, not a necessity. Your mom and I have gone out of our way, giving you everything you need. And most of everything you want. But maybe that's the problem. Maybe we've done way too much for you to begin with."

Charlotte watched and listened but still didn't say anything. Because to be honest, she wasn't in the mood for any of Curtina's drama this morning. What she *was* in the mood for was a relaxing glass of wine—even this early in the day. Something that would take her mind off her ungrateful daughter. But she knew taking a drink was a big risk that might cause a huge uproar in her marriage—that is, if Curtis found out about it. So maybe it was best to leave well enough alone. Maybe it was best to fight this terribly strong urge she had to drink again, the one she now found herself struggling with each waking hour of every day. Yes, that's exactly what she would do. Forget about alcohol and focus on something more constructive. Something that wouldn't bring unnecessary trouble into their household. Because if she didn't, she could only imagine the fallout that would result from her actions. Especially since Curtis despised all things alcohol, thanks to the awful way his drunken father had treated him as a child.

So, no, she wouldn't do this. To herself, to Curtis, or to their marriage. And most of all, she wouldn't ruin things for their family.

Chapter 6

After Curtina left for school, Curtis kissed Charlotte good-bye, and now he was back on I-90 east, heading to see his sister. But what he thought about more than anything—at least at this very moment—was how rude and disrespectful Curtina had become. She was so different, and Curtis wondered what was wrong with her. Why she was acting as though she hated them? He and Charlotte hadn't been perfect parents, but they'd loved her and taken care of her in every way they could. Yes, she hadn't been born into this world in the most honorable way, what with Curtis having an affair on Charlotte with Curtina's mother, Tabitha, but he and Charlotte had still given Curtina the best life possible. It was also true that, at first, Charlotte hadn't been too happy about taking in a two-year-old little girl who was a product of Curtis's cheating, but soon Charlotte had begun loving her as her own. So much so that Curtina had eventually become one of Charlotte's greatest blessings. She'd loved Curtina, doted on her, and treated her as though she'd given birth to her.

But for some reason, none of that mattered anymore, and Curtis couldn't understand it.

Curtis drove past the largest auto manufacturing plant in the area, crossed into the far-left lane, and accelerated a bit faster. Then it dawned on him that he still hadn't called Alicia to give her more details about her aunt. Actually, he hadn't told Matthew or Dillon either because when he and Charlotte had returned from visiting Trina, he'd been too mentally exhausted. He was still trusting God for his sister's healing, of course, but he was also still very hurt about all the years he'd lost with her, thanks to his own selfish decision to walk away from her and their mom. He'd done so and hadn't felt bad about it—until now—and he couldn't stop replaying the whole scenario. Worse, he cringed every single time he tried to accept his daunting truth: He couldn't change what he'd done, and he would always have to live with it. Forever.

Curtis dialed Alicia's number, and she answered on the second ring.

"Hey, Daddy. How are you?"

"I'm okay."

"You don't sound okay, but I certainly understand why you don't. I'm devastated, too."

"It just doesn't seem real."

"No, it doesn't. She was always so full of life."

"I'm really glad your mom decided to take you to meet your grandma and auntie," he said, remembering how he hadn't learned about that until the day his mom had died. His ex-wife, Tanya, had taken Alicia to see them behind his back, and while he'd been a little shocked about it, he was glad she had. "I'm also still sorry that I was never planning to do it myself. And I'm sorry that I lied and led you and Matthew to believe that your uncle Larry's mom and dad were your grandparents."

"We all make mistakes, Daddy, and I hope you'll eventually find a way to forgive yourself. I know you want Aunt Trina to forgive you, too, but you also have to find peace within."

"I know, and thankfully, Trina has forgiven me. She told me yesterday. And she also said the same as you, that I have to forgive myself."

"I'm so glad to hear that, Daddy."

Then Curtis told her everything that Jason had told him about Trina's illness and how she'd decided not to continue treatments.

"Gosh," Alicia said. "This is a lot. It's so heartbreaking."

"That it is, and it's the reason I've made up my mind to spend as much time with her as possible. I wasn't there for her in the past, but I will be from here on out."

"Are you going back to visit her today?"

"I'm on my way now."

"When you and I hang up, I'm going to call her. But Levi and I are also going to go visit her one day this week."

"She'll be so happy to see you. And hey, how is your writing going?"

"Fine, and I only have a few more chapters to write."

"I'm so proud of you, baby girl. I'm also very proud of Levi and glad to call him my son-in-law—well, actually, he's more my son than he is an in-law."

"Thank you, Daddy. That makes me so happy, because more than anything I wanted you and Levi to be close."

"I know, and he's a good man. Even when he was dealing drugs, he still had a big heart, but once he got out of prison he turned his life around for the better. And I have so much respect for him. So many people find God in prison and vow to become true Christians, but it doesn't always happen."

"That's very true."

"He's also doing a great job at the church. Our jail and prison ministry was already great, but now that Levi is heading it up, we're reaching so many more men and women. And we have a lot more volunteers."

"He did wonders with the addictions ministry at Dillon's church, too. So I'm not surprised about how seriously he's taking his dedication to helping people. He really cares about them."

"It's very noticeable, and on top of that, he genuinely loves you."

"He does, Daddy, and I love him, too. He's my heart and joy."

Curtis thought about his first two marriages and how he'd ruined them, and then he thought about the fact that Alicia had done the same with her first husband, Phillip. Likely as a result of the bad example Curtis had set for her. Then, if that hadn't been enough, she'd allowed her great desire to have lots of money and material possessions to prompt her into remarrying—this time to a deceptive but successful pastor named JT. He'd given Alicia everything she could want, but he'd also slept around on her behind her back and done other things that weren't worth mentioning ever again. But with Levi, even though Alicia had begun seeing him while she'd still been married to Phillip, she'd found true happiness. The two of them had made bad choices very early on, but now they were good.

"Well, baby girl, I have a couple of business calls to make, but I just wanted to fill you in a little more about Trina."

"I'm glad you did. You drive safely, Daddy."

"I will, and I'll see you soon."

"I love you."

"I love you, too, sweetheart."

Curtis rang Trina's doorbell, and seconds later a sandy-brown-haired thirtysomething woman opened the door, smiling. She was dressed in light blue scrubs, so Curtis knew she was the home health nurse that Jason had told him and Charlotte about yesterday. "Please come in," she said.

Curtis walked inside. "Thank you."

"I'm Denise," she said, reaching her hand out to him.

"It's very nice to meet you, Denise, and I guess you already know I'm Curtis."

"Yes, Miss Trina told me you were coming. She said she really enjoyed her time with you yesterday and couldn't wait to see you again today."

Denise's words warmed Curtis's heart. "That's really great to hear. And how is she doing this morning?"

"She's a bit on the tired side, but she's comfortable."

Curtis half smiled and hoped the word *comfortable*

41

didn't mean that Trina was now being given morphine. Jason hadn't said anything about hospice care being called in, but because of all the terminally-ill church members Curtis had visited over the years, he knew that this was normally what *comfortable* meant. So what if Jason had only claimed that Denise was from a home health agency because he didn't want Curtis to know the truth?

"So which agency are you from?" he asked before he realized it.

"Interim Private Home Care," she said, already heading down the hallway.

Curtis followed her. "Well, thank you for taking care of my sister."

"Miss Trina is one of the best patients I've had. She's so thoughtful and kind."

"She's always been that way. Even when we were children."

When they arrived inside the family room, Trina smiled. She was sitting in her recliner, watching Gwyn Shepherd, who was local, but also known as a prominent female evangelist nationwide.

Curtis leaned down and hugged her and sat on the sofa adjacent to her. "So you like hearing Gwyn. So do I."

"She's awesome. Over the years, I've listened to her from time to time, but these last few months I've listened to her daily. Then on Sunday mornings, I watch *Ever Increasing Faith*."

Curtis smiled. "Apostle Price is in a class all by himself. A true man of God who I wish I'd known in my younger years.

Because if I had, there's a chance I wouldn't have fallen astray the way I did."

Trina nodded in agreement. "And his wife, Dr. Betty, is special, too. I've never met her, but the first time I heard her speak, I knew right away that she loved God, her family, and mankind as a whole. And that says everything."

"They're really good people. Such great examples for pastors, first ladies, and well, Christians, period."

Trina reached for Curtis's hand. "You're a great example, too. I know you've had lots of problems over the years, something the media had no problem reporting. But I also know you've changed. I've watched some of your sermons on YouTube."

"Wow, so you were keeping up with your big brother after all."

"I was. I never told anyone, not even Jason, but how could I not? Sometimes I would browse your church's web site, and sometimes I would scroll through your social media pages. Just to see photos of you."

Curtis took a deep breath. "I know I keep telling you how sorry I am, but I really am. I'm sorry for everything."

"I know, and I believe you. So please don't feel as though you have to keep telling me. Because you don't. You and I are good. Really."

"I appreciate that."

"I'm glad," she said, turning down the volume on the television and changing the subject. "So how was Two Ninety-Four south?"

"Not bad. I-Ninety was fine, too, but I'm sure it was because rush hour was already over."

"That always makes a difference."

They sat in silence for a few seconds and then Curtis said, "Can I get you something? Do you need anything?"

"No, I'm okay. I'm comfortable."

There was that word *comfortable* again, and although he didn't believe Denise was from hospice the way he'd originally been wondering, the word still reminded him of how sick his sister was.

"Well, if you need anything I hope you'll let me know. Anything at all. Even if I have to drive somewhere to get it."

"I will."

Trina glanced back toward the television, and Curtis looked at the large bronze-framed family portrait above the fireplace. In it he saw Trina, Jason, Amber, and Eric.

"What a beautiful portrait," he said.

Trina gazed up at it. "We just took it a year ago...and little did I know it would likely be our last. At least when it comes to professional photos, anyway."

Curtis raised his eyebrows. "But you're still trusting God to heal you, though, right?"

"Yes, but if He decides it's my time to leave here, I'm very much ready. I have things completely right with Him, and I'm at peace about it. I mean, don't get me wrong. I certainly don't want to leave Jason or my children. Or *any* of you, for that matter. But if leaving here is God's will, then at least I can say without any doubt that I know where I'm going."

Curtis smiled. "I'm really happy to hear you say that. I'm so glad to know that you have such an awesome relationship with God, because that's what's important. It's the most important thing for any of us."

"It is. There was a time when my relationship with Him was lukewarm at best, but over this last year, I drew as close to God as I possibly could. I've gotten to know Him on a much deeper level, and I also know that I'll get to see Mom again. I'll get to see the best woman I have ever known."

Curtis understood every word she'd just told him because his mom had, in fact, been kind and loving to everyone she met. But sadly, he also couldn't help thinking about the terrible resentment he'd felt toward her when he was a child—because of the way she hadn't protected him from his evil father.

Curtis stood in the short hallway that led to his bedroom, his sister's bedroom, and his parents', peeking around the corner. As usual, he saw his father sitting in the box-sized living room, drinking. But Curtis was hungry and wanted to go into the kitchen, where his mom was, to see if dinner was ready. They were having a rare delicacy, spaghetti and meatballs, and he couldn't wait. So he darted through the living room as quickly as he could, and his mother smiled when she saw him.

"You dumb little idiot," Thomas yelled. "Stupid little bastard. You're nothing more than scum on the street, and I can already tell you'll never amount to anything."

Curtis looked at his mom and felt sick to his stomach.

But Pauline didn't say anything. She just kept stirring the pot of spaghetti as though his father hadn't said a word to Curtis—her firstborn child.

Curtis swallowed hard, becoming more nervous by the second, and wondered why his mother wouldn't defend him. Why she never defended him. She'd done this kind of thing all the time, and Curtis couldn't understand why she saw no reason to protect him. Because wasn't that what mothers were supposed to do? Protect their children from people who wanted to harm them? Even if one of those people was their own diabolical father? Curtis could tell how afraid of him she was, but why she wouldn't stop this monster from belittling him, and more important, beating him, well, Curtis just didn't get that.

"Bring your dumb behind in here," his father yelled angrily. "And grab a beer out of that icebox and bring it with you."

Curtis always hated doing that, because it made him feel as though he was helping his father get drunk. But he knew if he didn't do as he was told, there would be trouble. So he pulled a brown bottle of beer from the refrigerator and took it to him.

His father turned up the beer he was just finishing and reached it toward Curtis, who guessed it was so he could throw it away. But then he told Curtis to open the full one. Curtis cringed yet lifted the opener from the small wooden table next to his dad and flipped the top off the bottle. Then he passed it to Thomas.

"No, you drink some first," he demanded.

Curtis felt more nauseated than before and wondered why his father was asking him to do something like this. Because regardless of how much he drank himself, he'd never asked Curtis to consume alcohol. "Please, Dad, I don't want to."

His father sat up straighter in the worn-down olive-green crushed-velvet chair. "What did you say? Are you talking back to me?"

Curtis slowly backed away from him. "Uh…no…but I don't want any."

His father moved to the edge of the chair, squinting his eyes. "You do want it. And from here on out, you'll want whatever I tell you to want."

Curtis was terrified and wondered why his mom still hadn't as much as looked into the living room to see what his father was doing to him. She never even grunted, let alone said anything. So Curtis took another couple of steps backward from his dad.

But when he did, Thomas got to his feet, grabbed him by his neck with one hand, and yanked the beer away from Curtis with the other.

It was then that Curtis dropped the empty bottle to the floor.

"I said drink this, and I mean it!" his father yelled.

Tears fell down Curtis's face. "No, Dad. I don't want to."

Thomas's eyes grew angrier. "Don't you talk back to me. Don't you ever talk back to me," he said, and then forced the beer bottle into Curtis's mouth.

Curtis tried to move his head away, but soon, he had no choice but to swallow some of the alcohol, all the while choking on it and coughing uncontrollably.

His father released him and laughed hysterically. "You're

nothin' but an ignorant little wimp. A weak little punk who I wish had never been born," he exclaimed, pouring the rest of the beer on Curtis's head and face. "Now take this in the kitchen and get me another one."

Curtis tried to stop crying but he couldn't, and now his face was soaking wet—from tears and the beer his father had tortured him with. Still, as he dragged himself into the kitchen, all his mom did was gaze at him, seemingly with sad eyes and a look of sorrow. And it was at that moment that Curtis knew she would never protect him and that when he was older he would leave this house of terror and never look back. He was only thirteen, and Lord knows he wasn't sure how he'd be able to last living there another five years, but he would. He would trust the God that he'd been reading about and getting to know as much as he could, and he would work hard in school so he could graduate, go to college, and never be poor again. When he was older, he would buy his wife and children a big beautiful home, and they would never want for anything—he was going to make sure of it. Why? Because he was smart, and he made A's in every subject. And while Dr. Martin Luther King Jr. had passed away four years ago, Curtis thought about his "We Shall Overcome" speech. He thought about it a lot, because he, too, would overcome someday. Deep in his heart, he knew he would.

He just had to.

Chapter 7

Charlotte pressed the phone button on the center console of her vehicle, searched through her contact list, and scrolled down a few lines. When she saw her best friend's cell number appear on the dashboard, she selected it. She'd almost called Janine at her office, but since it was just after noon, she knew Janine was probably already heading out to lunch.

Janine answered right after the second ring. "Hey, girl."

"Hey, yourself. How are you?"

"I'm good. Just on my way down to the parking lot so I can go grab a sandwich. What about you?"

"I'm okay. I'm actually heading to get something to eat as well."

"Really? Are you nearby?"

"No, almost in Schaumburg."

"Oh, okay. Are you going shopping, too?"

"Yeah, maybe. But mostly I just needed to get away for the afternoon."

"Is everything okay?"

"Not really. Yesterday, Curtis found out that his sister has cancer."

"Oh no. I'm so sorry to hear that."

"Thanks."

"Did she call him? Because I know they haven't spoken in a while."

"No, her husband, Jason, did. He called Curtis right before the first service began, and we drove over there to see her in the afternoon."

"How wonderful."

"Yes, definitely. Curtis is so happy about their reconnection. He's really hurt about her illness, especially since her prognosis isn't good. But he's very glad to have her in his life again."

"I can only imagine, and I'm sure his sister really needs him right now."

"She does. Which is why I'm glad Curtis drove back over there this morning."

"But is that all that's bothering you? Your sister-in-law's illness? Because, to tell you the truth, you haven't seemed like yourself for a while."

"Well, for one, Curtina is driving us crazy. She's so mouthy and disrespectful, and Curtis and I are getting sick of it. Actually, we're past sick."

"I know you'd mentioned how distant she'd become, but I didn't know it was that bad."

"Girl, you don't know the half of it. And she stays on her phone nonstop. Texting her little girlfriends every chance she gets. Not to mention the C's she's bringing home now.

And the only reason she's getting those is because she's smart enough to pass her tests without studying. She's always been able to make a C without doing any homework, but C's are completely unacceptable. At least to Curtis and me they are."

"Maybe she's just going through puberty. When I was her age, I acted out a little myself."

"Yeah, so did I, but with the age of new technology, these children are much worse."

"Have you tried to talk to her?"

"All the time, and that's why I'm tired."

"Wow, I really hate hearing that, and now you've got me worried about Bethany."

Bethany was Janine and Carl's only child, and she was also Charlotte and Curtis's goddaughter.

Charlotte adjusted her sun visor. "Hmmph. As much as I hate to say it, you have a right to be. Bethany has always been a good girl, though. But then so was Curtina. Yet now, she's getting on my very last nerve."

"Gosh, that's really too bad. And I hope things get better soon."

"Me too, but I don't know. I mean, she's nothing like Matthew was. He was such a good child, all the way through his teen years, and he never talked back to us. He never thought he was grown."

"Every child is different, though."

"Very true," Charlotte said, remembering all the problems they'd had with their daughter Marissa . . . before she'd died. But then, Marissa hadn't been a normal child, either, and had inherited mental issues from her father, Aaron—the man Charlotte had slept with behind Curtis's back, yet Curtis had still accepted Marissa and treated her as his own.

"Maybe you should have Matthew talk to her. And Alicia, too. Maybe she'll listen to her big brother and big sister a little more than she's listening to you and Curtis."

"Maybe."

"I know this must be hard, but this too shall pass. The same as it does with all the other problems we have in life."

"I agree, but I just hope this passes sooner rather than later."

"I hear you," Janine said. "Well, girl, I just pulled up to the deli, but if you get a chance, call me later. I should be off work right at five."

"I will, and if not, I'll call you tomorrow."

"Sounds good, and you hang in there."

"Thanks for listening."

"Anytime. Love you."

"Love you, too."

Charlotte ended the call, turned her radio to SiriusXM's Heart & Soul channel, and enjoyed the rest of her drive into the northwest suburbs. Curtis loved listening to a few different gospel- and Christian-related channels, but sometimes Charlotte needed a change of pace—sometimes she didn't want to hear anything that reminded her of Deliverance Outreach. Because there were days and moments when she just wanted to be normal. Left alone and able to exist without so many moral pressures. Plus, she didn't see a thing wrong with listening to secular music, as long as it didn't include profanity or explicit sexual language.

Charlotte drove along, enjoying herself, and then several miles later, she pulled into the parking lot of a popular Italian restaurant. When she walked inside, the hostess escorted her to a nice, quiet booth, and she was sort of glad to see many of the customers leaving. This was actually part of the reason she hadn't wanted to arrive before one o'clock. Because by then, she'd known that most people would be heading back to work.

"Hello," a petite, beautiful young woman said, smiling. "My name is Charlotte, and I'll be taking care of you."

Charlotte smiled also. "Well, hello, and what a coincidence. My name is Charlotte, too."

"Oh my, then I guess we won't have any problems remembering each other's name, huh?"

"No, I guess not," she said, and they both chuckled.

"So can I get you something to drink?"

"How about a glass of Riesling wine?"

"Sure thing. I'll be right back."

Charlotte scanned the menu that the hostess had set in front of her, but soon she felt a little guilty. And she knew the reason. During breakfast, she'd decided that drinking alcohol would only cause problems for her and Curtis. However, once Curtis had left for Chicago, she'd realized that having one glass of wine wasn't going to hurt anyone. It wouldn't cause a single bit of harm; hence the reason she'd driven sixty miles away from Mitchell. Of course, she certainly didn't believe that drinking alcohol was sinful, not if a person didn't overdo it or cause danger to others. But she'd still known it was probably best to find a restaurant far enough away that she wouldn't run into some of their church members. Or residents of Mitchell, period.

There were definitely people in the Chicago area and in most other states who knew what she looked like, thanks to her husband's nationally known ministry and bestselling books, but she still had a better chance here in Schaumburg of not being recognized. At least on a weekday, anyway, because many out-of-town people did tend to frequent the area on weekends.

Charlotte's waitress returned to the table, setting down a long-stemmed glass and filling it halfway with the wine she'd ordered. "Will you be having more than one glass? If so, I'll leave the bottle on the table."

"No, I think this will be all."

"Sounds good. And for lunch?"

"Mmm…" Charlotte said, taking one last glance at the menu. "I'll have your house salad and the mushroom ravioli with white sauce for my entrée."

"The ravioli is very tasty, and I'll get this ordered for you right away."

"Thanks," Charlotte said, smiling and then eyeing the glass of Riesling that sat in front of her. She'd been so sure that having a drink wasn't going to cause issues for Curtis and the rest of her family, but now she couldn't help thinking about the time she'd drank uncontrollably. That had been eight years ago, but it wasn't as though she'd been an alcoholic. She had just found a way to deal with the many marital problems she and Curtis had been struggling with. Today was different, though, as she was only drinking casually, the way any normal person would.

Charlotte lifted the glass, took a couple of sips, and closed her eyes. The wine tasted as good as she remembered, so she took another couple of sips, and it wasn't long before she felt the relaxing effects of it. In the past, she'd had to drink at least two glasses to feel the way she felt now, but maybe drinking on an empty stomach was making all the difference. That and the fact that she hadn't consumed alcohol in a very long time.

Charlotte set the almost-empty glass down and then looked across the room and saw a handsome gentleman smiling at her. But all she did was smile back at him and quickly turn away. He was sitting with another man, likely a business associate, and she hoped he wasn't planning to approach her.

Charlotte finished the last of her wine, and then her phone vibrated. When she removed it from her purse, her stomach turned flips. But she pulled herself together and answered it.

"Hi, baby," she said to Curtis.

"Hey, how's it going?"

"Fine, and how is Trina?"

"About the same, but she's taking a nap right now. What are you doing?"

"Having lunch at the deli down the street," she lied.

"Ritchie's?"

"Yep."

"I'm sorry I can't be there with you, and thank you again for understanding my need to spend as much time as possible with my sister."

"Of course. And please don't apologize for that. Take all the time you need."

"I love you for that, and once Jason gets home from work, I'll be on my way back to Mitchell."

"I'll see you then."

"I love you, baby."

"I love you, too, honey."

Charlotte pressed the End button on her phone and dropped it back in her bag. She so hated lying to Curtis. For years, she'd done this pretty regularly, but not recently, and she hoped she wouldn't have to make a habit of it.

After the waitress brought her salad to the table, she took a couple of bites of it, looked up, and saw the handsome man watching her again. They made eye contact, and then he continued conversing with the man he was having lunch with. There was a time when Charlotte would have found herself interested in someone like him, but today she was a different woman. She loved Curtis with her entire being, and seeing another man was the last thing she wanted to do. And she was proud of that. She was happy that the husband and the life she had were finally enough. That is, with the exception of this first-lady business that she no longer wanted any part of. She still hadn't told Curtis that she wouldn't be attending church this coming Sunday, but she would. She wouldn't tell him her true feelings about wanting to step away completely, however, at some point, she would be honest about that, too.

She wished she could feel differently, for his sake and everyone else's, but she couldn't help how miserable she was. She was sorry, but this was her new reality—and it was time she did what made her happy.

Chapter 8

Charlotte walked inside the kitchen, closing the door leading from the garage and feeling a bit light-headed. Now she wondered if having three glasses of wine had been a good idea. She certainly hadn't planned on having more than one, but before she'd known it, she'd asked the waitress to refill her glass and then fill it again. Although, maybe she hadn't eaten enough, and that was the reason she felt somewhat weak. She had finished most of her salad but not all of her mushroom ravioli. She also hadn't eaten very much for breakfast this morning.

Charlotte set her purse on the island, and while she'd known Curtis wouldn't be home for another couple of hours, she sort of wished he would drive back sooner. Because if he did, she wouldn't have to deal with Curtina's nasty attitude. Their daughter usually arrived home around three thirty, and since it was now four thirty, Charlotte knew she was already upstairs *not* doing her homework, and instead texting on her phone like some addict. Though Charlotte *was* pleasantly surprised about Curtina having reactivated the security system, because even though she knew she was supposed to do so, even in the daytime, she usually didn't.

Charlotte walked into the hallway and down toward the front of the house near the staircase. "Curtina!"

She waited for a response but there wasn't one.

Charlotte frowned. "Curtina," she yelled again, "don't make me come up there."

Again there was no reply.

Charlotte hated when Curtina ignored her like this, and enough was enough. So she went up the stairs and down to her daughter's room. Strangely, the door wasn't closed, and when Charlotte walked in, Curtina was nowhere to be found.

Charlotte shook her head, wondering where she was, and then went back downstairs to grab her cell phone. She quickly dialed Curtina's number. Of course, she didn't answer.

Charlotte left her a voice mail message. "Curtina, where in the world are you? You know you're supposed to come straight home, and you'd better call me as soon as you get this message. And get your little behind back here. Now."

Charlotte ended the call and sighed heavily. What was this child going to do next? And why was she acting this way in the first place? Charlotte sat at the island for a couple of minutes and then called Curtis.

He answered on the first ring. "Hey, baby."

"Have you heard from Curtina?"

"No, why?"

"She's not here."

"What do you mean she's not there?"

"She didn't come home from school. She should've been here an hour ago, and she's not answering her phone, either."

"Maybe she went over to Taylor's. You know she's done that before, especially when it's Jackie's week to drive them to school," he said.

"Still, she knows she's not supposed to do that. She's not supposed to go anywhere without permission. Not even over to Taylor's or Lauren's."

"You're right, but you know how hardheaded she is now. Why don't you call Jackie to see if she's there?"

"I will, and I'll call you back."

Charlotte hung up and dialed Jackie.

"Hello?"

"Hey, Jackie, how are you?"

"I'm good, but I'll bet you're doing even better since this isn't one of your weeks to cart these grown little women around."

"Yeah, tell me about it, and actually, that's the reason I'm calling you. *One* of those grown little women isn't home."

"You mean Curtina?"

"Yes, is she there with you?"

"No, I dropped her off at home a little more than an hour ago. You haven't seen her?"

"Nope."

"Well, when we pulled up to the gate, she reached out of the back window and typed in the code to open it. Just like always. Then I drove her up to the front of your house and waited for her to go in. You didn't hear the door opening?"

"I didn't get here myself until just a little while ago."

"And your housekeeper didn't hear her come in, either?"

"Agnes is off on Mondays."

"Oh yeah, that's right. Well, then, I don't know what happened, and now I'm worried because I literally watched her unlock the front door and walk inside."

"I'm sure she's fine. Just somewhere she shouldn't be."

"Hold on a minute," Jackie said, and called out to her daughter. "Taylor, come here for a minute."

Taylor, Lauren, and Curtina were thick as thieves, so even if Taylor knew something, Charlotte doubted she would admit it.

"Do you know where Curtina is?"

"She's home, I guess," Charlotte heard Taylor saying.

"No, she's not. Her mom is on the phone right now. And if you know where she is, you'd better tell me."

"I don't, Mom. She didn't tell me she was going any-where."

"You'd better not be lying to me," Jackie told her. "And you can just wipe that ugly frown off your face, too."

Charlotte couldn't believe these twelve-year-old girls.

"Did you hear what she said?" Jackie asked.

"Yeah, but I wonder if she's telling the truth."

"You and me both. There was a time when I believed every-thing she said, but now she lies whenever she feels like it."

"We're dealing with the same thing over here with Curtina."

"Too much, girl, but I'll let you know if we hear from her."

"I appreciate that, and thank you."

"Talk to you later."

Charlotte pressed the End button and immediately called Curtis again.

"Hey," he said.

"She's not at Jackie's, but Jackie says she didn't leave until she saw Curtina come inside the house."

"I just tried calling her, but she's still not answering. So I hope nothing happened to her."

Charlotte rolled her eyes because even though Curtis didn't play games with Curtina, there was still a small part of him that wanted to believe the best about her. Curtina was his youngest child—the baby of the family—and there were times when he didn't want to accept how awful she could be.

"Curtina is fine," Charlotte said. "Trust me. She's just being grown and doing what she wants."

"Are you okay?" Curtis asked.

"What do you mean?"

"I don't know. You sound different."

Charlotte hoped he couldn't tell she'd been drinking, and now she wished she'd focused more on hiding that fact versus getting herself all worked up about Curtina. "No, I'm fine. Just upset about Curtina and wondering what we're going to do with her."

"Well, first we need to make sure she's okay."

"Like I said before, Curtina is fine. And part of the reason I know that is because she even reset the alarm system. She had to have turned it off and then back on so we would think she hadn't been here yet. Not knowing I was going to call Jackie. Probably thought she could sneak away and get back here before we realized it."

"I hope you're right."

"I am. You'll see."

"Let me get off and try her again," he said.

"Call me back."

Charlotte set her phone down on the island and sat in one of the chairs. The wine she'd had was still taking full effect, and just as soon as they found out where Curtina was, she was going to lie down and take a nap. That way, she'd be able to sleep off her little buzz before Curtis got home.

Charlotte turned on the television and flipped through a few channels until she saw an old episode of *Law & Order*. But then Curtis called her back.

"Did she answer?" Charlotte asked.

"No, but I finally got her to call me."

"Really? How?"

"I texted her and told her that if she didn't respond in the next two minutes, I was grounding her for a month. And that she could also forget about using her phone or going anywhere except school and church."

"That's so ridiculous. You had to threaten her before she called you? And where is she, anyway?"

"Down the street at the convenience store. She claims she was just getting some snacks, and that she's already on her way home."

"I don't believe that. Not when we have all the snacks a

person could want right here. She's gone down to that store a couple of other times for some so-called snacks."

"Yeah, I know. Which is why we're going to have to keep a closer watch on her. For a while you're going to have to try to be home before three thirty. She needs to know that you're going to be there waiting on her."

Charlotte agreed but didn't like the sound of what Curtis was saying. Why should she have to rush home five days a week, just because their wannabe-grown daughter needed monitoring? It was true that they didn't want her there alone for more than an hour or so, but now Charlotte would have to schedule every single weekday around a twelve-year-old? She loved Curtina with all her heart, but this crazy-preteen drama was becoming too much.

Still, she told Curtis what he wanted to hear. "You're right. And I'll be here from now on."

"Okay, well, I'll see you in a couple of hours or so. Just depends on how bad traffic is."

"Drive safely."

"I will. Love you."

"I love you, too."

Chapter 9

Agnes set two cups of coffee down on the table, one in front of Curtis and one near Charlotte. "I really am sorry to hear about your sister, Mr. Curtis, and my prayers are with her. My prayers are with all of you."

It was the following morning, and Curtis had just told her what was going on and why he was heading back over to Chicago.

"I really appreciate that, Agnes, because prayer is exactly what we need."

"Can I be excused?" Curtina blurted out.

Curtis stared at her. "Why? Because it's not like your ride is here yet."

Charlotte lifted her cup, sipped some of her coffee, and looked at Curtina. And while Curtis knew Charlotte wanted to say something, she didn't.

Curtina folded her arms. "I just want to go to my room until Miss Jackie gets here."

"Why can't you just sit here with us?" he asked. "Why do you need to go back upstairs?"

"No reason. I just want to go to my room."

Charlotte half laughed, shook her head, and drank more of her coffee, and it was at this moment that Curtis knew his wife was completely fed up with Curtina. He'd known she was beyond frustrated and tired of their daughter's attitude, but now she seemed totally put out about it.

Now Curtis picked up his own cup of coffee. "No, just stay right where you are."

Curtina leaned back in her chair with more force than normal, pouting and pretending to watch one of the news programs.

"And I'll tell you something else," Curtis told her. "From now on, when either of your carpool moms drops you off, we expect you to come inside and *stay* inside. Do I make myself clear?"

"Yeah."

Curtis raised his eyebrows. "What did you say?"

"Yes."

"That's what I thought, and if you know what's good for you, you'll fix that face of yours."

Curtis and Charlotte looked at each other, and then at their housekeeper.

Agnes walked over and wrapped her arm around Curtina's shoulders. "Young lady, what's gotten into you? What's wrong with you these days?"

"Nothing, Miss Agnes," she said in a much more pleasant tone than she had to Curtis, something he wasn't that surprised about, because for some reason, Curtina had the utmost respect for Agnes.

"Well, it sure doesn't seem like it's nothing. You spend all your time in your room, and you pretty much never talk to your mom or dad unless you have to."

Curtina didn't say anything, but now Charlotte did.

"She acts like she hates us. Like we're the most awful parents in the world. Like she's twenty-one years old, living on her own, and paying her own bills."

"I never said I hated anyone."

"You didn't have to," Charlotte exclaimed. "Your actions say everything."

"They really do, baby girl," Curtis said. "You're not the same, and we're just trying to find out what the problem is."

"You guys treat me like a baby. You keep me locked up in this house like some prisoner."

Charlotte laughed out loud. "Wow, you can't be serious. I mean, what is it that you expect to be doing, Curtina—and at twelve years old, no less?"

"Go visit my friends whenever I want, spend the night with them, and stay up past midnight on the weekends."

"We already let you go visit your friends, and sometimes you do stay overnight with them," Curtis reminded her.

"Very rarely, and only when you feel like it."

"No young girl needs to be away from home all the time," Curtis said.

"Or staying up past midnight," Charlotte added. "Not on a weekday or the weekend."

Curtina looked at her mother. "And why not? All my friends get to stay up as late as they want. On Fridays and Saturdays. And their parents don't say a word to them about it.'

Curtis was finally through debating this topic. "Look, we're not your friends' parents. We're yours. And as long as you live in this house, you'll do what we tell you."

Curtina cast her eyes back toward the television, ignoring him.

Agnes shook her head with disappointment. "Curtina, you really don't know how good you have it, sweetheart. Your parents love you with all their heart, they take care of you in ways that some children can only imagine, and you have brothers and a sister who love you, too. You're a very blessed young lady, and it's time you remember that. Okay?"

"Yes, ma'am."

Curtis and Charlotte made small talk, and twenty minutes later, Curtina left for school and Agnes went upstairs to change their bedding.

"It just doesn't make sense," Curtis said to Charlotte.

"What? The way Curtina's acting?"

"Yes. I fully understand that most children go through that I-don't-want-my-parents-telling-me-what-to-do stage, but Curtina seems irritated and angry all the time. And for no reason."

"And she's getting worse by the day."

"Well, if she disobeys either of us again, I meant what I said. I'm taking her phone and she can forget doing any outside activities."

"I agree."

"And hey," he said, sounding as though something had dawned on him out of nowhere. "Are you okay?"

"I'm fine, why?"

"I don't know. You look tired, and you didn't have much to say when Curtina was sitting here, either."

"I'm just sick of talking about the same thing with her, and then nothing changes. And if I look tired, it's only because all this drama with her is really starting to take a toll. I'm to the point where I wake up in the middle of the night thinking about it and wondering where we went wrong with her."

"I feel the same way, and all I can hope is that she settles down soon."

"So, how was your sister when you left yesterday? We were so focused on Curtina last night that I never got to ask you."

"I don't know. She seemed a little weaker than she was on Sunday, but I'm sure some days will be worse than others. She wasn't in any pain, though."

"That's good."

"But you know what?"

"What's that?"

"The one thing I'm most happy about right now is that she was finally able to forgive me. Because otherwise I never would've been able to spend this kind of time with her. We talk about things we didn't know about each other, and we also talk about our past. Although, I will admit, some of my conversations with her are hard to have."

"Really? Why?"

"They force me to think about the awful things that happened to me when I was a child. Some of those things I'd buried so deep, I really had forgotten about them. Some things I've never even told you, yet now I'm having to relive them."

Charlotte caressed his back. "Sweetheart, I'm so sorry to hear that, and I hope you can eventually find peace with all of it."

"I do, too," he said, and then he smiled at Charlotte.

"What?" she said, smiling back at him.

"I have no idea what I would do without you. You know that?"

"I don't know what I'd do without you, either. Which is the reason I don't like thinking about it."

"Over the years, you and I went through a lot. We made a lot of mistakes, and we did and said hurtful things to each other. Yet, in just a couple of months, we'll be celebrating twenty years of marriage."

Charlotte nodded. "I know. Two whole decades, and it's hard to believe that so much time has passed. We finally got things right, though."

"That's the best part of all...but I still regret the way I treated my sister and mother," he said, suddenly wanting to cry.

And he did.

Charlotte rested her hand under Curtis's chin. "Baby, what's wrong?"

"I lost so many precious moments with them. Special times with my sister that I'll never be able to get back. I lost years and years, and there's nothing I can do about it."

Charlotte stood up from her chair and held him in her arms.

Curtis wrapped his arms around her waist and laid his head against her chest.

"I know this is tough," she said, "but everything is going to be fine. I know you lost a lot of years with Trina, but God has still given you an opportunity to spend time with her. He's allowed the two of you to come together again, and that's what counts."

Curtis wept and didn't say another word. He just didn't have the will or desire to do so.

Chapter 10

C urtis drove his SUV down their driveway, through the iron gates, and onto the main street. He did feel somewhat better than he had an hour ago, but there was still a certain sense of sadness that consumed him. He almost cried again but then his car phone rang. It was his youngest son, Matthew, calling, but before Curtis could answer, the call ended. So maybe Matthew had accidentally dialed him, especially since he was likely at work by now.

Just the thought of Matthew made Curtis smile, because even though Matthew had dropped out of Harvard in the middle of his freshman year—a result of his deciding to marry his girlfriend, Racquel, who had recently given birth to their son—he'd gone back to finish his bachelor's degree in business administration. This had occurred not long after he and Racquel had separated and divorced. Their union had been tumultuous and short, but the good news was that they'd become great friends and were co-parenting in a way that Curtis wished all divorced couples could.

Then, after Matthew had finished his four-year degree,

he'd continued his education and earned a master's in human resources locally at Mitchell University. Curtis and Charlotte had encouraged him to stay at Harvard for graduate studies, especially since they hadn't minded taking care of MJ for another year and a half or two. But Matthew hadn't wanted to spend any more time away from MJ. Then, when Curtis and Charlotte had realized how serious he was, they'd tried talking him into going to Northwestern, which was only ninety miles away from them. But Matthew had told them no to that suggestion as well. Still, not going to Harvard or Northwestern for grad school certainly hadn't hurt his career, as he was already earning six figures from a top telecommunications company right there in town. And he was only twenty-six years old, so Curtis was beyond proud of him.

Curtis drove another mile, then stopped at a red light, and when his phone rang, he saw that Matthew was calling again.

He pressed the button. "Hey, son, how are you?"

"I'm good, Dad. What about you?"

"I'm good, too, and actually I was just thinking about you."

"Oh yeah? What were you thinking?"

"About how proud I am of you. And how happy I am that Stacey stood by you the way she did. I know I've said this many times before, but Stacey was a Godsend for you and MJ. She hung in there the whole time you were at Harvard, and then you guys still made your relationship work while she was finishing her MBA down in Champaign at U of I. And she knew all along that you were divorced and had a child."

"She's definitely the best, Dad. A great wife and a great mom for MJ."

"That she is."

There was a slight pause and then Matthew said, "So, I hate to change the subject, but Alicia told me about Aunt Trina and how sick she is."

"I meant to call you yesterday, but by the time I got home and had to deal with that baby sister of yours, the evening got away from me."

"What's going on with Curtina?"

"You name it, she's doing it. She's so rude and hard to deal with. And she thinks she's grown and on her own."

"Wow, Dad. That's too bad, and maybe I should talk to her."

"I think you should. Because she's certainly not listening to me or your mom. She's angry all the time about nothing."

"Then I'll just plan on coming by there tonight or tomorrow."

"Sounds good."

"Okay, Dad, well, I'd better get back to work, but Aunt Trina is in my prayers, and please tell her that Stacey, MJ, and I will try to get over to see her very soon."

"I will, and you have a good day."

"You too. Love you."

"I love you, too, son."

Curtis relaxed further into his office chair, and Miss Lana took a seat in front of his desk. A few minutes ago, she'd called to see if he had some time to review his schedule for the next month.

"So how is Trina doing?" she asked.

"About the same. Although, she did seem a bit weaker yesterday than she did on Sunday. But it's like I was telling Charlotte earlier, I'm sure some days will be worse than others."

"Well, I have already been praying for her, her husband, their children, and you, and I'll continue."

"I really appreciate that, Miss Lana, because Trina's illness has really knocked the wind out of me. I never saw it coming, and the amount of guilt I'm feeling is sometimes too much. You know my whole story when it comes to my family and why I walked away from them, but now I'm losing sleep over it again. I'd somehow tried to come to terms with it, but I just keep thinking what if. What if I'd handled things differently? What if I'd realized a long time ago that no amount of hurt or animosity should ever be enough to end your relationship with your own mother? The woman who gave birth to you. Or to completely cut off your only sibling."

"I hear you, Pastor, and I understand how you feel, but it's too late to change any of that. I wish you could, but you and I both know you can't. And as painful as that particular truth must be, you have to focus on the present. You have to leave the past in the past and keep your mind on the time you have with your sister now."

"I know. That's the same advice I give hundreds of members all the time throughout any given year when I'm counseling them. But it's a lot harder to do when…well, when it's you."

"You'll get through this, though. You just stay prayerful and trust God to give you the peace you need."

"I will, and thank you for listening. And for always being like a mother to me. After all these years."

"You know how I feel about you and your family."

Curtis smiled with tears in his eyes, but he didn't let them fall. "So, what's the deal with my calendar?"

Lana passed him a copy of it and kept another for herself. "You have a lot of speaking engagements next month, both at churches and conferences."

Curtis sighed. "And they couldn't be coming at a more inopportune time."

"I was thinking the same thing. Over the last three months, you haven't traveled more than once or twice, but April is pretty full."

"Well, unfortunately, I'm going to have to cancel all of them. So can you call each contact person to let them know?"

"Of course."

"Please apologize for me and let everyone know that my sister isn't doing very well."

Lana nodded. "Don't you worry about a thing. I'll get it all taken care of."

"Plus, to be honest, even if Trina hadn't become ill, I still would have needed to reschedule a few events."

"Why is that?"

"Curtina is very much not herself right now. She's unruly, she pouts about everything, and yesterday she left the house without permission."

"To go where?"

"She says down to the convenience store, but she doesn't usually go places without us knowing about it."

"Mm-mm-mm. Sad to say, but this is pretty much the norm with a lot of these kids today."

"Yeah, I know, but no matter how many times you hear about it, you never expect to have to experience it yourself."

"No, definitely not, and I hope that whatever little Miss Curtina is going through will pass soon. You and Charlotte have raised her to know and honor God, and you've taught her right from wrong, so I'm sure she'll come around."

Curtis leaned forward, resting his hands on his desk. "I hope so."

"Okay, well," Lana said, standing up, "if that's all, I need to get busy with making all these phone calls."

"Thank you for everything."

"Anytime," she said, and left. But right after she closed the door behind her, Dillon walked in.

"Hey, Dad, how's it going?"

"Hey, son. I'm hanging in there. Have a seat."

Dillon sat in the same chair Lana had. "I know this is a hard time for you, so let me know if there's anything I can do. Either here at the church or wherever you need me."

Curtis smiled at his son, his firstborn child, and was grateful to have him in his life. While Curtis had been driving home from Trina's yesterday, Dillon had called him about church business, and this was when Curtis had briefly told him about his aunt. But what made Curtis smile was how concerned his son had sounded on the phone then and how sincere he was being now. And just watching him warmed Curtis's heart, because only two years before, they'd had one of the worst father-son relationships ever. They'd been cordial at best, and sometimes that hadn't even been the case. Yet now, they'd forgiven each other, and life was good between them.

"I appreciate that, son, and I'll probably have to take you up on your offer, as I do plan to spend as much time as I can over in Chicago with Trina."

"I'm so sorry about what she's going through."

"Me, too."

"Well, I'll do what I can, and Dad . . . I won't let you down. I know I have in the past, and that I did a lot of dirty stuff. To you and Matthew, but I'm not like that anymore. Partly because I lost everything. Including my wife and my church. And partly because Porsha has helped make me a better man. She's made me see how great life can be if you just do the right thing."

"I'm really glad to hear that, son, but let me say something to you. Number one: When it comes to the strain in our relationship, I wasn't completely innocent myself. And number two: You don't have to spend the rest of your life telling me that I can trust you. It's easy for anyone to say what he or she will or won't do, but what matters to me is that for two whole years, you've shown me that I really *can* trust you. That you have my back, and that you want to be a good person."

"I do, and while I'm not trying to make excuses, all I wanted was to be close to you. I wanted us to have the same kind of relationship that you have with Alicia, Matthew, and Curtina. I know now that I was wrong for trying to compare myself to them, but that's exactly what I did, and I was really lost."

"Yeah, but now you're found," Curtis said.

"Exactly," Dillon said, laughing.

Curtis laughed with him. "And you have a good woman in your life."

"I do, Dad. After that whole Raven fiasco, she was almost done with me. But thank God, she decided to give me another chance."

Curtis thought about the way Dillon and Porsha had first begun seeing each other—how they'd had an affair behind Raven's back. How Porsha had made a point to tell Raven everything, and how she and Raven had started a successful ministry together—for all the wrong reasons. But then, as anyone should have expected, that highly unlikely friendship had ended in mass destruction. Still, Porsha had repented and come clean about all her wrongdoing, and Curtis could tell she was a genuine person with a good heart. She showed every bit of that to be true, both as Dillon's girlfriend and as the director of women's ministry at New Vision Christian Center, the church she and Raven had founded.

"God is good, son, and you just keep treating her like the wonderful woman of God she is."

"I plan to. Always."

"That sounds pretty permanent. So do I hear a proposal coming in the future?"

"Yes, but not for another few months. Not until she

knows beyond a shadow of a doubt that I really do love her, and that she can trust me to do what I say I'm going to do. She says she does, but I want her to know that I'm not playing games or just pretending to be a better person."

"I understand, and good for you."

Curtis and Dillon chatted a bit more, and then Dillon left to go prepare for a meeting they both had with several staff members that afternoon. Dillon was Deliverance Outreach's VP of broadcasting, and to say he was doing an amazing job would be an understatement. Curtis was hoping that Alicia would take a position at the church, too, but for now, he knew she wanted to focus on writing, and he respected that.

Curtis thought about Trina and called her.

"So how are you feeling this morning?" he asked.

"A little tired, but I'm good. What about you? How are you doing?"

"I'm fine. Just trying to get some work done here at the church, but now I wish I'd come to see you."

"No, you're exactly where you're supposed to be. You already drove over here two days in a row, and all I'm planning to do today is get some rest. Plus, Denise is taking very good care of me."

"I'm sure she is, but I'll be back tomorrow."

"Sounds good. But only if you don't have anything else you need to be doing. I know the kind of responsibility you must have running such a large ministry, and I'll totally understand if you can't."

"Like I said, I'll be back tomorrow."

"I love you, big brother."

"I love you, too, sis."

"See you soon."

Curtis set his phone on his desk and rested his elbows on the arms of his chair. He wasn't sure why, but at this very moment, thinking about how weak his sister had just sounded on the phone reminded him of the time his mom had been ill and bedridden for more than a week.

"How long is your sorry behind going to lie up in that bed?" Thomas yelled at his wife.

Trina hurried into Curtis's room, horrified, and sat next to him on his bed.

The door to their parents' bedroom was closed, courtesy of their dad slamming it shut, but Curtis and Trina could still hear every word they spoke.

"Now get up and make me some dinner, woman. And I mean get up now!"

"Thomas, I'm sick," they heard Pauline say almost in a whisper. "I've got a bad flu, but I know I'll be better tomorrow. And I'll make you a nice breakfast in the morning."

Curtis wondered how she was going to do that. How she was going to cook anything when all he'd seen an hour ago was a quarter loaf of bread on the counter, some peanut butter in the cupboard, and a half jar of grape jelly in the refrigerator. There wasn't even a can of broth or tomato soup to be found. And they certainly didn't have any meat, not even those canned Vienna wieners they were sometimes lucky enough to have.

"You haven't cooked anything in two days! Two whole

days! Now, I want you to get up and fix me something to eat."

Pauline burst into tears, and so did Trina. Curtis pulled Trina into his arms, trying to be strong for his sister, but it was taking every ounce of willpower he had not to cry like a baby.

"You're about as worthless as some of those whores on the street," Thomas ranted. "You know that? And not only aren't you doing anything around here, you've missed two days of work."

"Thomas, please try to understand."

"I do understand," he said, hitting the wall so hard with his fist, it shook. "What I understand is that I should've married a real woman when I had the chance. I never should've let my mama and daddy talk me into marrying somebody like you. You're ugly, dumb, and useless, and I deserve better."

"Thomas, please don't," Pauline begged him. "The kids can hear you."

"Do I look like I care about that? Well, I don't, and I will *always* hate you for getting knocked up with that little idiot, Curtis. And for tying me down the way you did. Then you had that little heifer, Trina, when I told you I didn't want another kid. I had so many big plans and dreams, and you ruined all of it. My uncle was going to get me on at the aerospace company he works for in California, but you snatched all of that away. I had my whole life ahead of me, but because you schemed and trapped me, I haven't been able to do a single thing worth talking about. And just look at this dump that we can barely afford. I can't enjoy my life even a little. And now you're lying up in some bed pretending to be sick."

"I'm sorry I'm sick, Thomas. But I know my fever will be gone tomorrow. You'll see."

"It better be or else."

Curtis didn't hear any more conversation and prayed his dad was preparing to leave the house.

But then he heard him speak again.

"You know what? I wish you would just die. Because at least then I'd be able to collect on that life insurance policy we have on you. And I'd also be free to get me a woman I really want. A fine, classy woman who knows how to treat a man. A woman much better than you and better than that little heifer, Trina, will ever be when she finally grows up."

Trina cried harder, and Curtis took her hand and placed it over her mouth so their father wouldn't hear her.

"Don't cry, T," he whispered, and pulled her even closer to him. "Please don't cry. He'll be gone soon," Curtis said as tears fell down his own cheeks.

Then they heard their parents' bedroom door opening, and Curtis squeezed his eyes shut, praying that their father wouldn't bother them. *Please, God, don't let him come in here. Please, God, let him leave and be gone for the rest of the night. Please, God.*

Curtis silently prayed again, and in seconds, they heard the front door opening and their father leaving. Curtis finally breathed normally, and both he and Trina rushed out of Curtis's room and into their mom's. She was crying, but gazed at both of them and said, "I'm so sorry. I'm so, so sorry."

Trina leaned down and hugged their mom, weeping loudly, but Curtis just stood there, wondering why his mom wouldn't stand up for herself. Why she wouldn't pack them up and take them far away from this mini-penitentiary. Because what reason did she have to stay? His father never brought his money home, anyway. Not a single dime Curtis could think of. So it wasn't like they needed him for anything.

But instead of asking his mom why she wouldn't leave his dad, Curtis watched her with a blank stare on his face. He stood in his parents' room hurting from the bottom of his soul—worse than ever before—because now he knew the truth. His father truly did hate him and wished he'd never been born—just as he'd been saying to Curtis all along. He wholeheartedly believed that Curtis was the reason he was stuck in a loveless marriage that he didn't want to be in. He believed that Curtis had destroyed all his dreams.

But what his father didn't know was that the feeling was mutual, because Curtis was just as unhappy as he was. He was miserable, and he wished his mother had gotten pregnant by someone else. Any man at all would have worked, just so long as it hadn't been Thomas Black. But that was okay, because all Curtis had to do was bide his time. Hang in there for another five years and make his escape. Hold on until he turned eighteen and could leave this awful place for good.

Chapter 11

Two. That was the number of times Curtis had asked Charlotte if she was "okay." First yesterday, and then again, this morning. Was her drinking that noticeable to him? Had it been noticeable to others in the restaurant? If so, she would definitely need to be more careful. Maybe it would be better if she drank only one glass every now and then. That way she would never have to worry about overdoing it. She wasn't an alcoholic, not by any stretch of the imagination, but she couldn't deny that she did sometimes become a little tipsy when she had two or three drinks in one sitting. Especially, if she hadn't drunk liquor of any kind in a good while. That was normal for anyone, though. Wasn't it?

Agnes was downstairs fixing dinner and watching her afternoon talk shows, so Charlotte walked over to her bedroom door and closed it. So much was going on, and the only other person besides Janine who she could speak to openly was her mom.

Charlotte sat in her bed, picked up the cordless phone

on her nightstand, and drew her knees into her chest. Then she muted the television, which was turned to the Hallmark Channel, and called her mother.

When it rang four times, Charlotte wondered if maybe she was busy.

But then Noreen answered. "Hey, sweetheart."

"Hey, Mom. How are you?"

"I'm good, and you?"

"I'm okay. How's Dad?"

"He's fine, too."

"So what are you doing today?"

"Not a lot," Noreen told her. "Your dad is on his way back from his quarterly men's retirement luncheon, and I was just sitting here reading a couple of magazines."

"I'm really glad Dad likes going to those. I'm glad he stays in contact with the guys he used to work with."

"I am, too, and he really does love it. A lot of the women I retired with have so many other things going on with family and volunteer work that it's hard for us to schedule get-togethers. A few of us keep saying we're going to make it happen, though. But what's going on with you? When you called me last night, you didn't sound like yourself. I know you're worried about your sister-in-law, but is that all?"

Charlotte sighed. "No, it's not. Curtina is causing us all kinds of drama, and we really don't know what to do about it."

"What is she doing?"

"Yesterday she left the house without permission, and it took her forever to respond to our phone calls."

"Where was she?"

"She claims she was down at the convenience store getting snacks, but I don't believe it. It just doesn't make sense, and this is the first time she's done something like this. I've let her walk down there before, but she's never gone without asking."

"So she left the house while you were there?"

"No, Taylor's mom dropped her off after school, but I didn't get home until an hour later. And she was gone when I got here."

"This isn't good, and you guys need to put an end to this now before something bad happens. I know it may not seem likely, but sex trafficking is on the rise. And not just near our borders."

"I don't even want to think about anything like that. I can't even imagine someone taking Curtina away from us."

"Neither can I, but she stays on that phone way too much. You and Curtis have been saying that for a while, and your father and I have noticed it, too. Whenever we come for a visit, she's up in her room. Or if she does decide to come downstairs, she's texting or scrolling through social media. And there's no telling who she's actually communicating with."

"Well, the other day, I took her phone before she could delete anything, and she was texting with Taylor. She said awful things about me and her dad, and I still can't get over it."

"Like what?"

"That we make her sick."

"You make her *sick*? Why?"

"According to her, we're always trying to control her."

"Oh really? Well, what is it that she expects, when she's only twelve years old?"

"I don't know. Suddenly she's decided that she's grown and old enough to do whatever she wants."

"Then it's like I said, you guys need to put an end to this. And soon."

"Curtis has already told her that if things don't change, we'll be taking her phone and grounding her. She won't be able to go anywhere except church and school."

"Good. That's precisely what she needs."

Charlotte switched her phone to her other ear. "And then, Mom, there's something else I need to tell you. Something else that's really bothering me."

"What's that?"

"I need a break from church."

"Church as in Deliverance Outreach, or church in general?"

"Both. I mean, right now, I need a break from all aspects of the physical church. Sunday morning services, Bible study, and women's ministry meetings. But more than anything, I need a break from being first lady. I need some time away from all of it."

"Oh my. I had no idea you felt this way. Is there a reason?"

"I'm just tired, Mom."

"Of what?"

"All the expectations that come from the entire congregation and even strangers who don't attend Deliverance

Outreach. The pressure on me is so great, the same as it is with most other first ladies I know, and I just need some time off."

"I hear what you're saying, but how does Curtis feel about all this?"

"That's just it. He doesn't know."

"Hmm. Well, I definitely think you need to tell him."

"I know, but I'm not sure how. I also don't want to upset him. Not with everything that's going on with Trina."

"I understand, but in the meantime, what are you going to do? Continue with everything as is?"

"No, and I've already made up my mind to not attend service this coming Sunday."

"And you're not going to tell him ahead of time?"

"No, for now, I just think it's best that I tell him I don't feel up to going."

Noreen didn't say anything.

And Charlotte knew why.

"I know what you're thinking, Mom. That I shouldn't start lying to Curtis again, but—"

"That's *exactly* what I'm thinking, and you know I'm right. You and Curtis have been down this road many times before, sometimes because of you and sometimes because of him. But you finally got past all that. You made a commitment to be honest and faithful to each other, and life has been good for both of you. It's been good for your entire family."

"I just can't tell him that I don't want to be at church anymore. And plus, it's not like I'll be away forever. I just need a short sabbatical. Three or four months at the most. That's all."

"Three or four months is a long time."

"Not to me. Not when I've been doing this for nineteen years."

"Yes, and you know the anniversary committee is already planning a huge twenty-year celebration for next year. Just last week, I heard Curtis talking about it to your dad."

"I know, but right now, he's not thinking about it or talking about it. He's worried about Trina."

"I still think you should tell him the truth. He might not understand—at first. But it'll save you both a lot of unnecessary disagreements down the road."

"I guess," Charlotte said. Then her cell phone rang, and she got up and went over to the dresser where it was lying. "Mom, this is Curtina's school calling."

"Okay, I hope everything's all right. Let me know."

"I will," Charlotte said, praying Curtina hadn't gotten into serious trouble.

Charlotte sat next to Curtina in the principal's office, livid. "Is this true, Curtina? You actually dared your science teacher to call us?"

Curtina pursed her lips and looked out of the window, ignoring both Charlotte and Mr. Norton.

Charlotte grabbed Curtina's chin and turned it toward her. "You look at me when I'm talking to you."

Curtina did what she was told, but the look on her face screamed annoyance.

"Did you dare Mrs. Gaynor to call home?"

"Nope."

Mr. Norton clasped his hands together. "Mrs. Gaynor says that you told her that if she took your phone, you were going to make sure your parents stopped giving money to the school. And that they transferred you to somewhere else."

"Whatever."

Charlotte shook her head. "So I'm going to ask you again. Is this true?"

"I already told you, no. Mrs. Gaynor just doesn't like me, and that's why she's lying. She lies all the time."

Mr. Norton looked at her. "But two of your classmates confirmed the entire story. According to them, you were texting on your phone, Mrs. Gaynor asked you three times to put it away, and then when she tried to take it, you jerked it away from her. Then you started threatening her about your parents' financial contributions."

"Curtina?" Charlotte said with disappointment. "Why would you say something like that? Your dad and I have been regular supporters of Mitchell Prep for years. Even when your brother went here."

"Can we go?" Curtina said matter-of-factly.

"Yeah, but not until you apologize to Mrs. Gaynor."

Curtina rolled her eyes toward the ceiling.

"Do you think she'll be here soon?" Charlotte asked Mr. Norton.

"Yes, I'm sure she's on her way."

Charlotte turned to Curtina again. "Give me your phone."

Curtina snapped her head around like she'd heard a gun being fired. "Why?"

"Because I said so. Now, give it to me."

"Mom, please don't take my phone," she spoke in a panic. "I'm sorry. I didn't mean it. I won't talk to Mrs. Gaynor like that again. I won't use my phone at all. Not until I get home. Mom, please."

Charlotte squinted her eyes. "Open up your backpack and give it to me. Or if you want, we can get your father on the phone."

"Mom, why are you doing this?"

Charlotte reached down to the floor, picked up the brown leather bag, unzipped it, and pulled out her daughter's phone.

"Mom, I'm begging you," she said, speaking quickly and nervously. "I'm really sorry. I'm sorry for everything. I'll do whatever you want."

Charlotte dropped the cell phone into her handbag and crossed her legs. She was done talking to Curtina, and she couldn't wait to get her out of there. She was being so disrespectful, and it was taking every ounce of tolerance Charlotte had not to snatch her out of that chair.

"I'm really sorry about all of this," Charlotte told Mr. Norton.

"I'm sorry, too," he said, "especially since we're going to have to suspend Curtina."

Charlotte was through. "For how long?"

"Two days."

Today was Tuesday, and since it was already afternoon, this meant she couldn't return until Friday. "This is crazy, Curtina. So uncalled for."

They sat for another couple of minutes, and then a thin sixtysomething woman walked in.

She shook Charlotte's hand. "I'm so sorry we had to call you. I only do this when it's absolutely necessary."

"No, Mrs. Gaynor, I'm the one who's sorry, and I can assure you this won't happen again. Curtina knows better."

Mrs. Norton nodded. "We've made it very clear to all the students that their phones are to remain off and put away during all class periods."

"Which is completely understandable," Charlotte said, "and at this point, I'm beginning to wonder if they should be allowed on the premises at all."

Curtina sucked her teeth.

But when Charlotte gave her the *look*—the one most children didn't want to be on the receiving end of—she didn't say anything.

"We've considered that," Mr. Norton chimed in. "But because of all the school shootings and everything else going on in the world, many parents want their children to be able to call them if something happens. And to be honest, I do, too."

"Well," Charlotte said, standing up, "until Curtina learns how to obey both your rules and ours, you won't be seeing hers."

Mr. Norton pushed his chair back and got to his feet. "I completely understand."

Curtina shot her mother a dirty look, but Charlotte couldn't have cared less.

"Again, Mrs. Gaynor, I'm very sorry."

"Thank you so much for coming in."

"Yes, thank you," Mr. Norton said, shaking Charlotte's hand.

Charlotte glanced down at Curtina, who was still sitting. "Let's go."

Curtina grabbed her bag, stood, and walked over to the door.

Charlotte raised her eyebrows. "So you think you're going to walk out of here without saying anything to your principal and teacher?"

Curtina sighed in a huff. "Good-bye, Mr. Norton. Good-bye, Mrs. Gaynor."

"And apologize to both of them," Charlotte told her.

Curtina barely looked at them but said, "I'm sorry."

"Apology accepted," Mr. Norton said.

Mrs. Gaynor nodded. "Yes, apology accepted, and we'll see you on Friday."

"Yes, ma'am," Curtina said, half smiling.

Charlotte wondered why Curtina's attitude had suddenly turned for the better, then quickly realized the reason: Curtina was now trying to play nice, thinking it would persuade Charlotte to give her phone back to her.

Charlotte wanted to laugh out loud, but the only problem was, she didn't see anything funny. As a matter of fact, after dealing with yet more unnecessary preteen drama, she needed a full, tasty glass of wine. That or something stronger.

Chapter 12

There's my favorite grandson," Curtis announced as soon as MJ, Matthew, and Stacey walked into the kitchen, and Charlotte smiled. Matthew hadn't lived with her and Curtis for a while now, yet he still used his own key and walked right in whenever he visited. Out of respect, though, he never did this unless he'd told them ahead of time that he was on his way. Still, Charlotte loved the fact that, regardless of how many years had passed, Matthew felt as though his parents' home was also his.

"Hi, Paw-Paw," MJ said, hugging Curtis, and then he hugged Charlotte. "Hi, Nana."

"How are you, sweetie?" Charlotte said, squeezing him tightly. "Nana is so glad to see you."

Matthew and Stacey hugged Charlotte and Curtis, too.

"Have a seat," Curtis told them, and MJ sat where he always did whenever they congregated around the island: between his grandparents. Matthew and Stacey sat on the other side, and for a second the empty chair next to Stacey made Charlotte a little sad. Because normally, Curtina would be sitting next to her sister-in-law or her brother. That was before she'd begun spending all her time up in her room, which was where she was now.

"So how was school today, MJ?" Curtis asked.

"Good."

"Did you learn anything?" he continued.

"Yes, we learned how to do more word problems."

Curtis raised his eyebrows. "In math?"

"Yes. We already learned how to do some easy ones, but now our teacher is giving us hard ones."

"When I was in second grade, I don't think I remember doing story problems," Curtis told him.

MJ scrunched his forehead. "What's a story problem, Paw-Paw?"

"It's a word problem, except when I was a small boy like you, we didn't call it that."

"Oh."

"So what else did you learn?" Charlotte asked.

"Ummm, we learned some new songs in music class."

"Well, that's nice."

"Uh-huh. They aren't the same kinds of songs that we sing at church, but I still like them. And my teacher might let me lead one of them for our family night program next month."

Everyone smiled.

"That's great, MJ," Charlotte said.

"Thanks, Nana. I told her I was leading a song at church this coming Sunday, and she was so excited. She said she might come just so she can hear me."

Charlotte forced another smile on her face, but she felt like crying. She'd totally forgotten about MJ's solo portion of the children's choir's upcoming performance. It was taking place during Sunday morning service, and there was no way she could miss being there. She'd decided that this would be her first week of not attending, but if she didn't show up, MJ would be crushed.

"That's right," Curtis said. "Paw-Paw's main little man is leading his first song."

"Yep," he said, grinning with a mountain of pride. "I've been practicing every day."

Stacey fist-bumped MJ across the island. "Yep, and you're definitely ready."

"Thanks, Mom," he said, and Charlotte smiled at the awesome relationship that her daughter-in-law had with her grandson. Not every stepparent and stepchild got along, but anyone who knew them could see how much Stacey loved MJ and how much MJ loved her. His love for Stacey had never undercut the love he had for his biological mom, but he certainly loved Stacey as though she'd given birth to him.

MJ reached toward the fruit dish, pulled an orange from it, and got down from his chair. "Where's Curtina? Is she upstairs?"

Charlotte knew MJ was only five years younger than his aunt, but whenever she heard him call her by her first name without "Auntie" in front of it, she was tickled. Because who would've guessed that Matthew would have a child only five years after his youngest sibling had been born?

Matthew stood up. "Actually, MJ, I need to go chat with

your aunt for a few minutes. But you can go up and see her right afterward, okay?"

"Okay," he said, now looking at his grandfather. "Paw-Paw, can I go watch TV in the family room?"

"Of course, just make sure you're watching something kid appropriate."

"I will. I'm going to watch a movie on Netflix."

Matthew left the room, and Stacey shook her head. "He loves watching movies he's already seen. Over and over and over again."

Curtis and Charlotte laughed, and then Charlotte said, "Can I get you something to drink? I meant to ask you guys that when you first walked in, so please forgive me. Although, it's not like you're company or anything like that."

"No, I'm fine, and actually, we grabbed a bite to eat on the way over here."

"Well, thank you guys for coming," Curtis said.

"Anytime, and I'm so sorry things aren't going well with Curtina."

Charlotte leaned back in her chair. "So are we. And this stunt she pulled today was the worst. Talking back to her teacher and threatening her? I just never expected her to go that far."

"Me neither," Curtis added. "And then when I got home and asked her about it, she acted as though it was no big deal. Almost like it hadn't happened."

"Gosh," Stacey said. "Well, maybe Matt will be able to find out what's going on."

"I hope so," Charlotte said, "because we're not getting

through to her. And now that I've taken her phone, she's angrier than ever."

"She loves her big brother, though," Curtis said, "so that's why I called Matt again this afternoon. He'd already told me this morning that he was going to come have a talk with her, but then when this thing happened at school, I wanted him to come even more."

"Do you think she's talking to boys?" Stacey asked. "You know—about things she shouldn't be."

"I sure hope not," Charlotte said, "but with Curtina you never know. Especially lately."

Curtis sighed. "The only text exchanges we've seen are with her friends, and no boys' phone numbers are listed in her contact directory."

Stacey rested her hands on the island. "Yeah, but nowadays, these kids are completely on top of their game. They delete everything. Text messages, private social media messages, emails, and even their Internet browsing history."

"Really?" Curtis said.

Charlotte was just as shocked as Curtis, and she felt like a gullible little child. Both she and Curtis were well aware that Curtina was deleting all her text messages, but not once had they thought she was communicating with boys. As a matter of fact, even though Taylor and Lauren giggled about boys at their school the way most preteen girls tended to do, Curtina never mentioned them around Charlotte and Curtis. And she certainly had never talked about anyone in particular.

"I just don't think she's acting like this for no reason,"

Stacey said. "And if she is talking to a boy, she probably wouldn't add his name to her contact list, anyhow. She would either attach a girl's name to his number, or she would just memorize it and not include it in her phone at all."

Charlotte knew this was a possibility, because men and women did this all the time when they were having affairs. In the past, she'd even done it herself. Still, she hadn't considered the idea that Curtina might be chatting it up with a boy. And if Charlotte had been that naïve, she knew Curtis had never entertained the idea of it, either. Which just went to show, most parents believed what they wanted to believe, saw what they wanted to see, and ignored anything that they were sure their innocent little child would never do.

"I hope she's not texting boys, talking to them on the phone, or doing any of that," Curtis said.

"I hope she's not, either," Charlotte told him, "but we also know it might be true."

"Well, as much as I hate saying this," Stacey said, "when I was twelve, I was liking boys, texting them, *and* talking to them on the phone. I had to sneak behind my parents' back to do it, but I did it all the time. So imagine what must be going on with this current generation of kids. Given all the new technology and social media usage, they have so many ways to communicate. More than most people realize. And parents just aren't checking every possible medium."

"She was such a good girl," Curtis said. "All the way until just a few months ago. But whether she's talking to boys or not, we're not putting up with all these problems. Or her awful attitude."

Charlotte agreed. "No, we're definitely not, and that's why I took her phone right in the principal's office."

"And I took her tablet as soon as I got home. It's already locked away with her phone in our safe. I took her laptop, too, and the only way she'll be using that is if she can prove that she needs it to do her homework."

Stacey's eyes widened. "Oh my. And how did that go over?"

"Not well," Curtis said, "but I don't care. Not when I know it's for her own good."

Stacey stroked her hair behind her ear. "I think you're doing the right thing, because sometimes cutting off all electronic communication is the only answer."

"It's so sad that we had to confiscate everything," Charlotte said. "But we need to turn things around before it's too late. Before she enters eighth grade in the fall and then high school."

"Exactly," Stacey agreed.

The three of them chatted for another half hour, and the only time they saw MJ was when he returned to the kitchen looking for an apple juice box. Charlotte and Curtis didn't drink them, and Curtina preferred mango juice, but they always kept a supply on hand for MJ, as though he lived there.

Soon, though, Matthew came back downstairs raising both his hands in the air and shaking his head. "I really don't know what to say."

"What happened?" Curtis asked.

"She normally talks to me about everything, but the whole time I was in her room, she gave me all these one-word answers. And when she wasn't doing that, she pretended she was watching television."

"She didn't say *anything*?" Charlotte asked. "Nothing about why she's causing so much trouble?"

"Only that you and Dad think she's a baby, and that you won't let her do anything or go anywhere."

Charlotte pursed her lips. "That's not true."

"She goes places all the time," Curtis confirmed.

"Yeah, but not everywhere she wants to. And not whenever she wants."

"Well, if that's the problem," Curtis said, "she's going to be miserable for a very long time. Until she's graduated and out of this house."

"And she's really mad at you guys for taking that phone and tablet of hers," Matthew said, laughing. "She's through."

"She'll get over it," Charlotte said.

"I don't know," Matthew said. "She's so stubborn and bratty."

"Did you ask her to come down here?" Curtis said.

"Yep, but she acted like she didn't hear me."

Curtis got up, walked into the family room, and yelled upstairs. "Curtina, get down here."

Charlotte wondered if she was going to respond. But her curiosity was answered when she heard Curtis bellowing again.

"Curtina, did you hear me?"

Charlotte knew she'd heard him, because even though Curtis and Charlotte's bedroom was near the front, winding staircase, Curtina's was very close to the back one.

"Curtina, either you get down here now or I'm coming up after you."

Charlotte, Matthew, and Stacey looked at each other in silence, and although they couldn't see MJ, they never heard a peep out of him, either.

But soon Curtina moseyed into the kitchen with a drab look on her face, with Curtis and MJ following behind her.

Stacey smiled. "Hey, little sis."

"Hi" was all she said.

"Sit down," Curtis told her.

"Why, Dad? Why can't I just go back up to my room?"

"Because I want you down here, spending time with your family."

Curtina plopped into the chair next to Stacey with her arms folded, pouting. "If I get an F for not turning in my homework, it won't be my fault."

Charlotte squinted her eyes. "You're suspended until Friday, remember? So you've got more than enough time to get your homework done. The assignments you already had for tonight and the makeup assignments they emailed me for tomorrow and Thursday."

Curtina stared at Charlotte strangely, acting as though she was shocked to hear about the makeup homework. Did she think she was going to sit around watching television for two days?

Curtina sat with a scowl on her face, but Charlotte turned her attention to Stacey. "So how are your mom and dad?"

"They're fine. I spoke to them on the way over here, and they said to tell you guys hello."

"We left church right after the first service on Sunday, so we didn't get to see them."

"I know, and I'm so sorry about Miss Trina. I've been praying for her ever since Matt told me she was ill."

"Thanks," Charlotte said, glancing over at Curtis, but he and Matthew were doing what they usually did on most visits: talking about basketball.

Charlotte looked at Curtina, but only for a split second, and then said to Stacey, "Actually, I haven't spoken to your mom by phone in a while, so I'll have to call her to catch up."

"Yes, please do, because she's just as excited about MJ leading a song as he is," Stacey said, laughing.

Charlotte laughed with her, but deep down, she didn't as much as want to think about having to sit inside Deliverance Outreach yet one more Sunday. She'd been so sure she wouldn't have to, but no matter how she tried to weigh things in her mind, she knew she couldn't let down her grandson. MJ, without a doubt, expected all of them to be there, so she had no choice but to take one for the team. She would attend service, pretend to be happy, and begin her sabbatical Sunday after next. She would do this for MJ. Anything for him. Even if it meant being miserable the whole time.

Chapter 13

Curtis wondered how many more times he'd be able to visit his sister. He wasn't giving up on God, because he would never do that, but the human side of him couldn't stop thinking, *What if?* What if God's will was different from his and the rest of his family's? What if Trina's time on earth was nearly complete? Yes, it was true that God never caused tragedy, suffering, or even death, and that this was all the work of the enemy, but He still had a certain will and destiny for every one of his children. God also didn't cause harm to anyone, however, He did allow certain things to happen—even if we didn't always understand the reason.

And there was another truth that Curtis thought about, too: Every person born into this world would in fact die one day. There was no getting around it, and there was nothing anyone could say or do to change it. Of course, none of us knew exactly when our time here would be up, but at some point, it would be, and it was best to be ready. It was important to have your life in order, just as he'd always told his congregation—just the way Trina had talked about herself only two days ago.

Curtis relaxed more comfortably into the seat of his SUV, took a deep breath, and continued down I-90 east, heading to see his sister. But just as he reached to turn up the volume of his radio, his phone rang.

He smiled when he saw that it was his father-in-law. "Good morning, Joe, how are you?"

"I'm good, Curtis, what about you?"

"Hanging in there."

"I'm glad to hear it, and I'm very sorry to hear about your sister. Noreen talked to Charlotte and told me what was going on. Such a shame."

"I know. It really was the last thing I was expecting to hear."

"I'm sure. And there's nothing they can do?"

"I don't think so. She's had a number of treatments, but she's decided not to try anything else. So, at this point, what we need is a miracle. We need God to save her life."

"Well, Noreen and I have already been praying, and we'll continue."

"I really appreciate that. Prayers are what we need from everyone."

"Indeed. Okay, then, I won't hold you. Just wanted to let you know that we're thinking about you."

"Thank you, and I or Charlotte will keep you posted on how Trina is doing. I'm actually on my way to see her now."

"Sounds good. And you be safe out there on the road."

"I will. Talk to you soon."

"Take care now, and I love you, son."

"I love you, too," Curtis said, pressing the Off button...and feeling emotional. At first, he wasn't sure why, but then he realized it was because of how far he and Joe had come.

Over the years, so much had happened—some truly awful scenarios—and it was amazing just how drastically their relationship had changed for the better. For one, Joe no longer hated Curtis, and he loved him like a son. Yes, Curtis was only ten years younger than him, which was the reason he couldn't bring himself to call Joe "Dad," but Curtis loved him, too, and respected him like a father. This certainly hadn't always been the case, though, as there had been a time when Curtis had disliked Joe just as much as Joe had disliked him. But Curtis knew he'd been completely in the wrong, and that Joe hadn't felt the way he had without reason.

Curtis still cringed at the idea that he'd gotten Charlotte pregnant when she'd only been seventeen and while he'd been married to Tanya. For a long time, he'd tried to tell himself that he hadn't committed a crime—no matter how many times Joe had threatened to have him arrested if he didn't end all contact with Charlotte and Matthew. But what Curtis had eventually learned was that while Illinois law considered seventeen to be the legal age for consensual sex, this didn't hold true for offenders who held a position of authority or trust over the victim—such as a coach, teacher, and yes, a church leader. For them, the legal age was eighteen. So there was no denying the fact that Curtis had committed a crime. He'd slept with a minor, and what no one knew was that the thought of it always made him sick to his stomach. He'd apologized profusely to Charlotte and her parents many times, but his actions still bothered him. All three of them had forgiven him, yet he sometimes couldn't fathom the legion of terrible things he'd done so many years ago. It was the reason he now begged people to do right by others. To do the right thing no matter what. To live according to God's Word daily. He knew most everyone had done something in the past that they were ashamed of, but what he wanted them to know more than anything was that there was always a chance to turn things around. He wanted them to see that change was always an option. That even if it took them a while to make things right, there was no time limit on doing so.

Curtis drove the rest of the way in deep thought, listening to gospel music, and before he knew it, he was pulling into Jason and Trina's driveway. When he saw that Jason's SUV was still parked in the garage, he got a little nervous. Still, he left his vehicle, walked up to the front door, hoping for the best, and rang the doorbell.

Jason opened the door almost immediately. "Good morning, Curtis."

"Good morning," he said, hugging his brother-in-law. "I expected you to already be at work."

"Normally I would be, but Denise wasn't able to come today. Her daughter isn't feeling well, and it sounds like a bad case of the flu."

"Oh no. I'm sorry to hear that."

"I do have a couple of afternoon meetings, though, so if you don't mind, can you stay until I get back?"

"Absolutely. You don't even have to ask."

"Thanks, man. I shouldn't be gone past five or six."

"Take all the time you need. Charlotte knew I was planning to stay most of the day anyway, so we're good."

"Denise should be back tomorrow, but if she isn't I'll just plan on taking the day off."

Curtis followed Jason down the hallway. "No, definitely not. I can drive back over tomorrow, and Friday, too, if need be. All you have to do is tell me."

Jason stopped and turned around. "Are you sure?"

"I'm positive. I want to spend as much time here as I can, and if I'm able to help you out in the process, that's even better."

Jason swallowed hard, and Curtis could tell he was fighting back tears. "You have no idea how much this means."

Curtis patted his shoulder and spoke a little quieter. "I know this is hard, but I'm here for you. I'm here for all of you, and don't you forget that."

Jason nodded and continued toward the master bedroom. The door was already open, so he and Curtis walked in.

"Well, sweetie," Jason said to Trina, who was sitting in bed against a stack of pillows, "I'm about to head down to the office."

She smiled. "Okay. And hey, Curtis."

"Hey, sis."

Jason kissed his wife on the lips. "I'll check in with both of you in a couple of hours."

"Sounds good," Curtis told him.

"Oh, and if either of you get hungry, there's a dish of

lasagna in the fridge. Amber made it last night before she went home."

"Okay," Curtis said, and soon he heard Jason leaving.

"So you just can't stay away, I guess, huh?" Trina teased.

Curtis leaned down and hugged her. "Nope, which means you're stuck with me. Like it or not."

"Sounds to me like you're trying to be the boss of me again. You know, the way you thought you were when we were kids."

Curtis sat down in the plush brown recliner next to the bed. "I didn't *think* anything. I *knew* I was the boss of you."

"Yeah, whatever. Think what you want."

"You know it's true. Especially when all those knucklehead boys thought they were going to date you."

"Don't remind me. You scared off every boy I liked. And for no reason."

"Big brothers are supposed to protect their little sisters, and I was no different."

Trina shook her head. "You were terrible. You acted like you were my dad or something."

"Somebody had to," Curtis said, and immediately regretted his comment.

Trina looked at him with sad eyes. "Yeah, I know."

"I'm sorry. I didn't mean to bring him up, and from now on I'm going to try my best not to."

"No, it's fine. Because maybe talking about him and our childhood will help you get past all the pain you're still dealing with. I have pain, too, but I've forgiven Daddy. I forgave him a long time ago, because if I hadn't, it would have killed me. And do you want to know why?"

"Why?"

"Because I had so much animosity toward you, too, and I couldn't handle despising two people at the same time. Two people who I loved...and almost hated."

"I'll never be able to make up for that, and I'm sorry. I wish I'd done things differently, but I couldn't see past my own feelings. I didn't think about you or Mom or how it would affect both of you."

"I already told you that I've forgiven you. And Mom forgave you many years before she died. At the time, I just couldn't, but now that I'm a mother I understand how unconditional her love was for her children. She couldn't stay mad at you or blame you for leaving."

"I will always regret not coming to see her. The last few years of her life, I sent her monetary gifts, but I remember when you told me the day of the funeral that she never spent any of it. And that she saved all of it for Alicia, Matthew, and your children."

"She still loved the fact that you thought about her on all the special days of the year. At the time, it made me angry, but she was always happy when your cards came in the mail."

"Really?"

"Yes. And I'm sorry I didn't tell you that when she died. But I just couldn't. I couldn't tell you anything that might give you peace about walking out of our lives the way you did."

"I understand. You had every right to feel the way you did."

"But thank God, I'm finally past those feelings. I know it's likely only because I became ill, but better late than never, right?"

"Exactly."

"And as much as I know you might not want to hear this, Curtis, you're going to have to forgive Dad."

Curtis looked at her and then away. Partly because he knew she was right, and partly because he could never see himself doing that. The man had beaten him more times than he could remember, and in order to forgive him, Curtis would have to relive everything. It was bad enough that his conversations with Trina were dredging up painful memories and opening raw wounds, but to have to face his whole childhood and then forgive a monstrous father? He just couldn't see it. He knew not forgiving every single person in your life, dead or alive, went against God's Word, but...

"I know how hard it'll be, but I really think it's best," Trina said. "And you'll feel so much better when you do. You'll be free. Just like I am, now that I've forgiven you."

Curtis heard what his sister was saying, and although he couldn't imagine doing any of what she was suggesting, he nodded anyway. He led her to think that he agreed with her, and all he could hope was that she wouldn't bring this up again. Especially when he wasn't planning to forgive their father—ever.

Chapter 14

Charlotte and Curtina walked into the sanctuary of the church, and as expected, Curtina was still pouting and not speaking to anyone unless they basically forced her. And even then, she answered all questions with as few words as possible and barely looked at the person she was responding to. Curtis still instructed her to look at him whenever he asked her something, but Charlotte no longer tried. It just wasn't worth it to her, and while she did love Curtina with all her heart, this whole preteen insanity wasn't something she'd signed up for. It wasn't something Charlotte had ever seen the need to prepare for, and she doubted most other parents had, either. Although, maybe she and Curtis were a lot more naïve than they were willing to admit. Maybe their little angel had always been a grown-acting drama queen in the making, and they just hadn't noticed the signs.

As they continued down to the front of the sanctuary, Curtina finally said something. "Mom, why can't I sit with my friends? I sit with them every Sunday."

Charlotte looked at her with a straight face. "You're sitting with me, and I don't want to hear another word about it."

Now Curtina slowed her pace, walking a couple of steps behind Charlotte, and as soon as they arrived at the middle section of the front row, which was reserved for the first family and their guests, Curtina sat in the third seat from the aisle. She left the first two seats open for Curtis and Charlotte.

But just as Charlotte prepared to sit next to her, one of the members of the church, Priscilla Brown, walked up to her.

"Lady Charlotte...how are you?" she said in a fake, singsong tone, even though Charlotte had recently made it known to the entire congregation that she didn't want to be called "Lady" anything. Sister Black or just Charlotte suited her fine.

"I'm good," Charlotte answered. "How are you?"

"I'm doing well, and thanks so much for asking."

Charlotte couldn't stand her, but she didn't want to act ugly. Not when all their members expected her to love and respect everyone—even if some of the women at the church, like Priscilla, wanted Curtis to be more than just their pastor. There had even been a time when Priscilla would go out of her way to speak to Curtis and then pretend she didn't see Charlotte standing only inches away from him. That is, until that day when Charlotte had decided she was going to end this game Priscilla kept playing once and for all. And she hadn't minced words with her, either. Instead, Charlotte had walked right between Curtis and Priscilla, even though they'd only been standing two feet apart, and told her, "From here on out, if you can't speak to me, too, don't bother speaking to my husband ever again."

"Hi, Miss Curtina," the woman now said. "How are you, sweetie?"

But Curtina seemed just as unenthused as Charlotte. "Hi."

Priscilla seemed uncomfortable and ultimately realized that neither Charlotte nor Curtina wanted anything to do with her. "Well, I'd better go find a seat," she said. "Oh, and by the way, I love that suit you're wearing, Lady Charlotte. Those colors look great on you."

"Thank you," Charlotte forced herself to say, all while wondering when Priscilla would end her phony commentary. And wipe that bogus smile from her face.

When she finally left, Charlotte shook her head, and seconds later, Sonya Miller approached her. Sonya was the vice chairwoman of Deliverance Outreach's women's ministry, and since Charlotte served as chairwoman, they worked closely together.

"Good morning, Sister Black."

"Good morning," Charlotte said, smiling and hugging her, because Sonya had proven time and time again to be both genuine and loyal, and Charlotte loved her for that.

"So, I know service is about to get started, but I was thinking yesterday how we really need to start discussing the church's twentieth anniversary. At least the early planning of it, anyway."

Charlotte nodded, but she didn't want to think about

something so far away. "I agree, but since it's not for another year, we have more than enough time to prepare."

"Yes, but a number of other ministries have already had their first meeting, and if nothing else, we need to figure out how the women of the church are going to contribute to the overall celebration. In the past, we've hosted a women's luncheon, a fashion show, a weekend retreat, and a ladies' night out event, so I was thinking that since this particular anniversary will mark such an important milestone, maybe we could do all of the above. Maybe we could do one event every month for the four months leading up to the final celebration."

To be honest, the church's anniversary was the last thing on Charlotte's mind. Even when her mom had brought it up the other day, she hadn't wanted to think about it then, either. But she didn't want to be rude to Sonya, so she said, "Maybe that's the way to go. Doing something four months in a row."

Sonya beamed. "Really? Because I wasn't sure you'd be okay with our having to plan and do so much work."

"We have a lot of women who probably won't mind helping, so I think we'll be fine. Why don't you call me on Tuesday, and we'll talk about it then."

"Sounds good," she said, smiling and then glancing over at Curtina. "Good morning, beautiful."

Curtina's face brightened, and strangely enough, she smiled. "Good morning, Miss Sonya."

"Okay, well, I'll see you later," Sonya told Charlotte.

"See ya."

Charlotte took her seat, surprised about how polite Curtina had been to Sonya. Curtina had always liked Sonya, of course, but with the way she'd been acting, Charlotte hadn't expected her to smile at anyone this morning. Although it just went to show that, no matter the situation, most daughters liked who their mothers liked and they didn't like who their mothers *didn't* like, too. Hence, the reason Curtina's greeting to Priscilla had fallen on the cool side and her demeanor toward Sonya had been a lot warmer.

A few more minutes passed, and Alicia and Levi walked in, as did Matthew and Stacey. They all hugged each other, and while Charlotte still didn't want to be there, seeing her family always made her feel better. It made sitting through service and dealing with women like Priscilla much less irritating.

"So how are you, little sis?" Alicia said to Curtina.

"Good."

Alicia stood in front of her baby sister. "Good? Is that all you have to say?"

Curtina hunched her shoulders.

"You and I need to talk," Alicia said.

Curtina looked at her dumbfounded. "About what?"

Alicia folded her arms. "I heard you were out of school last week."

Matthew stood next to his older sister. "She was, and she's been doing a few other things she shouldn't be, too."

Curtina frowned. "Whatever, Matt."

"You know it's true."

Curtina turned her body toward Charlotte and looked toward the pulpit.

"Are Grandpa and Grandma still coming?" Matthew asked.

"Yes," Charlotte said, turning to look behind her. She scanned all the members who had already arrived and saw her parents heading toward them. "Here they come now."

Charlotte stood up and hugged them, and once they'd said hello and embraced everyone else, they sat down. Joe took a seat next to Curtina, and Noreen sat between him and Matthew. Alicia and Levi sat on the other side of Stacey, and not long after, Stacey's parents walked in as well. Then Porsha joined them, too. Dillon was always behind the scenes directing the broadcast, so he rarely got a chance to sit with them during service.

When everyone was seated, Charlotte glanced across Curtina at her father. "Are you okay, Daddy?"

"Uh-huh. Why do you ask?"

"You look a little tired," she said, not wanting to tell him he was slightly sweating across his forehead.

"Well, as much as I hate saying it, I think your old dad is coming down with something. I never get sick, but I think I might be getting some kind of bug."

"Then how come you drove all the way here?" Charlotte asked. "You should be in bed before you get worse."

"And miss my great-grandson leading a song today? I wouldn't miss that for anything, and I would never disappoint him."

Charlotte and her mom made eye contact and both shook their heads, laughing.

Joe ignored them and looked over at his granddaughter.

"I've been getting some bad reports on you, young lady," he said, smiling. "But I know this is only temporary, right?"

"Nobody understands me, Grandpa. They don't want me going anywhere besides school, church, and home. And they took my phone away from me," she said with tears in her voice. "They think I'm a baby."

Joe placed his arm around his granddaughter. "I'm sure it might seem that way, because believe it or not, I was once your age, too."

Curtina sniffled but looked shocked.

Joe half laughed. "Hard to imagine, huh? But it's true. And so were your grandma, your mom and dad, and your aunt and uncles. We were all children who grew up thinking we should be able to do whatever we wanted. But in the end, what we found out was that our parents were right to be strict. We learned that it was their job to guide us, teach us, and discipline us as best they could."

"But I just want to hang out with my friends."

"I understand that, and you'll be able to in due time. In a few years, you'll be graduating and heading off to college. Then you'll be in your twenties, working, paying bills, and dealing with life on life's terms. You'll be an adult, and that's when you'll think back to these days. That's when you'll wish you were twelve again and living in the comfort of your parents' home with no responsibilities."

"I don't think so," she said proudly. "I can't wait to be in my twenties, so I can be happy again."

Charlotte was glad the parishioners were all chatting among themselves, because she would never want them to hear this nonsense Curtina was talking. Being a difficult, smart-mouthed child was bad enough, but being a difficult, smart-mouthed pastor's daughter was much worse. It shouldn't have been, but just as she'd learned that pastors' wives couldn't make the same mistakes as most other women—and gain the same kind of understanding—pastors' children had to stay on their best behavior more than any other child, too.

Charlotte crossed her legs and smiled when she saw her grandson strutting in from one of the side doors and down the front row.

"Hi, Nana," he said, hugging Charlotte. "Hi, Curtina. Hi, Grandpa Joe," he said, hugging them, too.

"How's my great-grandson doing this morning?"

"I'm good, Grandpa. And excited."

Joe laughed. "I'm sure you are, and we're all excited, too."

"And my music teacher is even here. I saw her a few minutes ago."

"That's great," Joe said. "I'm glad she could make it."

MJ hugged the rest of his family members—every single one of them—and then hurried back out the side door. Charlotte had heard Matthew asking him if he was even supposed to be in the sanctuary at all, but MJ had ignored the question, smiled, and waved good-bye to his dad. He was such a happy child. So intelligent, good-hearted, and loving. He was all that Curtina had been only a few months ago.

When another five minutes passed, the praise and worship team took their positions, singing beautiful, uplifting songs. Then one of the leaders prayed an awesome and very moving prayer, and Charlotte couldn't deny that it was during these kinds of moments that she didn't mind being there. She loved God and always would, but she just couldn't continue living her life the way she was. She needed an opportunity to be herself without having to defend her statements or actions against public opinion. She also didn't want to have to dread seeing women like Priscilla or even have wonderful women such as Sonya constantly asking her to do yet something else. Get on a conference call. Come to a meeting. Make a decision as soon as possible. Add another event to her already overloaded church calendar. Listen to complaints from members who would never be satisfied with anything, even if you made things absolutely perfect for them.

Just before praise and worship ended, Curtis walked in, stood next to Charlotte, and then walked into the pulpit.

"This is the day the Lord hath made, so let us rejoice and be glad in it."

"Amen," the members of the congregation said.

"As always, it is great to be in the house of the Lord just one more time. It's great to be alive and well. Great to wake up another morning in good health, both mentally and physically," he said, looking toward the ceiling, "and Father God, I thank You for Your unconditional love, Your mercy, Your grace, and Your favor upon our lives."

"Amen," everyone commented.

"By now, some of you may have heard that my sister is very ill, so I'm asking all of you if you would please pray for her healing. She has been diagnosed with a very aggressive form of cancer, and as of this month, she's decided to end all treatments."

"Oh my," Charlotte heard some of the members saying, while others shook their heads with sadness.

"This has already become one of the most trying times of my life, and I am asking that you please pray for me and my family as well. Especially my brother-in-law, niece, and nephew. I'm asking that you pray for our strength and the understanding of God's will. Because no matter what, we will still give God the glory. We will love and trust our Lord and Savior Jesus Christ through all of it."

"Amen," the congregation said again while nodding in agreement and applauding.

"Still, even as I stand here before you, trusting God, I can't deny how hard this is for me. Trina is my baby sister. My only sibling. And many of you have heard me talk about her over the years. You've heard me share about our es-tranged relationship and how I walked out on her and my mom as soon as I graduated high school. I've always been so ashamed of that, but now the guilt that I feel and the re-gret I can't seem to overcome . . . well, it's now taking all the prayer and faith I have just to be there for her without weep-ing or being sad the whole time. It's tough because I can't change everything that happened. Which is why my hope is that *my* mistakes will serve as an example to all of you of what not to do. My hope is that you will love your family members and friends, no matter what. And if you're sitting here right now, knowing that you haven't spoken to a loved one for years—or even months—all because you believe they betrayed you in some way, it's time you rethink your position. Or maybe they didn't support you the way you thought they should when you started your business. Maybe they borrowed money from you and never paid it back. Maybe your brother, sister, cousin, friend, or whomever it might be talked badly about you behind your back. Well, whatever your reason is, my advice to you is to stop, think long and hard, and then ask yourself if it's worth it. Because, church, I'm here to tell you right now, life is precious. It's short. It's delicate. And there might come a time when you won't get any do-overs. You won't have a chance to make up for lost time. You'll end up like me, trying to cram all the years I missed with my sister into every hour that I'm finally able to spend with her now. Or you could end up worse. You could go years being angry with and not speaking to your loved one and then discover that they've passed away. So I'm asking you . . . begging you . . . to please don't make the horrible mistake I made. Please do the right thing while you still have a chance, before it's too late."

Tears streamed down both sides of Curtis's face, and Charlotte and most everyone else cried with him. The pain her husband felt was heartbreaking, and Charlotte prayed that God would soon give him the peace he needed.

Curtis pulled a handkerchief from inside his suit jacket and wiped his face. He took a deep breath and grabbed the glass podium with both hands. "So now that I've preached a mini sermon," he said, smiling, and the congregation laughed. "I didn't mean to do that, but I just needed to share with all of you what I'm going through. Also, if you don't see me on some Sunday mornings or at Bible study, it will only mean that I'm spending time in the Chicago area with my sister. So I hope you all can bear with some of my absences."

Everyone nodded with their support and approval.

Curtis always gave what he called his pastoral observations before the choir sang, but today his heart was full, and Charlotte was glad he'd spoken to the congregation the way he had.

"Before the children's choir comes in, I want to acknowledge two very special people who are here visiting with us today: my father-in-law and mother-in-law, Joe and Noreen. I know they've been here many times, but I just want to take this opportunity to say thank you for being the best in-laws a man could ask for. And thank you for driving over to see your great-grandson lead one of the songs this morning, because for the past two weeks he's been acting as though he was getting ready for a Broadway solo debut. And he wanted everyone in the world to be here."

The entire congregation laughed, as did Joe and Noreen, who also nodded and mouthed the words *Thank you* to their son-in-law.

Curtis spoke a few more words, left the podium, and the children's choir director led them into the sanctuary and into the choir section of the church. They were all smiles, and Charlotte couldn't be prouder. None of MJ's family members could be prouder, and when it was time for him to sing his part of Hezekiah Walker's "Every Praise," he sang straight from his soul. His voice was beautiful and powerful, and now Charlotte wondered if singing might be the purpose God had for him. As a matter of fact, all the children sang brilliantly, and while the adult choir had sung this song many times before, this was the first time the children's choir had performed it.

Many of the members, including all of MJ's family, stood and clapped along with the choir, and Charlotte couldn't help crying. Curtis looked at her and then pulled her close to him as they continued admiring their only grandchild. Charlotte hadn't wanted to be there, but now she was glad she'd come to witness such a joyous occasion. It was a good day, and she was happier than she'd been in a while—but then her father suddenly grabbed his left arm, squeezed his eyes shut, and dropped back down in his seat. He looked to be in total distress, and Charlotte couldn't move. Not even when she heard Curtis yelling for someone to call 911 and then for any doctors who were in the building.

She watched as Curtis, Matthew, and one of the elders carefully transferred her father from his seat onto the carpeted floor. She gazed in terror and wondered if her father would be okay. He just had to be, because she couldn't imagine life without him.

Chapter 15

*I*t just didn't seem real. Charlotte's father had collapsed out of nowhere, and while they still hadn't seen the ER doctor yet, all signs were pointing to a heart attack. Which didn't make a whole lot of sense, because Charlotte's dad had always eaten well, and he walked every single day of his life. Even during the winter months, he either walked on the treadmill in his home gym or went to one of the nearby malls and got in a mile or two there.

Charlotte held her mom's hand, and although they looked at each other, sighing, they didn't say anything. They didn't have words, not to mention they didn't understand why this was happening. Curtis sat on the other side of Charlotte with his arm wrapped around her shoulders, and MJ lay across the bench-like leather seating with his head resting on Stacey's lap, drifting off to sleep. Matthew, on the other hand, was beside himself, and Charlotte wasn't sure she'd ever seen her son so sad or worried. He was her parents' only living grandchild, and he had always been very close to them. To be honest, Joe and Noreen loved Matthew and MJ more like children than grandchildren.

Alicia, Levi, Dillon, Porsha, Curtina, and two of the leaders at the church, Elder Jamison and Elder Dixon, quietly spoke among themselves, but the overall atmosphere was very grim. There were other families waiting as well, either to be seen by a doctor or to hear the diagnosis of a loved one.

Curtis looked at his watch. "They've been in there for a little while."

Charlotte nodded. "I know, and I just wish they'd come tell us something. Anything."

"I'm sure it won't be much longer," he said.

"I should've known something was wrong," Noreen said. "I should've known something wasn't right."

"Mom, why do you say that?"

"Because for the last few days, your dad has seemed a little tired. He still walked every morning, and remember I was just telling you last week that he'd gone to his retirees' luncheon. But now when I think back on it, he wasn't as energetic as he normally is."

"Well, he didn't look the greatest at church this morning, and that's why I asked him if he was okay."

"I'd asked him the same thing before we left home, but when he told me he was maybe coming down with a cold or the flu, I never thought much more about it."

"Wow, and knowing Daddy, even if he'd been feeling bad for days, he wouldn't have said anything. He would have blown it off like it was no big deal."

"When he called me last week, he sounded fine," Curtis said.

"I just don't know what I'd do without him," Noreen said, sniffling. "I don't even want to think about it."

"And we're not," Curtis said. "We've already prayed for God to heal Joe, and we're going to trust and believe that."

"Exactly," Charlotte agreed. "Daddy is going to be fine, Mom. You'll see."

Noreen pulled a couple of tissues from her purse and dabbed her cheeks and the corners of her eyes.

Charlotte wondered how much longer the doctors were going to take, and then it hit her. What if her dad's illness was punishment for all the complaining she'd been doing about the church—God's sacred house? About her role as first lady, and how she no longer wanted any part of it? What if she was reaping all that she had sown? She didn't believe that God would bring harm to her father, but she did believe that He allowed certain things to happen. He sometimes allowed the enemy to cause problems and destruction, and the reason she knew this was because God had the power to prevent anything from happening if He wanted to. So when He didn't prevent bad things from happening, Charlotte believed there was a reason. Not everyone would agree, but sometimes when all was good in a person's life, they became too comfortable. They spent less time talking to God and less time asking Him for direction. They became lax with their overall relationship with Him, and Charlotte knew she was guilty of all of the above.

They sat for a few more minutes, and finally a thirtysome-

thing nurse with a very compassionate smile told them that
Dr. Simmons, the cardiologist on call, wanted to give them
an update. So Noreen, Charlotte, Curtis, and Matthew followed her through two wide automatic doors, down a short
corridor, and into a conference room.

Shortly after, the cardiologist walked in, shut the door,
and introduced himself. "Hello, I'm Dr. Simmons," he said,
shaking everyone's hand. "So, we've done a lot of tests on
Mr. Michaels, and we've discovered that he definitely went
into cardiac arrest. And on top of that, he has seventy percent blockage in his main artery."

Noreen covered her mouth. "Oh dear Lord."

Dr. Simmons nodded. "I'm so sorry that I don't have better news, and given the fact that the blockage is already
at seventy percent, we really need to get him ready for an
angioplasty. That way, I can go in and insert a stent."

"Is this our only option?" Curtis asked.

"Well, normally we would consider trying medication
and lifestyle changes, but when the blockage is this severe,
I always suggest having the angioplasty done as soon as
possible. Which is a lot less invasive than bypass surgery.
I've even spoken briefly to Mr. Michaels, and while he's fine
with having the stent inserted, he also wanted Mrs. Michaels
and his daughter to make the final decision."

Charlotte swallowed hard. "So once you do this, will he
be okay?"

"He should be fine. Your dad is in great health otherwise,
so that's a plus, but he will need to make some changes in
his diet and likely take meds for his heart and cholesterol

and a baby aspirin daily from now on. He can still live a normal life, though."

"Can we see him before you take him for the procedure?" Matthew wanted to know.

"Yes, but only for a few minutes. We need to begin prepping him right away."

"Is there anything else we need to know?" Noreen asked.

"No, I think that's about it, and I really do expect everything to go fine. Of course, there are always risks with any surgery or procedure, but as long as we don't find any other major blockages we should be good."

"Thank you, Doctor," Noreen said.

Dr. Simmons stood up. "You're quite welcome, and if you'll all follow me, I'll take you to see him."

"Would it be okay if I go get my son?" Matthew asked. "MJ is my grandfather's only great-grandson."

"Of course. Normally we can't allow so many people in all at once, but as long as you only stay for five minutes or so, we can certainly make an exception. And if it were me, I know I would want to see my little great-grandson, too."

When they left the conference room, Matthew went to wake up MJ, and Dr. Simmons escorted them to the room where they were holding Joe. As expected, there were all sorts of monitors, and an IV in his arm, but more than anything, Charlotte noticed how pale he looked.

One of the two nurses smiled and moved away from the side of the bed.

Noreen moved closer. "Hi, honey. How are you feeling?"

Joe half smiled and spoke in a weak voice. "I've been better."

Noreen kissed him on his forehead. "Well, you're going to be fine. Dr. Simmons is going to fix you right up."

"He sure is, Grandpa," Matthew said, grabbing MJ's hand and standing next to Noreen.

Joe looked at both of them. "My two favorite young men in the whole wide world."

MJ reached out and touched his great-grandfather's hand. "Are you going to be okay, Grandpa?"

"I sure am. You just wait and see."

MJ smiled. "I love you, Grandpa, and when your surgery is over, I'll be waiting for you, okay?"

"Sounds good to me, and I love you, too."

"And even though Curtina didn't want to come in with us, I'll tell her you said you love her, too," MJ told him.

"Yes, please tell her for me," Joe said, and Charlotte wished Curtina had in fact come in to see her grandfather. When Matthew had gone to wake up MJ, Charlotte had heard him asking Curtina if she wanted to join them, but she'd shaken her head no. At first, Charlotte hadn't been happy about her response, but then she'd seen the terrified look on Curtina's face and tears rolling down her cheeks. She was afraid that her grandfather was going to die, and knowing Curtina, she didn't want him to see how upset she was.

Matthew leaned over and kissed Joe on the forehead. "I love you, Grandpa, and we'll be right out in the waiting area."

"I love you, too, Matt."

Charlotte and Curtis switched places with Matthew and MJ, and Charlotte burst into tears.

"Now, now, sweetheart," Joe said. "I'm going to be fine. You hear me? I'm not going anywhere."

Charlotte hugged her father and cried even more. "I love you so much, Daddy."

"I know you do, and I love you from the bottom of my heart. And I want you to stop crying."

Curtis held Charlotte close to him and then said, "Before we have to leave, let's have a word of prayer."

They all joined hands, and Curtis laid one of his hands on Joe's head. "Dear Heavenly Father, we come before You with humble hearts and great faith. We ask that You would guide the hands of Dr. Simmons, and that You will make this procedure a successful one. We ask that You would prevent any and all complications, and that You will keep Joe safe from start to finish. We ask that You would bless the hands of all the other staff members who will be providing care for Joe, before, during, and after the procedure, and that You will allow Joe to experience a very fast and full recovery. Please take care of him, dear Father, and bring him through this trying time. We ask You for these and all other blessings in Your mighty Son Jesus's name. Amen."

"Amen," everyone said.

"Thank you, son," Joe said. "And you take care of my family, you hear me? And tell my granddaughter to remember what we talked about before service started. And that I love her."

"I will," Curtis said. "But you'll be up and about and able to do all of that in no time."

Charlotte wondered why her father was telling Curtis to

take care of them, and she quickly pushed the thought of him dying from her mind. She refused to think about anything of the sort, because she knew her dad was going to be fine, just the way Dr. Simmons had told them. In a couple of hours, he would be in recovery and all would be well. Life for each of them would return to normal, and soon this entire day would become nothing more than a distant memory. It would seem as though it had never happened at all.

Chapter 16

*I*t was early evening, and while everyone else had gone home, Charlotte, Curtis, and Noreen sat waiting to see Joe. His procedure had ended a while ago, and Dr. Simmons had just finished giving them an update. Everything had gone as well as he'd expected, and he'd told them again that with a few lifestyle changes, Joe would be fine. However, it was the "lifestyle changes" comment that Charlotte still couldn't understand.

Noreen crossed her arms. "It's been a really tough day, but thank God, everything turned out well."

"Indeed," Curtis said. "God is as good as always."

Charlotte nodded. "That He is, and I'm so grateful. But, Mom, there's something I don't get."

"What's that?"

"Dr. Simmons saying that Daddy needs to make lifestyle changes."

"Hmmph. Well, I'll just say this: Your daddy doesn't eat the way you remember. He stopped doing that right after he retired."

Charlotte scrunched her forehead. "Really? Because it never seems that way when you guys drive here for dinner or we come to Chicago."

"I know, but that's only because you haven't paid much attention to it. He's made a lot of unhealthy changes, and I've been on him about it for more than a year. Remember how he always ate oatmeal for breakfast? And one scrambled egg?"

"Uh-huh."

"Well, now he eats three scrambled eggs, three pork sausage links, two pieces of toast, and a huge glass of orange juice."

"No way. I had no idea."

"I'm sure you didn't, and remember how he almost always ate tuna for lunch or a chicken Caesar salad? With no croutons?"

"I do, and he's always done that."

"Well, not anymore. Now he wants very little to do with a salad and would much rather fry two large patties of ground beef in a skillet, top them off with two slices of cheese, and place them on a ridiculously sized bun. Then he either deep-fries frozen French fries or he cuts up a white potato and fries those instead."

"Mom, are you kidding?"

"No. And no matter what I say to him, he doesn't listen. He even gets angry if I talk about it too much."

Curtis half laughed. "I can't believe what I'm hearing. Joe cooking cheeseburgers and French fries?"

Noreen shook her head. "Mm-hmm. Double cheeseburgers, too. So really we shouldn't be all that surprised about his having a blocked artery. If anything, we need to be happy it wasn't worse."

Charlotte was stunned. None of this made any sense, and she still couldn't wrap her mind around any of it. "Well, by the time he eats all of that for breakfast and lunch, what does he have for dinner?"

"I'm almost afraid to even hear," Curtis said.

"And you should be, because dinner is sometimes his biggest meal of the day. Pot roast, fried chicken, fried pork chops, spaghetti and meatballs. You name it, and your father-in-law has probably had it sometime within the last week or month. I even suggested a while ago that if he was going to have spaghetti, maybe we could try whole-grain pasta and turkey versus ground beef."

"And?" Charlotte said.

"He looked at me like I was crazy and never said a word."

"Mom, this is awful, and why hadn't you told me?"

"To be honest, I didn't know this would be the result. At least not this soon, anyway. I also hadn't fully thought about how terribly he eats seven days a week. But things are going to change big time now. He can get mad all he wants, but I'm not losing my husband to food."

"Exactly, Mom," Charlotte agreed. "I'll be staying on him, too."

Curtis crossed his ankle over his knee. "I'll talk to him, too."

"I don't know how he eats that way and never gains weight," Charlotte said. "I mean, he might be maybe ten pounds heavier than, say, a couple of years ago, but that's it."

"Your dad has a very high metabolism," Noreen told her. "He always has, and walking every day helps him, too. So that's why I think he believes he can eat whatever he wants with no consequences. But even the skinniest person can have a heart attack or stroke. Especially if they're loading up on fatty and sugary foods all the time. Plus, you know your dad has always struggled with high blood pressure. Eating healthy, walking, and taking his medication every morning has always kept it under control, but his new eating habits must have changed everything."

"This should be a wake-up call for all of us," Curtis said. "I've always tried to eat pretty well, but now I'm going to make sure of it. I'm not saying I won't ever have red meat, anything fried, or a large piece of cake every now and then, but moderation will now mean a lot more to me."

"I agree," Charlotte said.

"Me too," Noreen added. "I do pretty okay, anyway, but now I'm going to become even stricter so your dad can get better. I'll be cooking for him and eating the same things."

They chatted a bit more and then Curtis's phone rang.

"Oh, this is Trina," he said, getting up and heading closer to the entrance of the surgical waiting area.

Charlotte watched as he smiled and walked farther away, and although she would never say out loud what she was thinking, she wondered why Trina was now calling all the time. Even more, she wondered why Curtis dropped whatever he was doing when she did so he could talk to her. Charlotte fully understood how ill Trina was and that she and Curtis were trying to make up for lost time, but over the last three days, she'd called multiple times *every* day—and today was no different. Curtis had gone to visit her again on Wednesday, but not on Thursday. Then, because he and the elders had an important meeting scheduled on Friday and he'd wanted to write his sermon, he hadn't gone then, either. And yesterday, he had attended the men's annual breakfast. So maybe not seeing her brother for four days was bothering Trina. At first Charlotte hadn't thought much of it, but Trina had called Curtis three times yesterday, and then again this morning while they were getting dressed for church. Then she'd called while Charlotte's dad was having his angioplasty, and now she was calling again. And actually, the more Charlotte thought about it, Trina had called Curtis on Friday evening, even though he'd already spoken to her earlier that afternoon.

Charlotte sighed but didn't say anything.

"What's wrong?" Noreen asked.

"Nothing."

"I'm your mom, remember? So what is it?"

"I'm good. We should just be focusing on Daddy."

"Your daddy is going to be fine. But you, on the other hand, seem upset about something."

Charlotte looked toward the entrance, where Curtis was standing and still talking on the phone. "She calls all the time, Mom."

"Who, Trina?"

"Yes."

"And you have a problem with that? Why?"

"I know it sounds bad, but she calls him multiple times

a day, and especially since Thursday. It's almost as if she doesn't understand that he still has a family here in Mitchell and a church to run."

"But you said yourself that she's terminal, right?"

"Yeah, but it's not like Curtis can drive over to Chicago every single day."

"Even if he did, I could understand why. They hadn't talked in years, and now he doesn't know how much more time he'll have with her."

"And I get all that. And I like Trina. But just a few hours ago, I heard Curtis telling her that Daddy had had a heart attack, so you would think she wouldn't call back so soon. That she would let him focus on me and you instead."

"I'm sure she's just concerned. She knows what it's like to be ill and probably wants to see how things are going."

"Maybe."

Charlotte looked over at Curtis again, and finally he walked back toward them and sat down.

"Trina sends her love, and says she's still praying for your dad."

"Oh, okay," Charlotte said. "Please thank her when you speak to her again."

"I will. I told her it was very nice of her to call."

Charlotte didn't say anything else, because maybe her mom was right. Maybe Trina meant well, and Charlotte was reading too much into all the phone calls Trina was making. Or maybe Charlotte was just stressed about her dad and was overthinking everything.

A nurse they hadn't seen before walked over to them. "Mrs. Michaels?"

"Yes," Noreen answered.

"They're taking your husband up to his room now, so if the three of you will follow me, I'll show you to the elevators. He'll be on the seventh floor."

Noreen grabbed the blazer to her skirt suit, and Charlotte grabbed her own. They both wanted so badly to take off the heels they were wearing, but they also hadn't wanted to leave the hospital until they had a chance to see Joe.

As they followed the nurse down the first corridor and then around the corner and through another, they strode along in silence.

"Here you are," the nurse told them. "When you get off the elevator, just stop at the nurses' station, and they'll direct you to your husband's room."

Noreen smiled and touched the woman's shoulder. "Thank you for all your help."

"You're quite welcome."

"Yes, thank you," Charlotte said.

When they arrived on the seventh floor, they stopped at the desk and then walked down the hallway. Joe's door was half-closed, so Noreen knocked once and opened it.

A middle-aged male nurse smiled. "Are you Mrs. Michaels?"

"Yes. And this is our daughter and son-in-law."

"Nice to meet all of you. I've just finished getting your husband situated, and I'll be right outside. He was already asking for you, so you came at the perfect time."

Noreen moved closer to the bed. "Thank you so much."

Charlotte and Curtis went around to the other side of it.

Noreen held Joe's hand. "It's so good to see you awake, but you know you gave us quite a scare, though, right?"

"I'm sure I did, and I'm sorry," he said, speaking in a quiet tone.

"We were worried to death, Daddy," Charlotte said, rubbing his arm. "We were so afraid."

"I'm really sorry about that, but the doctor says I'm going to be fine."

"Yeah," Noreen said, "but you're going to have to make a lot of changes. Big changes."

"Oh, there you go," he said, "being the food police. But I love you anyway."

Charlotte was thrilled to see her dad being so humorous. It set her mind just a little more at ease. "She means it, Daddy, and so do I. You're going to have to change all your bad eating habits."

Joe turned his head completely toward his daughter. "Not you, too."

"Yes, me too."

"And me three," Curtis chimed in. "Normally I stay out of things like this, but unfortunately, Joe, I'm going to have to agree with them this time. You have to take better care of yourself."

"So they've conned you over to the other side, too, I see."

"No, we just want you to be okay. You're the closest thing to a real father that I've ever had, and I need you to be here."

Joe stared at Curtis, and Charlotte saw tears welling up in Curtis's eyes. She'd heard him say similar words to her father before, but today, they'd made him more emotional than usual. Probably because of all the time he'd been spending with his sister and talking about their childhood.

"I really appreciate hearing that, and you're the closest thing I've had as far as a son. Even though I'm way too young to have a son your age."

They all laughed, including Joe, but then Joe coughed a few times.

"I think we need to let you rest," Noreen said. "But I'm not going anywhere. I'll be staying the night right in this room with you, if they say it's okay."

"I'm staying, too, Daddy. Even if I have to spend the night in the waiting room."

"Both of you go home and get some sleep. I'll be fine, and you can come back tomorrow."

Noreen shook her head. "It's not happening. I'm staying, and that's that."

"Whatever you say, woman."

"Exactly," she said. "Now you try to get some sleep."

"I'll see you tomorrow, Joe, okay?" Curtis told him.

"See you then."

The three of them walked out of the room, and Noreen said to Charlotte, "Are you going home to change?"

"Yes, but I'll be right back. Do you want me to bring you a sweat suit or something?"

"Please."

"What about shoes? Because you know my feet are a little bigger than yours. And the mall has already closed."

"Just stop by Walmart or Target and get me a pair of gym shoes there."

"I will."

"Well, you hang in there, and try to get some rest yourself," Curtis said, hugging his mother-in-law.

"I will, and thank you for being here."

"I wouldn't have been anywhere else."

Charlotte hugged her mother. "I'll be back soon, Mom, and call me if you need anything before then. I love you."

"I love you, too, honey."

Charlotte and Curtis headed toward the elevator, and Charlotte thanked God for saving her father's life. But for some reason, she felt like having a drink. She'd been fine most of the day, even while her dad's procedure had been in progress, but now she needed something to calm her nerves. Something to relieve all the tension she'd been feeling. And she would find that something before she returned back to the hospital.

Chapter 17

Charlotte, Curtis, and Curtina walked inside the house, and oddly enough, Curtina sat down at the island. Normally she went straight upstairs, not wanting to be bothered with them, but not tonight. As a matter of fact, right after they'd picked her up from Alicia and Levi's, she hadn't ignored them, and she'd even asked how her grandfather was doing.

Curtis pulled off his suit jacket and laid it across one of the chairs, gazing at Curtina. "What's wrong?"

Curtina hunched her shoulders. "Nothing, I guess."

"Are you sure?" Charlotte asked.

"Is Grandpa really going to be okay? Because he didn't seem okay at the church."

"Yes, the doctor says he's going to be fine," Charlotte assured her again, because she'd already told Curtina in the car that all was well.

Curtis sat across from his daughter. "Why? You don't believe us?"

Curtina hunched her shoulders again.

"Well, it's true."

Charlotte pulled off her four-inch pumps. "Your grand-father will need to change some of his eating habits and take medication, but he can still live a great life."

Curtina just stared at her mother.

"Maybe you'll feel better about it once you see him," Charlotte said. "And actually, I'm a little surprised you didn't go in to see him before they did his procedure."

"I was afraid, because he looked like he was dying."

Charlotte walked over to her and placed her arm around Curtina's shoulders. "That's understandable. We were all a little worried and afraid."

Curtina leaned her head toward Charlotte's side, and at that very moment, Curtina seemed like her old self. Charlotte knew it might be wishful thinking, but had her father's heart attack opened Curtina's eyes? Had it made her realize how precious life was and how nothing was more important than family?

"I'm glad he's not going to die," Curtina said.

Charlotte looked at Curtis, but then agreed with their daughter. "We all are."

"I'm really tired, so I'm going to bed," Curtina said.

Charlotte released Curtina. "I need to head upstairs, too, so I can change and pack a bag for Mom."

Curtina removed her cross-body bag and stood up. "Good night, Mom and Dad."

"Good night, sweetheart," Curtis said.

"Good night, honey," Charlotte added.

Curtina still hadn't hugged them the way she'd done

every single night for as long as they could remember—that is, until the last few months—but just the idea of her talking to them cordially and saying good night was a total turnabout.

"Wow," Charlotte said when Curtina was gone. "That was different."

"Very."

"Maybe tomorrow we can take her to see Daddy. But only if she wants to go."

"That's a good idea," he said.

"So what time are you coming back to the hospital in the morning?"

Curtis got to his feet, stretching. "Pretty early. That way I can be on my way to Chicago to see Trina before noon."

"What?"

Curtis looked at her strangely. "You don't have a problem with that, do you?"

"Well, in case you've somehow forgotten, Daddy just had a heart attack. He also just had a stent inserted."

"Yeah, and that's why I'm going to stop and see him on my way out."

"Really? And you don't think you need to be there most of the day. For him, of course, but also for me and Mom?"

"I do want to be there, but baby, I also haven't seen my sister in four days."

"I understand that, but can't you at least wait until Daddy is released? Until we know for sure how well he's doing?"

Curtis sighed. "I'll be back in plenty of time to see him again tomorrow afternoon."

"How, Curtis? Because each time you've gone to see Trina on a weekday, you haven't gotten home before six or seven o'clock. And what about the day her caregiver's daughter was ill? You didn't get here until sometime after eight."

"I know, but that was a special situation. Tomorrow will be different."

"I don't believe this," Charlotte said. "But I guess I shouldn't be surprised."

"What is that supposed to mean?"

"Just forget it," she said, turning to walk away.

Curtis grabbed her hand and pulled her back. "Baby, what are you talking about? And why are you so upset about me going to see my sister? You know how ill she is."

"Yeah, but you need to get your priorities in order. I have no problem with you spending as much time as you want with Trina, but right now, I need you here."

"But what's so wrong with me doing both? Going to see Trina *and* being here for your dad?"

Charlotte pulled away from him. "I don't want to talk about this anymore. You do what you want."

"Baby, please try to understand what I'm saying. The doctor believes your dad is going to be fine, but my sister is terminally ill. Yes, I will say a thousand times that I know God can heal her, but I also want to visit with her as many times as I can, just in case."

"Like I said, you do what you want. I'm going upstairs to change."

Charlotte left the kitchen and never looked back at him. She was hurt and livid all at the same time, and she couldn't believe how disloyal Curtis was being. He was choosing his sister over her and her dad, and she would never do something like that to him. To her, and also usually to Curtis, it was the two of them against the world. They were ride-or-die, for better or worse and till death do us part—always. So she wasn't sure why things were suddenly changing. But then, she knew how to ease her pain. How to fix everything. And she would, just as soon as she left here.

An hour ago, Charlotte had driven into the parking lot of a small-town liquor store located about thirty minutes away from Mitchell. She certainly hadn't expected to see anyone there that she knew, but to be safe, she'd made sure to remove all her makeup, and she'd also put on a baseball cap. Then, when she'd stopped by one of the superstores to get her mom a pair of athletic shoes, she'd bought a pair of clear black-framed glasses. Her vision was totally fine, and although she didn't need them for seeing purposes, she did need *these* so-called fashion eyeglasses for her disguise. They were perfect, and unless someone stared at her and knew her personally, she was totally unrecognizable. Which was what she'd needed to be so that she could freely purchase a small cooler, a bag of ice, plastic cups...and of course, a bottle of red wine.

Now she sat in the dark parking lot of the hospital, as far away from the building as possible, enjoying some of it. This particular wine tasted wonderful, and she was already starting to feel at ease. She wasn't sure why, but there was just this certain sense of peace that wine and other alcoholic beverages tended to give her, something she so desperately needed after what had happened with her father—and with Curtis making very clear who was more important to him. Charlotte certainly understood his desire to see his sister, and she even applauded it, but not when it made him forget about his own wife, father-in-law, and mother-in-law.

Charlotte poured herself another half cup of wine, leaned back in her seat, and closed her eyes, savoring the moment. Then, when she'd drunk the rest of it, she debated pouring another half cup but decided that this might not be such a good idea. So instead, she placed the bottle back in the cooler, hid it in the trunk of her car, grabbed the bag of clothing and shoes she'd brought for her mom, and went into the hospital. But not before she ate the cheeseburger with extra onion she'd picked up from a fast-food restaurant. She'd read online that onions and garlic did wonders when it came to eliminating the smell of alcohol on a person's breath, and she hoped this was true because the last thing she wanted was for her mom to suspect that she was drinking. It was the reason she would also be popping a couple of peppermint Altoids on the way inside and then chewing two or three pieces of gum behind it. She hated all the sneaking around, but it was just best to keep all of this to herself. It was better not to worry her mom or send Curtis into a complete frenzy.

Chapter 18

Curtis walked toward his father-in-law's room the following morning, and Charlotte just happened to be returning from the restroom. At first she considered ignoring him, pretending she didn't see him, but she knew that would be childish and uncalled for.

"You're still not speaking to me?" he said, stopping in front of her.

"Should I be?"

"Baby, let's not do this."

"Fine. How was Curtina this morning? Was she still in the same great mood she was in last night?"

"Yeah, but that only lasted for a few minutes."

"Why?"

"Right after we finished breakfast, she asked me for her phone again, and when I told her no, she got upset."

Charlotte frowned. "That's really sad, and something needs to be done."

"I agree, but what? Counseling, maybe?"

"I don't know, because the only way that will help is if

she's honest about what's bothering her. Versus only saying what she thinks a therapist will want to hear."

"Very true," Curtis said. "Maybe we can let her have her phone back, but only with some very strict conditions. There are a lot of control features that the cell phone companies offer now, so we would definitely be able to limit some of the things she does. If nothing else, we'll be able to read her text messages and see what web sites she's browsing."

"Maybe, but I still think we should keep it from her for the rest of this week. At least."

"That's fine with me," he said as they walked into Joe's hospital room.

"Hey, how are you this morning?" Curtis asked him.

"I'm hanging in there. No pain, and they've even had me walking through the hallway. Actually, they started that late last night, after you left."

"Good. And did you rest well?"

"I did. Well, as much as I could, given how many times my nurse kept coming in to check on me. She was only doing her job, though."

"That she was, and I so appreciate that," Noreen said. "She was very kind and hands-on."

"So when are they letting you out of here?" Curtis asked.

Joe sat up in bed a little straighter. "I'm hoping today."

Noreen shook her head. "Yeah, but I think it'll be a while longer."

Joe rolled his eyes toward the ceiling. "I don't see why. I feel fine. Just like brand-new."

Charlotte laughed. "Daddy, you just had a heart attack less than twenty-four hours ago."

"I know, but the doc fixed me right up, and I'm good. So I'm ready to blow this camp."

Curtis, Charlotte, and Noreen laughed, and then Dr. Simmons walked in.

"Good morning to all of you, and how's my patient?"

"Good morning," everyone said, then Joe added, "We were just talking about you and how I'm ready to get out of here."

"Is that right?" Dr. Simmons laughed. "Well, you do seem to be doing well, but I think to be safe, we shouldn't count on releasing you until Wednesday. And that's at the earliest."

Joe half frowned. "Wednesday? Doc, that's two days from now."

"I know, but you didn't just have an angioplasty, you also went into cardiac arrest."

"Yeah, but I feel well enough to leave, and I can walk around the house and rest at home."

"I'm sure you can, but why don't you just hang out here. Only for another couple of days."

"If you say so, and I guess you're the doctor," Joe said.

"That he is," Noreen said. "And I'm glad you're listening to him."

Dr. Simmons smiled at Noreen and then at Joe. "I've reviewed your bloodwork from this morning, and everything looks great. Your vitals are good also. The one thing I did want to mention, though, is that your blood pressure was very high when you came into the ER. We were able to get it down, but what this also tells me is that the medicine you've been taking isn't doing what it needs to. Especially since you told me you took it like clockwork. And that means that it's either not strong enough or you need a different kind altogether."

Charlotte looked at her dad and noticed that he wasn't saying anything. From the time Dr. Simmons had come in, he'd been talking nonstop, yet now he barely blinked or moved.

But Dr. Simmons continued. "So over the next two days, I'm going to see how things go. I'm trying two different pills now. Lisinopril, which is an ACE inhibitor that will work to keep your blood pressure down and help keep your heart healthy. And the second is a diuretic called spironolactone."

"Did you know your blood pressure was high, Daddy?" Charlotte asked. "Were you having headaches or anything?"

"Sometimes," he said.

Noreen looked shocked. "Then why hadn't you said anything? Or gone to the doctor?"

"I didn't think it was any big deal. Everyone gets headaches from time to time."

"Yeah, but not you," Noreen said. "You never complain about those."

"Well," Dr. Simmons said, "the important thing now is that we're aware of it, and if these two meds don't keep your pressure down where I want it, I'll add a third pill."

Charlotte watched her father, and something didn't seem right. He looked as though he was hiding information.

"Daddy, were you really taking your medication every single day?"

"Pretty much."

Noreen squinted her eyes. "What does 'pretty much' mean? Either you took it consistently or you didn't."

"My pressure was fine. Every time I went to the doctor it was fine. So sometimes I might've missed taking it."

Dr. Simmons raised his eyebrows. "But that's not what you told me, Mr. Michaels. Remember when I asked you about it right before we put you under?"

"I do. But sometimes I missed a few days. You know...here and there."

"A few days?" Charlotte said, louder than normal. "Why would you do that, Daddy?"

"And how *long* have you been doing it?" Noreen asked.

Curtis stood in silence, not saying anything at all, and Charlotte knew it was because he didn't want to side with them against his father-in-law. Siding with them about their wanting Joe to eat healthier was one thing, but this topic was much too tense.

Joe looked at this wife but didn't respond.

"Daddy, how could you? Why would you put your life in danger like this? You could've died."

"But I didn't die. I'm here, alive and well. Breathing and feeling just fine."

"That may be, Mr. Michaels," Dr. Simmons said, "but a blood pressure patient should never stop taking their meds without monitoring. You should have been taking your pressure daily, and more important, you should've spoken to your primary care physician first to make sure it was okay."

Joe was irritated and noticeably embarrassed. "Well, it won't happen again."

"I'm glad to hear that, and now that we know you hadn't been taking your original medication the way you should, it might work fine. So again, we'll monitor this new regimen I have you on and will go from there. You're going to need to take lisinopril anyway, for your heart, so I may just keep things as is. I'll also call your primary doctor and discuss it with him."

"I appreciate that," Joe said. "And I didn't mean to cause so much ruckus this morning. Goodness gracious."

"Maybe now you'll do the right thing, then," Noreen told him.

"Exactly," Charlotte said. "You have to take better care of yourself, Daddy."

"Yeah, yeah, yeah. I will. I won't miss another pill," he said, and then glanced over at Curtis. "You see how your wife talks to me? So when you leave, maybe you should take her with you."

Curtis laughed and so did Joe.

Charlotte couldn't get over her dad's carelessness. He knew he had high blood pressure problems, so there was no reason at all why he should have stopped taking his pills. Charlotte could tell how upset her mother was, too.

Dr. Simmons chatted with them for a few more minutes, but when he was ready to physically examine Joe, Charlotte and Curtis walked out of the room.

"Your dad is funny," Curtis said.

"Yeah. Funny not funny."

"Well, at least he won't likely try something like this again."

"We can only hope."

Curtis stood against the wall but looked at his watch.

"So you're still going to Chicago?"

"I know you don't understand, but yes."

"You know you're wrong for this, right?" Charlotte said.

"I'm not trying to hurt you or not be here for you, and I've already tried to explain that."

"You can explain until the end of time, and it won't make any difference. You could easily go see Trina tomorrow or the next day."

"Baby, I'm really surprised that you feel this way. Knowing what my sister's situation is."

"And I'm surprised you're not staying here with us, knowing what my father's situation is."

Curtis stepped closer to her. "Look, all I can say is that I'm sorry. And if I thought your father wasn't doing well, I wouldn't go. But he is."

"You can say whatever you want. I'm still not okay with it."

"Well, I'm sorry," he said, "and I guess I'll see you later. I should be back by five or six."

"Bye."

Curtis stared at her for a few seconds and then turned and headed down the hallway.

Charlotte watched him, but mostly she wished she could somehow get away to have herself a drink.

* * *

"Mom, can you believe Daddy?" Charlotte said, taking a bite of her scrambled eggs. She and Noreen had just sat down in the hospital cafeteria for breakfast, and Charlotte was still upset about what her father had done.

"Not really, but then a part of me can. A lot of people decide to stop taking their medication, even though they really need it."

"I don't get it. Daddy could've had a massive stroke or the kind of heart attack that could've taken him out of here."

Noreen drank some of her orange juice. "I know, but thank God he didn't."

Charlotte ate more of her food and looked around at staff members and other patients' loved ones and friends.

"So how is Curtis's sister doing?" Noreen asked.

"I don't know. About the same, I guess."

"You haven't asked him?"

"I did last week."

"Charlotte?"

"Yeah?"

"Why are you so upset about Curtis and his relationship with Trina?"

"I'm not upset about it at all. I just know he should be here with me. And for Daddy."

"But you heard Dr. Simmons. Your daddy is doing fine."

"Well, I can't help how I feel, Mom. I've never been okay with Curtis putting anyone before me. Not when I really need him."

"But you did hear what he said during service yesterday,

right? Talking about how short life is. How precious and delicate it is."

"I heard him."

"Then you also know that very few things are worth being mad about. But more than that, you know how much Curtis loves you and how much he's given you. And I'm not talking about the financial part of your marriage. That's all great and wonderful, but I'm talking about the emotional and loving aspect. You and Curtis have been through a lot, sweetheart. But no matter how bad things got, he's always been there for you. And you've always been there for him. But honey, this is different, and there's no way he can be here for you and be there for his dying sister."

Charlotte didn't want to disrespect her mom, so she changed the subject. "So if Daddy is released on Wednesday, do you want to stay with us for a while? Maybe even just until the weekend?"

"Oh, so does that mean you don't like what I'm saying?"

"I'd just rather not talk about Curtis right now. I'm sorry, Mom."

"It's fine. And to answer your question, we'll see. Because if the doctor says that he's strong enough to take a ninety-minute ride, then I'd rather go home. That way I can get him completely situated, do some grocery shopping, and begin cooking him three healthy meals every day."

"Well, I'll at least drive over with you so I can stay with Daddy while you go to the store and then help with anything else you need."

"Yes, that will be good."

Noreen and Charlotte talked and kept eating, but then Noreen set her fork down and asked Charlotte a question.

"Is something bothering you? Something you're not telling me?"

"No, why do you ask?"

"Because when you came back to the hospital last night, you seemed different. You were very talkative, and I can't remember the last time I saw you go out in public without makeup. You've always been beautiful even without it, but still..."

Charlotte already had the perfect lie ready, and she didn't hesitate. "I'm tired of having to worry about what people think of me. Going out of my way, trying to satisfy members of our church—and even nonmembers who expect me to look a certain way in public."

Noreen rested her elbows on the table and clasped her hands together. "I'm really sorry that you feel this way. That you're so miserable being first lady at Deliverance. Have you still not spoken to Curtis about it?"

"No. And while I know you think I should, Mom, I just can't. Not right now."

"I really think you're making a mistake, but I can't force you to do something you don't want to do."

"It'll be fine, Mom. I'll take a step back, and in time, I'll be ready to return to the church with the same enthusiasm I had years ago."

"I hope that's true."

Charlotte hoped it was, too. But to be honest, she just couldn't guarantee it. There were so many things relating to the church that she didn't want to have to deal with anymore, so she wasn't sure how any of that would ever change. Then, to add insult to injury, Curtina was still causing drama, Charlotte's father was in the hospital, and she and Curtis had argued both last night and this morning. So whether she wanted to or not, she was dealing with what seemed like every problem imaginable, and she felt like screaming.

Which was the reason she looked at her mother and lied again. "Oh no. I was supposed to call Curtina's principal first thing this morning to see how things went last Friday. You know that was her first day back from being suspended. So once we finish here I think I'll head outside to get some fresh air and call him."

"That sounds like a good idea."

Charlotte felt awful about what she'd just told her mother, but she had to figure out a way to get out of there. Alone. That way, she could go to her car and drink in peace. She needed to rid herself of all the troubles that were floating around in her head. Not later, not tomorrow, but as soon as possible.

Chapter 19

I'm so glad your father-in-law is doing well," Trina said, making herself comfortable at the end of the sofa in the family room.

Curtis sat adjacent to her in a chair. "We are, too. He had us worried for a while, but God brought him through just fine, and he's recovering well."

"I know Charlotte and your mother-in-law must be so relieved."

Curtis and Trina both turned their attention to a rerun of *Good Times* that was playing in the background. Trina actually seemed a little more energized today, which he was happy about, but he also couldn't stop thinking about Charlotte and the way they'd argued. He couldn't deny that there was a part of him that felt guilty about not being at the hospital with Joe today, but he also hadn't wanted to miss another day of seeing his sister. He still didn't know how long she had, so he'd decided last week that he was going to spend all the time he could with her. Plus, he wondered why Charlotte had seemed so agitated and angry. She was acting as though he'd done a lot more than drive over to Chicago, and he couldn't understand it. Curtis knew she was stressed about her father, but it almost seemed as though something else was going on. Something she wasn't telling him.

"Do you ever think about Daddy's family?" Trina asked. "Because I sort of hate we never got a chance to meet any of them."

"Sometimes. Especially our paternal grandparents."

"I know. And we didn't get to know Mom's parents, either. Mom's dad died when she was a child, and her mom died when I was still a baby. But I never stopped wishing we could've had them in our life."

"I wished for that, too, and now that Charlotte and I have our first grandchild, I'm very much aware of what you and I missed. There's nothing that compares to a grandparent-grandchild relationship. Nothing I can think of."

Trina's face turned sad. "I've heard that from so many people, and I'm sorry my grandchildren won't ever get to know me."

Curtis stared at her.

"And no, I still haven't lost my faith in God—if that's what you're thinking. But I'm also being realistic. I know how sick I am, and so do you."

"I know" was all Curtis said.

Trina smiled. "But hey. At least we got to meet Uncle Bradley and Aunt Samantha," she said, referring to their mother's brother and his wife.

"True, and we met Mom's two first cousins from Ohio, too. Etta Mae and Rayzene."

"That's right. You met them at Mom's funeral. I'd forgotten about that."

"Yep. I'd first met them when we were kids, but I didn't remember them all that well."

"They've both gotten up in age, but I do still talk to them a few times a year," Trina said.

"That's really good. I'm glad you keep in touch with them."

Trina smiled again. "Do you remember all those times Uncle Bradley and Aunt Samantha came over and brought us clothes for the summer? They always came right after the school year had ended. Usually the next day."

"I do remember that. Wow."

"I was always so excited and grateful."

Curtis nodded. "I was, too. They bought us clothing every summer and again when school started back up, and those were the only two times we ever got to wear something new. Well, actually, they always got us a few pieces at Christmastime, too."

"And they gave us money on our birthdays."

"Yep. I remember, and it's so hard to believe they're gone now."

Trina turned her attention back to *Good Times*, but Curtis thought more about Uncle Bradley and Aunt Samantha. He thought about one day in particular when they'd come over to bring some clothing—a day Curtis would never forget.

"Do you like your short sets?" Aunt Samantha asked Trina.

"I sure do," she said, hugging her aunt and uncle. "Thank you so, so much."

Aunt Samantha was a large happy woman with smooth, beautiful skin and an equally beautiful smile. "And two summer dresses and two pairs of sandals are in the bag, too."

Trina pulled out the rest of her things, and so did Curtis.

"*I* picked out your stuff," Uncle Bradley proudly announced. "I know what us men like to wear."

Pauline and Aunt Samantha laughed, and so did Curtis.

"Thank you, Uncle Bradley. Thank you, Aunt Samantha," he said, hugging both of them.

Uncle Bradley patted him on his head. "You're quite welcome, son. We're glad to do it."

"You all didn't have to do this," Pauline said tearfully.

"We wanted to," Aunt Samantha said. "We don't mind at all."

Pauline wiped her eyes. "Well, God bless you both."

"And anyway," Uncle Bradley said matter-of-factly, "somebody's gotta do it. Because that lowlife you're married to sure isn't."

Pauline looked mortified. "Bradley!"

"Well, you know I'm telling the truth, Pauline. He's a worthless, good-for-nothin' lunatic. And he'd better not be putting his hands on you," Uncle Bradley said, and then looked at Curtis. "Is he putting his hands on your mama? Because if he is, I can put a stop to that. Just like I did before."

Curtis shook his head. "No, sir, he doesn't."

Uncle Bradley looked at his niece. "Trina?"

She shook her head, too. "No, sir, he doesn't."

"And what about the two of you?"

Curtis and Trina immediately glanced over at their mother, who was standing slightly behind Uncle Bradley, and she subtly shook her head.

"No, sir," Curtis told him.

"No, sir, he doesn't," Trina added.

"Well, he'd better not be, and I mean that. And if he ever does, I want you children to call me as soon as possible. You hear me?"

"Yes, sir," they both answered.

Pauline seemed nervous and spoke quickly. "Bradley, you leave my babies alone. Curtis and Trina, don't you pay your uncle any mind. Now, take your things and go to your rooms, okay?"

"Yes, ma'am," they both said, gathering their clothing and shoes and leaving.

But as soon as they both entered Curtis's room and shut the door, they heard their mom and Uncle Bradley arguing.

"I don't know why you stay in this ol' crazy situation," he said. "No man is worth all the madness he puts you through. And he's not doing a doggoned thing for these children, either. It's a crying-out-loud shame, and for the life of me, I don't know how you can live with yourself."

"Bradley, please," they heard Aunt Samantha say. "Please don't do this. Just leave it alone."

"Well, I can't help it. This is my sister, and I want better for her. I want better for my niece and nephew."

Curtis and Trina looked at each other, and as usual, tears fell from Trina's eyes.

"Why does Mom take up for Daddy all the time, Curtis?"

"I don't know, and now she's making us lie about the way he treats us."

Trina cried harder, and Curtis tried to console her. It was true that their dad never touched their mom, but he had definitely roughed up Trina a few times, and he flat-out beat Curtis whenever he felt like it. Their father did whatever he wanted, and there wasn't a single thing they could do about it. It was the reason Curtis wished he were dead. Or that he would simply leave and never come back again.

Trina was still watching *Good Times*, but Curtis couldn't stop thinking about his uncle Bradley and how angry he'd gotten with their mother. Until now, Curtis hadn't thought about this particular day in years, and interestingly enough, he still wondered what his uncle had meant when he'd said, "Just like I did before." Curtis had even asked his mom about it later that evening, but she'd told him that she had no idea what her brother had been talking about. Curtis hadn't understood why she was lying about it, because he'd been able to tell from the look on her face that she was. But what hurt him more was the fact that she'd nonverbally told him and Trina to tell Uncle Bradley that their father wasn't abusing them. Curtis hadn't understood that, either, and this single incident had given him yet one more reason to resent his mother. Because even though she wouldn't protect her own child, she seemed to have no problem protecting the monster she was married to. This was, of course, something Curtis had never been able to accept, and truth be told, he still hadn't accepted it today. He likely never would.

Chapter 20

*C*urtis unlocked the door separating the garage from the
kitchen entry area and walked in. But he wasn't looking forward to facing Charlotte. Unfortunately, Jason
had been called into a mandatory emergency meeting at four
thirty, and Curtis had told him he would sit with Trina until he
arrived home. Or he would at least stay until Amber or Eric got
there. Normally Denise wouldn't have minded staying late if
she needed to, but she'd already made plans with her daughter
and parents for the evening. Of course, Curtis didn't mind
staying longer, either, but when he'd called Charlotte she'd listened and then hung up without saying good-bye.

Curtis strolled farther into the kitchen, pulled off his
sweat jacket, and laid it across one of the chairs. Charlotte
stood by the sink staring at him.

"Baby, I know you don't want to hear it, but I'm sorry. I
really am," he said, waiting for her to respond and wondering why she still wasn't wearing any makeup. This morning,
he hadn't thought much about it when he'd seen her at the
hospital, because he knew she was worried about her father.

But at the same time, he also knew that Charlotte almost never went out in public with a bare face. No matter what she was doing or how she was feeling. "So you're not going to say anything?" he asked her.

"There's nothing to say. You did what you wanted, and that's that."

"But you know it's not like that. You know it couldn't be helped."

"Of course it could have. Because had you not driven over to Chicago in the first place, Jason would've found another option. He either would've missed his meeting or gotten someone else to come sit with your sister. Or one of their children would've taken off work. People always figure things out when they have to."

"Yeah, but why should they have to do that when I was already there? Jason has a lot on his plate. He knows how sick Trina is, yet he still has to go to work. They've been down to one income for a while, so it's not like he has a choice."

"And I'm sorry about what they're going through. But we're going through something, too. And you should've been here."

Curtis was starting to lose his patience. "And I was. I spent the entire day and night at the hospital yesterday, and I stopped there again this morning before I left."

"You still should've been there with me today."

Curtis frowned. "Do you know how you're sounding right now? I mean, are you really that cruel?"

"What do you mean, cruel?"

"You are. And you're acting like a selfish little child."

Charlotte raised her eyebrows. "Excuse me?"

Curtis meant every word he'd just said, but he was sorry that he'd allowed his thoughts to leave his mouth.

"Wow. So that's how you feel, huh? That I'm a selfish little child?"

"I'm sorry. I shouldn't have said that."

"You're right. You shouldn't have, and how dare you. But let me just say this: I know your sister is dying, Curtis, but my father could've died, too. So the very least you could be doing is spending time with your *real* family. The family who's been here for you all along."

Now Curtis raised his eyebrows. "You can't be serious. I know you don't mean that."

"I do mean it. Every . . . single . . . word. I have no problem with you going to visit Trina, but what was so wrong with you missing one more day? Why couldn't you have stayed here to support my dad? And what about me and Mom? So you're very wrong for that, and you know it."

"No, you're the one who's wrong for trying to compare my sister to your dad, and also for insinuating that Trina isn't my real family. She's my sister. My own flesh and blood. And nothing will ever change that."

Charlotte rolled her eyes at him and grabbed her jean jacket from the chair. "I'm not arguing about this anymore."

"Where are you going?"

"Back to the hospital to see my father. Remember him?"

Curtis laughed. "And you think that's funny?"

"Nope."

"Well, it sure sounds that way to me, and you really need to stop it."

"And you need to get your priorities straight."

"They are straight."

"Whatever you say," she told him while lifting her purse from the island.

"Does Curtina have any homework?" Curtis asked.

"Yep."

"Is she working on it?"

"I guess. At least that's what she claimed when I asked her."

"And you didn't check to make sure?"

"Nope. And had you come home when you said you were, you could've checked on her yourself."

"Why are you acting like this? What's wrong with you?"

"Nothing, Curtis. Nothing at all," she said, walking past him and out the door to the garage.

Curtis watched as she slammed it shut, and was stunned. Was Charlotte actually jealous of his terminally ill sister? She couldn't be. The reason he knew that was because only a heartless, self-centered person could feel that way about someone who might be dying any day. It simply didn't make sense, and this made Curtis wonder again what was going on. But nonetheless, he hated that his relationship with his sister was causing problems between him and his wife. He didn't want that, and he never wanted Charlotte to think he was putting anyone before her, but he also wasn't about to stop visiting Trina. He didn't want to go against Charlotte's wishes, but her reasoning was completely out of line and pointless.

Curtis went upstairs, strolled down to Curtina's room, and knocked.

"It's open," she said.

Curtis walked in, and strangely enough, she was sitting at her desk, doing her homework. "Hey," he said.

She turned and looked at him "Hi."

"I was just checking on you."

"Daddy, can I ask you something?"

"Of course."

"Why doesn't Mom want you to go see Aunt Trina?"

"I don't know, and I'm sorry you had to hear us arguing about it. Maybe she's just upset about your grandfather."

"Oh."

"Is that all?"

"No."

"Well, what else?"

"Are you ever going to give me my phone back?"

"For now, we want you to focus on your schoolwork and getting your grades back up," Curtis said.

Curtina didn't seem happy about it, but she didn't say anything.

"We know what you're capable of, and so do you. So is there some reason why you all of a sudden stopped getting A's?"

"I just don't like school all that much anymore, and I miss my real mom. I mean, I know I don't really remember her, but I think about her all the time. And sometimes I just wish I could see her."

Curtis wondered where all this "real" stuff was coming from. First Charlotte had talked about who his *real* family was, which she obviously didn't believe included Trina, and now Curtina was missing her *real* mother? Still, Curtis didn't question Curtina, and instead, he tried to be as understanding as he could. "Honey, I know you must be curious about her and that seeing photos of your mom isn't the same as having her here in real life, but at least you didn't have to grow up with no mom at all. Because a lot of children do."

"I still wish I had my real mom."

"I'm sure you do. And maybe Charlotte didn't give birth to you, but she's been every bit of your real mom ever since you were two years old. And that says a lot."

Curtina just looked at him.

Curtis folded his arms. "Is there a reason you're all of a sudden feeling this way?"

"No, I just wish I could have my own mother back. That's all."

"Well, sweetheart," Curtis said, sighing, "as much as I wish you could, that's just not possible."

Curtina looked away from him with tears in her eyes.

Curtis moved closer to where she was sitting and placed his hand on her back. "Sweetheart, what's wrong? Where is all of this coming from?"

"Nowhere," she said, wiping her eyes and sniffling. "Sometimes I just think about her, and it makes me sad."

Curtis rubbed her back. "I'm sorry you feel that way, but the one thing you can be sure of is how much your mom really loved you. You were everything to her, and the hardest part about her having to pass away was knowing that she was going to have to leave you. And I hope you also know how much your mom, Charlotte, and I love you. You mean the world to us. You always have. So are you going to be okay?"

Curtina sniffled again but nodded. "Yes."

"Well, why don't you finish your homework and just maybe I'll let you call one of your friends."

Curtina's eyes lit up like Times Square. "Really, Daddy?"

"Yes, but from my phone, though, not yours."

Curtina's upbeat attitude fizzled almost on cue.

"Oh, so does that mean you don't want to use it?" Curtis said, already turning to walk away from her."

"No, I do, Daddy," she hurried to say.

"Okay, well, you'd better get busy, and just let me know when you're finished with your homework. And I want to see it, too."

"Thanks, Daddy."

"You're welcome."

Curtis left the room, but he couldn't shake the conversation he'd just had with his daughter. She'd brought up Tabitha before and asked questions about her, but she'd never referred to her as her "real" mother. And until recently, she'd always had a very close and loving relationship with Charlotte. So much so that Curtina had never seen Charlotte as some awful stepmother who didn't care about her. Instead, she acted as though Charlotte was, in fact, her biological mother.

Now Curtis wondered if there was some specific reason that Curtina suddenly felt this way. But unless she made up her mind to tell him, there wasn't much he could do to help her. He certainly couldn't tell Charlotte how Curtina was thinking, because as it was, Charlotte was already teed off about his visits to Chicago. So, for now, he would simply hope for the best and pray that God would work things out for all of them—in every area they were struggling in.

Chapter 21

When Charlotte's cell phone rang, she glanced at the number on her dashboard and frowned. It was Bonnie, president of one of the local pastors' wives organizations, and Charlotte knew the reason she was calling. They were planning a fall conference, and a few weeks ago, Bonnie had asked Charlotte to serve as chairperson—something that was the last thing Charlotte wanted to do. She did like most of the women who were members, but there were a select few who had talked badly about her when she and Curtis had been having problems several years ago. Many of them had judged Charlotte and looked down on her—Bonnie included—and it was the reason she'd stopped attending most of their meetings and events. She did attend on occasion, but she certainly had no interest in chairing an event for them, not when she was already trying to distance herself from her own church and anything that reminded her of being a first lady. So hopefully, when Bonnie realized that Charlotte wouldn't be returning her calls, she would ask someone else to volunteer for the job. Plus, right now, even if one of Charlotte's loved ones or her best friend, Janine, called her, she wouldn't be answering. The reason: She didn't want anyone interrupting the new bottle of wine she was enjoying.

Right after leaving the house in a fury, she'd traveled to that same liquor store outside of Mitchell and then driven here to the hospital parking lot. She'd even found a great spot toward the very back of it again, and she felt so relaxed. So at ease and at peace about everything that had gotten her upset. Actually, about three hours before Curtis had come home, she'd finished off the bottle from last night, but it had barely been enough to give her a buzz; hence the reason she'd blurted out things that she maybe wouldn't have said to Curtis had her nerves been calmer. In particular, she was sorry for implying that Trina wasn't his real family. From the time those words had left her tongue, she'd known how cruel they were, but because she'd been hurt, she'd wanted Curtis to hurt, too. She'd wanted him to pay for spending the day in Chicago and not standing by her the way he should have. Then, when she'd thought about all the drama and mistreatment she'd had to endure because of Curtis's position as senior pastor, she'd become angrier. She'd taken a lot and done a lot of things she hadn't wanted to, simply because she was Deliverance Outreach's first lady. She hadn't been perfect, but she'd gone over and above, making sure she made Curtis and the church her top priorities. For her, it was God, Curtis, her family, and the church—in that order—but there were also times when church business and the people inside it tended to supersede Charlotte's time with her family and other personal obligations. Yet Curtis now thought it was okay to place someone before her? A sister who hadn't as much as given him the time of day until a week ago? A sister who he'd begged to forgive him, over and over, even though she wouldn't even talk to him by phone?

Charlotte leaned back in her seat and took another couple of sips of her wine. Then she thought about Curtina and how rude she had been again this afternoon. Here Charlotte had hightailed it home, making sure Curtina had something to eat as soon as she got there—once Curtis had informed Charlotte that he wouldn't be home until after eight—yet Curtina had acted as though she couldn't have cared less. She'd barely even spoken to Charlotte, and with the exception of the one slice of pizza she'd eaten, she hadn't touched anything and had gone upstairs to her room and shut the door. She was so ungrateful, and daughter or not, Charlotte wouldn't continue catering to a twelve-year-old and kissing her little behind.

Charlotte finished off her second cup of wine, ate the burger with onions that she'd picked up from a drive-through restaurant, and got out of her car. She opened her trunk, placing the cooler back inside it, but then flinched when another vehicle pulled into the space next to her. Since Charlotte was parked far away from the hospital, she had a feeling it was someone she knew, and she was scared to death it was Curtis. Still, she took a deep breath, pressed the button to lower the trunk, and looked over to see who it was. She almost jumped for joy when she saw that it was her best friend, Janine. But that didn't stop her from quickly pulling the box of Altoids from her purse and tossing four of them in her mouth.

Janine turned off her car, stepped out of it, and hugged Charlotte. "Hey, dear. And why are you parked all the way in the last row?"

"I just needed a moment to myself. Away from everything and everybody," Charlotte lied. "I needed some time to think about my dad and the problems we're still having with Curtina."

"Well, I really wish you would think twice before strolling through this dark parking lot. It's not a good idea."

"I know, and I won't do it again," she said as they began walking toward the hospital.

"So how is your dad doing, anyway?"

"He's coming along fine, and both his cardiologist and primary care doctor are happy with the way he's recovering," Charlotte said, but she felt a bit tipsy. Until now, she hadn't thought she'd drunk the same amount as last night, but maybe she had.

"Oh, and Carl sends his love and so does Bethany."

"Please thank them for me."

"I will. They both wanted to come, but Bethany has this big science project she's working on, and her dad is helping her."

"I totally understand, and I'll have to give our little god-daughter a call. Maybe she could even serve as an example for her godsister. And she's three years younger than Curtina."

Janine chuckled. "Things have to get better, though, and I'm sure they will."

Charlotte and Janine walked inside the hospital and took the elevator up to the floor her dad's room was on.

Joe put on a big smile. "There's my other daughter."

"Hey, Dad," Janine said, hugging him. "It's great to see you doing so well."

"It's great to be seen, my dear."

Janine went around the bed and hugged Noreen. "How are you, Mom?"

"I'm good, honey, and thank you so much for coming."

"Of course," she said, "and I'm here for whatever you need."

"You're a great friend," Noreen told her, "and like Joe just said, our other daughter."

"I was just telling Charlotte that Carl and Bethany send their love. She has a science project that she needs to finish up, but they're definitely thinking about you and praying for you, Dad."

"I really appreciate that. I need all the prayers I can get."

Noreen agreed. "Yes, and thank God for everyone who has been doing just that," she said, turning her attention to Charlotte. "Not long ago, a few members from the church came by, too. It was very kind of them, and they asked where you were."

Charlotte didn't say anything, but she could already imagine what some of them were thinking. That she should've been there with her father nonstop. Charlotte knew how some of them thought because it had only been two years ago that some women had complained that Charlotte didn't visit the sick and shut-in the way she should—or as much as they believed she should, anyway. Never mind the fact that the church had a very capable and dedicated sick-and-shut-in ministry, and that Charlotte did try to see as many people as she could; these women still didn't feel she was doing enough. Then there was the time when other women had thought she should host a lot more women's events than she had over the last few years. What they wanted was for her to give her absolute all to them and the church, even if it meant sacrificing time for herself and her family. They never thought about things like this. They merely saw her as first lady of a prominent church and assumed that she wanted nothing more than to make each of them happy, even if it left her miserable and empty.

Just as Charlotte finished her last thought, Matthew, Stacey, and MJ walked in.

"Hey, Grandpa," MJ said, walking right past Charlotte and over to the bed. He leaned over and hugged his grandfather.

"Hey, great-grandson, how are you?"

"Good, how are you?"

"Wonderful, and now that you and your dad and mom are here, I'm even better."

"Hey, Grandpa," Matthew said, hugging him, and so did Stacey.

"So what happened to you, Grandpa?" MJ wanted to know. "Why did you get sick?"

"Well, MJ, your grandpa wasn't quite taking care of himself the way he should. But God still took care of me."

MJ wrinkled his forehead. "Why weren't you taking care of yourself?"

Noreen laughed. "Good for you, MJ. Ask him anything you want."

Joe tossed Noreen a playful eye roll.

"Tell me, Grandpa," MJ continued. "Why weren't you taking care of yourself?"

"I just wasn't. I made a mistake, but I won't do that again."

"You promise?"

"I promise, and I'm so sorry I got sick on your big singing day."

"That's okay, Grandpa. I was already finished anyway, remember? So you still got to hear me sing the whole time. Everybody did."

Everyone laughed.

MJ smiled but looked dumbfounded. "Why are all of you laughing?"

"No reason," Matthew said.

"Well, you did an awesome job," Joe told MJ, "and I can't wait to hear you again."

"We all can't wait," Noreen said.

"Thanks, Grandma. Thanks, Grandpa."

They all chatted about one thing or another, and then Matthew looked at Charlotte. "Are you okay, Mom?"

"Yes, I'm fine. Why do you ask?"

"You look tired."

"That's because I am," Charlotte said, trying to appear as though she were completely sober, because now she knew for sure that she wasn't. And her realization had nothing to do with her son asking her a question. Instead, it was because of the way her mom had just looked at her. Noreen hadn't said anything, but Charlotte could tell that she knew her daughter was drinking again. Charlotte could see it in her mother's eyes, and she was ashamed of herself. And for this reason, she wouldn't drink any more after tonight. She would finish the rest of the wine that was sitting in her trunk, and that would be it. For good.

Chapter 22

As expected, Joe had been released from the hospital on Wednesday, and since Noreen had decided to drive him home to Chicago that same afternoon, Charlotte had followed behind them. She'd then spent the night, making sure her parents had everything they needed, and returned home on Thursday. Of course, before she'd left Mitchell, she and Curtis still hadn't been on the best of terms, but by that evening, they'd been so glad to see each other, they'd made up in more ways than one. So, needless to say, life had been good for them for two whole weeks.

But so much for marital peace and harmony, because Curtis had sort of started slipping back into his old ways. He wasn't completely ignoring Charlotte, but to her, he was still being insensitive when it came to her dad, and she didn't like it. Take yesterday, for instance. They'd gotten up like they would on any normal Saturday, but when Charlotte had asked Curtis if he was planning to spend the day at her parents' with her, he'd told her that he'd already invited all the children to drive over to Trina and Jason's. Charlotte hadn't seen anything wrong with that, except for the fact that he hadn't told her about it beforehand. Curtis had simply made plans and assumed she didn't have any of her own. But even after they'd experienced this small misunderstanding, she'd heard him out, understood his reasoning, and had told him and Curtina to have a good time.

She'd also spoken to Matthew and had thought it was great for him, Stacey, MJ, Alicia, Levi, Dillon, and Porsha to go as well. With the exception of Alicia, none of them had gotten a chance to know their father's only sister, and she believed the visit would likely make Trina happy. And as it had turned out, they'd all ended up staying for the entire day. To be fair, though, Curtis had asked Charlotte again if she wanted to come with them, but since she'd already gone with him to see Trina the previous Saturday, she'd told him she would see her another time.

So as far as she was concerned, all had been well—until early evening had rolled around, and not a single one of them had found the decency to drop by to see her father. Not even for a few minutes. She'd just assumed that when they all left Trina's they would come by her mom and dad's. Especially since her parents didn't live more than twenty to thirty minutes from Jason and Trina. Charlotte had been so upset about it, but she did have to admit, that during her drive home last night, she couldn't help wondering if maybe she was overreacting. Her mom and dad had certainly thought she was, and maybe they were right. Maybe she was dead wrong for having any problem at all with the amount of time Curtis was spending with Trina, because it was like he kept telling her, his sister was terminally ill. Maybe her anger toward Curtis had nothing to do with Trina and had everything to do with how miserable *she* was. Maybe she was the essence of that old cliché "misery loves company." Because in all honesty, she truly was unhappy, and she didn't know what to do about it.

Yes, Curtina was acting somewhat better, but that was mostly because she'd been doing all she could to get her phone back—and even more so now that they'd actually returned it to her yesterday morning on a trial basis. She, of course, had no idea that her father had installed tracking software on it, and that he'd already read all of her text message communications from the last twenty-four hours—and reviewed her Internet browsing activity. But the good news was that she hadn't texted anything disrespectful or age-inappropriate, and she also hadn't visited any adults-only kind of web sites.

Still, she wasn't the same child from a few months ago, and she continued to be distant. Not so much with Curtis, but her loving relationship with Charlotte wasn't nearly back to where it should be.

Then there was this church sabbatical she had already begun—the one Curtis still didn't know about. Last Sunday, when she'd told him that she wasn't going to service, he'd wanted to know why, but when she'd explained that she was driving back over to see her father, he had fully understood. He hadn't questioned any other possible motives, and he had also told her he thought it was a good idea.

But that was a whole week ago, and Charlotte wasn't sure

how he would respond to her not going again today. She was about to find out now.

"Why are you still in your pajamas?" Curtis said, strolling out of their walk-in closet and over to the dresser. He stood in front of the mirror wrapping his tie around his neck and under his shirt collar.

"I'm not feeling well," she lied. "I don't know if I'm getting a cold or if I'm just run down from making so many trips back and forth to Chicago. And of course, worrying about my dad."

Curtis pulled his tie through its first loop. "Really? Then maybe you should go to the immediate care clinic."

Charlotte hadn't been expecting him to suggest anything like that, but she kept a straight face and said, "If I feel any worse, maybe so."

"I'm a little tired myself, so once the last service is over, Curtina and I will just plan on coming straight home."

Charlotte didn't say anything, but today was the one day when she'd been hoping that he would leave church and head straight over to Chicago to see his sister. She'd also been hoping that he would take Curtina with him, because that way she'd be able to enjoy her time at home in peace. She'd be able to do what she wanted without either of them seeing her.

"So what do you want me to pick up for dinner?" he asked.

"I don't know. Pretty much anything will be fine."

"Okay, but if you think of something you really want, just text me."

"I will."

"And does Curtina know you're not going to church?" he asked.

"No."

"Well, then you should probably let her know, because I'm sure she thinks she's riding with you and coming a little later."

Charlotte knew he was right, and although she'd never told him this before, she missed the days when they sometimes rode to church as a family. She knew Curtis liked arriving well before anyone else so he could pray, meditate, and review his sermon notes, but when she, he, and Curtina rode together, Sunday morning service seemed a lot more enjoyable. She wasn't sure why exactly, although she suspected that it had a lot to do with the fact that their entire lives were centered around the church. She didn't mind their lives being centered on God and His Word, but sometimes the church seemed to mean a lot more to Curtis than family. He didn't purposely mean for that to happen, and she was sure that if someone were to ask him he would say he never did. But as his wife, Charlotte knew different. She also wondered how many other pastors' wives—how many veteran first ladies—felt the same as her. If she had to guess, there were probably hundreds and maybe thousands. Many like her who hadn't shared their misery with anyone, not even their husbands, and were painfully suffering in silence.

Charlotte got up, went to Curtina's room, and knocked on the door.

"Yes?"

"Are you getting dressed?"

"Not yet."

"Well, since I'm not going to church today, your dad needs you to be ready in about twenty minutes. Have you already showered?"

"I just finished."

"Okay, well, you need to be ready very soon."

Charlotte waited for Curtina to respond, but of course she didn't, probably because she was sitting in her bed texting. Even if she was, though, Charlotte didn't have the energy or desire to open the door and find out. Today was going to be a great, relaxing day, and she wasn't about to let Curtina or anyone else ruin it for her.

After about thirty minutes, Curtina rushed downstairs—something that happened only after Curtis had yelled up to her room with a bit more bass in his voice than he had the first two times. So now Charlotte stood looking out of her bedroom window, watching them back out of the garage, maneuver around the circle driveway, and head down to the street. Charlotte waited for the wrought-iron gate to open and close, and when it did, she smiled.

She hadn't felt this free and relieved in years, so she quickly left her bedroom, strolled down to one of the guest bedrooms, went inside, and walked into the closet. She squatted down, reached toward the very back of it, moved a couple of shoe boxes to the side, and pulled out a small, fluffy brown blanket. She unfolded it and grabbed the pint of vodka that she'd purchased in Chicago yesterday before heading back home. Two weeks ago, when she'd realized her mother knew she was drinking, she'd made a vow to quit again. But it had been more of a struggle than she'd counted on. Still, she'd prayed and fought through her bouts of fiending until yesterday, when Curtis and the children hadn't come by to see her dad. She'd allowed herself to become too upset, and the next thing she'd known, she'd been stopping at a neighborhood liquor store in the suburb where her parents lived. She'd had on full makeup this time, but she'd still pulled her fake glasses and baseball cap from her trunk and put them on before going inside.

Charlotte stood up and went back to her bedroom. There was no one home, and she'd already placed her cell and home phones on silent. What she wanted was to enjoy her vodka in peace and watch a good movie.

Charlotte got in bed, crossed her legs Indian style, turned on the television, and opened her liquor. She took a nice, long swig, straight, no chaser, and half coughed, but boy was it good. She'd told herself that if she ever drank alcohol again, she would stick to wine, but yesterday she'd felt she needed something else. She hadn't wanted to drink and drive or get drunk before Curtis and Curtina had arrived home last night, so she'd waited until she'd pulled into the driveway to take a few sips. And she likely would have taken more, but by the time she'd walked into the house and gotten undressed, Curtis and Curtina had pulled up. So all she'd had time to do was run and hide the bottle in the guest bedroom closet, rinse her mouth with mouthwash, and pull two pieces of gum from her purse.

But now she didn't have to rush or worry about anything, because with Curtis and Curtina attending both services, it would be early afternoon before they returned home. That would give her at least five hours, which was the reason she smiled again, removed the top from the bottle, and took another drink.

But just as she did, Curtina knocked and opened the door all at the same time. "Daddy forgot his—"

Charlotte jumped and nearly dropped the pint of vodka from her hands. "I thought you and your dad were gone," she said, securing the top on the bottle and laying it to the side of her on the bed.

Curtina looked at her like she'd stolen something.

Charlotte wasn't sure what to say, although she wanted to tell her daughter that a child was supposed to knock and wait until a parent told them to come in. Just like Charlotte and Curtis did when they knocked on her door.

"Mom, why are you drinking? You said you would never do that again."

"Um, I know, but it's just this one time."

"Does Daddy know?"

"No, and we're not going to tell him, right? You know how he feels about drinking, Curtina, and this is my last time doing this. I promise."

"Daddy hates drinking because of his father," Curtina said, as if Charlotte didn't know the entire story.

"Exactly, and that's why I'm not going to drink anymore. And the reason you and I are going to keep this to ourselves. Right?"

Curtina ignored her mother's words and walked around to the short hallway in their bedroom where their closet was. "Daddy forgot his phone in his leather jacket."

Charlotte's stomach turned multiple somersaults. What if Curtina told her father everything? What if she squealed about Charlotte's drinking just for the sake of it? Just to be mean?

Charlotte's heart raced, and she could kick herself for not setting the alarm system after Curtis and Curtina had left. Rarely did they arm it when Charlotte or Curtis was home, but if she had, she would have heard Curtina coming back into the house. And why hadn't she just left her bedroom door open after all?

Curtina returned from the closet with her dad's phone and looked at her mom on the way out.

Charlotte swung her legs over the side of the bed. "Curtina?"

Curtina stopped but still had an *I caught you in the act* look on her face. "I don't want to upset Daddy, so I'm not telling him anything. He's already sad about Aunt Trina."

"I know, and again, I'm done with this. I'm even going to pour the rest of this out when you leave."

Curtina still showed no emotion and clearly didn't believe her.

"I have to go," she said. "Daddy's waiting for me."

Charlotte watched as her daughter left the room, praying she would keep their secret. Because if Curtis found out Charlotte was drinking again, life as she knew it would be over. Their marriage would suffer greatly, and there was a chance he would file for divorce. She knew this because he'd threatened to do it before. He'd told her in no uncertain terms that he wouldn't tolerate being married to a drunk. He'd been very serious, and if there was one thing Charlotte knew about her husband, it was that he was a man of his word.

Chapter 23

Charlotte hadn't drunk anything since late yesterday morning, right after Curtis and Curtina had left for church, but then she'd ended up sleeping until they'd returned home. She'd sort of been afraid that Curtis might notice what she'd been doing, but thankfully Matthew, MJ, and Dillon had come over to watch the Bulls play, so he'd spent the rest of the afternoon with them in the theater room. The game hadn't started until five o'clock, but they'd ordered food and hung out together starting two hours beforehand. During basketball season, they tended to do this a lot, and Charlotte loved how close Curtis was with his boys and grandson.

Charlotte stirred the small saucepan of oatmeal that she'd just finished cooking and set it on a cast-iron trivet next to the scrambled eggs, toast, turkey sausage, and juice that she'd already arranged at the center of the island. She knew Curtis was still getting dressed and would be downstairs shortly, but Curtina would likely have to be summoned the same as always. Or at least that was what Charlotte had thought until she saw her walking in with her headphones on, singing. She sat down in a chair, removed the headphones from her ears, and laid her phone on the island.

"Good morning, Mom," she said, and Charlotte wondered who this smiling, cheery stranger was. She hadn't shown this kind of normalcy in months, and it made Charlotte nervous.

Charlotte sat down in front of her. "Good morning."

Curtina took food from each dish and glanced up at the news program on the TV screen.

Charlotte fixed her own plate, but still felt a little uneasy. Yesterday afternoon, while the guys had been watching basketball, Curtina had assured her again that she wouldn't tell her dad what she knew. But Charlotte wasn't fully convinced that she could trust her. Not to mention, this new, happy attitude of hers was making Charlotte doubly skeptical.

"Mom, is it okay if I go to a sleepover at Taylor's this Saturday? She invited me, Lauren, and three other girls from school."

"You'll have to check with your dad, too, but I'm sure it'll be fine. Especially if you bring home good progress reports this week."

"But I don't want to just go to the sleepover, I want to stay until noon or early afternoon like everyone else."

Charlotte ate some of her oatmeal. "You know your dad won't like that."

"Well, I get tired of going to sleepovers and then getting up before seven just so I can come home to get dressed for church."

"Maybe so, but you know your dad doesn't want you missing service."

"I don't know why not, because it's not like I do it all the time."

Charlotte had wondered when rude Curtina was going to show back up, and it hadn't taken more than a few minutes. "I hear what you're saying, but you also know what your dad's response is going to be."

"Yeah, but you can get him to let me do it."

"No, I don't think so, and why can't you guys have your sleepover on Friday night instead?"

"Because Taylor's parents have plans that evening."

"Then you'll just have to wait until another time."

"Why?"

"I just told you. Your dad doesn't like you missing church."

Curtina sat back in her chair. "He doesn't like for any of us to miss church, but you haven't gone for the last two Sundays."

"Curtina, that's because I went to see my dad, remember?"

"Not yesterday. And you weren't sick like you said you were, either."

Charlotte was in shock. Maybe she shouldn't have been, not with all the disrespectful things Curtina had said to her as of late, but she was.

Curtina drank some of her juice. "I want to go to Taylor's sleepover, and I'm not missing it, Mom," she said in a quiet, demanding tone.

Charlotte still didn't comment, mostly because she wasn't sure what she should say or how she should say it. So they both sat in silence, yet the serious look on Curtina's face told Charlotte everything she needed to know: Curtina was already blackmailing her, and Charlotte would have to find a way to convince Curtis to let her go to that sleepover and miss church the next morning. She didn't want to, but she knew she had to or risk having Curtina tell Curtis everything.

Chapter 24

*C*urtis was a bit surprised at how supportive Charlotte had been this morning about his going to see Trina today. For the last couple of weeks, she'd done nothing but complain and act as though he was putting his sister before her, so this sudden turnabout seemed odd. Which made him wonder if there was some special reason for her change of heart. But nonetheless, he was glad she was okay with his spending time in Chicago, because he was tired of arguing about it.

Curtis walked inside Trina's home, and Denise closed the door behind him.

"She's already up, ready and waiting for you in the family room," she said.

"Sounds good," Curtis said, following her down the hallway and into the family room, and when he entered, he smiled at his sister. "Wow, don't you look beautiful."

She smiled back. "Why thank you. I feel pretty good today, so I asked Denise to help me do my hair and put on my makeup. Then she helped me pick out something to wear," she said, looking down at her silk sweater and dress pants.

"What're you so dressed up for?"

"I probably should've given you some warning, but I want you to help me make videos for Jason and the children. I know I could easily do them by myself from my phone, but I thought it might be nice if you helped me. That way, you'll always have a special memory of something we did together as adults."

Curtis looked at her, swallowing hard but refusing to shed tears. He certainly wanted to, but he also saw great joy and happiness on Trina's face, and he didn't want to ruin her idea.

"Okay," Curtis said, sitting next to her on the sofa. "Just tell me what you want me to do."

"Can you get two chairs from the dining room? That way you can sit one of them in front of me and lean my phone against the back of it. And you can sit in the other one right to the side of it."

Curtis did what she asked. "Is that it?"

"Pretty much. I just need you to start and stop it from time to time. We should probably check to make sure the lighting is okay, though. Otherwise I can move to another spot."

"What's your passcode?"

"Zero two zero one."

Curtis smiled. "Mom's birthday."

"Yep."

Curtis clicked on the camera icon, switched the setting

to video, and pressed Record. He let it run for about twenty seconds, hit Stop, and then pressed Play. "It looks fine to me."

"Me too."

"Okay, then," he said, standing the phone up on the chair and leaning it against the back of it. "Let me know when you're ready."

Trina took a deep breath. "I think I'll start with Amber."

"Now?"

"Yes."

Curtis hit the Record button again.

Trina smiled the way mothers do when they are exceptionally proud of their children. "My dearest Amber. My firstborn baby. My heart and joy. My beautiful daughter. To be honest, I wasn't exactly sure of what I should say to you first, but then it came to me. So thank you. Thank you for being the first person I shared unconditional love with—as a mother giving birth to her child. Because of you, I learned what it was like to love someone so deeply that you will go without everything for them if you have to, and you will even die for them...without giving it a second thought. I have certainly always loved your father unconditionally and with all my heart, too, but when you were born, my whole outlook on life and my reason for living changed drastically. It changed as soon as I saw your sweet, precious little face, and I knew then that I had fallen in love like never before. When I saw you, I knew that nothing in this world could ever compare to the love a mother has for her child. I knew from that moment on that you would become my priority, and that I would do everything in my power to take care of you, be here for you, protect you, and give you not just the things you needed but even some of the things you wanted. My goal from the start was to give you a much better childhood than I had. But what makes me smile even more is the fact that you are going to be an even better mother to your children. You are innately one of the most nurturing young women I have ever met in my life—even more so than me—and my grandchildren are going to benefit greatly because of it."

Curtis saw tears welling up in Trina's eyes, but she didn't let them fall.

"But back to what I was saying about my goal of giving you a better childhood than mine—well, that was your dad's goal, too. We both decided that we would make every opportunity we could available to you, but little did we know that you would end up graduating at the top of your high school class, and you would go on to earn both a bachelor's degree in political science and a law degree from Yale. And now you work for one of the most prestigious law firms in downtown Chicago. If that weren't enough, you graduated summa cum laude both times. So to say that I am very proud of you is an understatement, but I truly am. You have been a parents' dream, not just educationally and professionally, but also as a loving, caring, and respectful daughter, and I love you for that. I'm grateful that God gave you to us, and that I was here long enough to raise you up and see some of the many accomplishments I know you will have for years to come.

"I also want to thank you for going to your bosses, handing over your cases, and taking a leave of absence just so you could take care of me. My chemo treatments, radiation treatments, and just the emotional toll that my illness began to take on me, well, sometimes it was harder than I thought imaginable. But when you took off six whole months last year and spent every single one of those days with me, it was the highlight of this entire experience. And as much as I don't want to leave you, and as hard as I know it will be for you as well, I'm not sure we would have spent so many days in a row together during your adult years—that is, if I hadn't gotten sick. We might not even have gotten to say everything we wanted to say to each other while we still could. So thank you again for being such a wonderful daughter and blessing.

"I then want to thank you for being more of a second mother than a sister to your baby brother, because little did we all know he will need you to be exactly that from now on. And the other thing is this: No matter what, always remember that regardless of what kinds of disagreements you have, never turn against each other. And never, ever allow yourself to become so angry that if you do have a disagreement and your brother comes to you apologizing, you won't forgive him. I did that very thing with your dear uncle Curtis, and I now regret it. It is also the reason that this time I've had with him recently has been another awesome highlight of my journey, and I am grateful that God brought us back together when I needed him most. He brought him here when you, your brother, and your dad will now need him most, too, and that gives me peace. And since you have always been just as protective of your dad as you've been with me and your brother, I know you'll be there for him even more than you already are. And that gives me more joy than I can explain. So from the bottom of my heart, my sweet Amber, know that it has been my great honor and privilege to be your mom, and that I will remain in your heart, soul, and spirit always. I will never stop loving you, and neither will God, so remember to keep Him first at all times. Turn to Him, trust Him, and keep your faith in Him...during both the good times and bad...and all will be well. I love you dearly. Always."

Curtis pressed the Stop button, and while he'd told himself that he wouldn't cry, it was becoming tougher by the minute.

Trina blinked back her tears and repositioned her body on the sofa. "I knew this would be hard, saying good-bye to my babies, but it's much harder than I thought. I'm not going to lose it, though. Not before I get a chance to at least finish my message for Eric. Then I might have to wait and do Jason's tomorrow, if you don't mind coming back again."

"Not at all. Whatever you need me to do I'll do."

"I really appreciate you doing this with me."

Trina took a few moments and then took another deep breath.

"Ready?" Curtis asked.

Trina nodded her head, and Curtis pressed the Record button.

"My dearest Eric. So what does a mother say about her second baby, only son, and baby of the family? Although maybe that says it all, as you have certainly become an amazing young man. You were also an amazing baby who hardly ever cried, and a sweet little boy who cared about anyone who was just a little less fortunate than you. Your heart has always been huge, and even today, your dad and I talk about all the times you came home asking if we could buy one of your schoolmates a pair of shoes, or if we could pay for their school supplies, or if we could take them shopping to get a winter coat. The list was infinite, but what you taught us was that if a child could spend so much time trying to figure out what he could do for others, then it was the very least we could do to help you. But more than that, the reason we ended up helping so many children and people of all ages is because of you. You were our child, and we were the adults, but you showed us how important it was to focus more on others than we did on ourselves. So, my precious Eric, we are better human beings because of you, and don't you ever forget that.

"Then, there is the beautiful relationship you have with your sister, and no matter how many times I see the two of you together, it still makes me smile. You have always looked up to her, and I'm glad because now she'll be able to give you what I no longer can. I mean, don't get me wrong, the same as I will continue to be with her, I will also continue to be with you in your heart, soul, and spirit. But how great is it to know that you have a sister who treats you like her son? To me, it just doesn't get much better than that, and I thank God for the bond the two of you have. Then, as for your father, I don't think I'd ever seen him happier than when the ultrasound showed that we were having a boy. Your dad was, of course, thrilled out of his mind when we became pregnant with Amber, but I guess nothing can compare to the love a father has for a son. Your dad was so proud when you were born, and you'd barely become a toddler when he began taking you to see the Cubs, the White Sox, the Bears, the Bulls, and the Blackhawks. Actually, I'm sure this is the reason you have such a great love for just about all sports. And you know what? I pray for the day when you have your own son, and the three of you can go to games together. I also pray for the time when Amber's children and your children will get to grow up together like siblings rather than first cousins. I won't be here in my earthly body to see it, but I will be watching from the arms of our Heavenly Father. And I'm also glad that you have finally gotten a chance to spend some time with your uncle, Curtis, and with all of his children and his grandson. Family means everything…and I do mean everything, so please never forget that, son. Please be there for your sister, through good times and bad, and take great care of your father. But I already know that you will, and that makes me smile.

"I also want to say that having the great honor and privilege to become a mother to such a very handsome and special son has meant the world to me. Many times, I've had friends of mine ask me what Jason and I did to raise such an honorable and respectable young man. And years ago, I used to wonder what they meant. But then I started to pay more attention to the things you said, and more important, the things you did. Opening doors for all ladies from the time you were four. Cringing at men who walked in front of their girlfriends or wives at the mall or in the movie theater. Helping the elderly every time you had the opportunity, even if you didn't know them. So again, you have made us proud, and none of us should have been surprised when you chose to major in public administration in college, for both your bachelor's and master's degrees. And though you are only twenty-six, we're also not surprised about you being the youngest executive director that Chicago Charities, Inc., has ever hired. Your purpose in life has always been to help people who need it the most, and I know you'll continue to do even more good work for decades. All you have to do is keep God in your life and make Him a priority over all else. Allow Him to guide you, my dear son, through every storm and obstacle. Go to Him first, even when you have others to turn to. But then . . . you already do that now, and that makes me happy. And finally, I want you to remember something else. The most important thing of all. I love you with all my heart . . . and I always will."

Curtis turned off the recorder and looked at Trina. The smile she'd managed to display for Eric was gone, and she was crying massive tears. She'd held her emotions together until the very end, but now the reality of saying good-bye to her children was too much. And as Curtis sat next to his sister, holding her, he thought about how much he loved Charlotte, his children, and his grandson, and how he would never want to leave them, either. But more than anything, he grappled with another reality: Unless God decided differently, his sister's time was winding down very quickly. A lot quicker than he wanted it to.

Chapter 25

Charlotte poured herself a glass of brandy and drank almost half of it. She certainly hadn't planned on driving out to her favorite liquor store, but since Curtis was in Chicago, Curtina was at school, and Agnes was off on Mondays, she didn't see a reason not to. Plus, for some reason, she had been kind of bored and had thought it might be nice to buy brandy instead of vodka this time around. She hadn't purchased brandy in years, but it tasted good, and it relaxed her just as well as her vodka did—although vodka was still her drink of choice, and always would be.

After Charlotte finished the rest of her liquor, she rinsed out her glass and then went upstairs to hide her bottle in the guest bedroom closet. It was the one place she knew she didn't have to worry about anybody snooping around in—namely Curtis or Curtina—but she'd also told Agnes years ago that there was no need to clean the closets of the guest bedrooms. Maybe a dusting or two every now and then was fine, but that was it.

Charlotte went into her bedroom and stretched her body

across the bed, face forward. She felt so at peace and wanted to enjoy this feeling for as long as she could. Then she would simply take a nap, making sure to sleep it off before Curtina got home. Curtis wouldn't be back until evening, and she would definitely be sober by then. Or close to it.

Charlotte lay there for another five minutes, nearly dozing off, but then her phone rang.

"Ugh. Who is it?" she said, sitting up and looking at the caller ID on their home phone, and saw that it was her mother.

"Hey, Mom," she answered, trying to sound as though she hadn't been drinking.

"Hey, dear. How are you?"

"I'm good. And Daddy?"

"He's doing great, and believe it or not, he's going along with everything I tell him to do. No arguments about anything."

"Wow, that's really good to hear."

"I know, because I'd sort of thought that, by now, he'd be tired of eating fruits, vegetables, and only baked, broiled, or grilled meat."

"Yeah, me too. But maybe his heart attack really scared him."

"I think it did. He'll never admit it, but it definitely got his attention, and that's a blessing."

"Yes. For sure."

"So how's Curtis?"

"He's fine, and actually he's over there."

"Oh, okay, and how's his sister this week?"

"I haven't spoken to him since he left, but it sounds like she was about the same on Saturday. She's a very strong woman, though. She's handling her illness a lot better than I probably would."

"That's good. Especially for her husband and children, because sometimes the person who's dying can end up being the inspiration for the loved ones they'll be leaving. It's almost as if they find a certain peace about dying and know that they'll be okay. Yet they worry about the people who will miss them."

"I can't even imagine having to leave my children, MJ, or Curtis, or you and Dad. I can't imagine dying so young."

"That does seem to make it harder, and I'm very sorry this is happening. It's so very sad."

"It really is."

"So what's going on with Miss Curtina?" Noreen wanted to know.

"She's about the same," Charlotte said, knowing that things were actually worse now that Curtina had caught her drinking and was using it as leverage to get what she wanted.

"I think she's just going through something. No different than other eleven-, twelve- and thirteen-year-olds."

"That might be, but it's getting on our last nerve, and we weren't prepared for this. We were very naïve in thinking that we would never have to deal with this kind of drama. I was talking to Alicia one day last week, and she reminded me of the time she started communicating with a guy online. Back when she was fourteen."

"Curtis was married to his second wife then, right?"

"Uh-huh. We didn't have social media back then, but she

still met him online and somehow he talked her into meeting him somewhere after school and he raped her."

"I remember you and Curtis talking about that."

"It was awful for Alicia, and I just hope Curtina doesn't start texting and sexting with boys. I hope she's not even thinking about it."

"I hope not, too. But you know what?" Noreen said. "There's someone else I'm more worried about."

"Really, who?"

"You."

"Why?"

"Because I know you've started drinking again."

Charlotte wasn't sure whether to lie or keep quiet. Finally, she chose the latter.

"Are you there?"

"Yes."

"Why are you doing this again, and how did it even start?"

"I'm not, Mom," she said, and knew she didn't sound very convincing.

"Charlotte, you are. I know you are. I knew it when I saw you at the hospital, and I could tell some of the other times I've talked to you on the phone."

"Does Daddy know?"

"I don't think so, but that's neither here nor there. What's important is that you stop."

"I'm not overdoing it this time. I have total control over how much I drink, and it's not like I drink all day."

"But you know you had a problem with alcohol before, right? More than once."

"Yes, but I'll never go back to being drunk all the time. I'm only doing it as a way to relax."

"Honey, I know you believe that, but if you keep drinking, pretty soon you'll be drinking every day again, and then every day will become multiple times a day."

Charlotte didn't want to have this conversation with her mother or anyone else, and she wished Noreen would somehow realize that having a few drinks wasn't that serious. As a matter of fact, the only reason Curtis made such a fuss about it was because of how violent and cruel his father had been to him when he drank. But Charlotte wasn't Curtis's dad, and she wished he would understand that. She wished she could make him see that not every drinker was a chronic alcoholic. Not everyone had an addiction problem, and she didn't, either.

"Well," Noreen said when Charlotte didn't respond to her last comment, "I really wish you would quit."

Charlotte pursed her lips. "Okay, fine, Mom. I will."

"You mean that?"

"Yes."

"I hope you do."

"Mom, I'm really going to stop. You'll see."

"Good, because I've been worried to death about you driving around and about what it could mean for your marriage."

"Everything will be fine. I'll stop drinking, and that will be that."

"Okay, then, well, I'll let you go."

"I love you, Mom, and kiss Daddy for me."

"I will, and I love you, too."

Charlotte set the phone on its base, went into the guest

bedroom, and pulled out her brandy. She didn't even head downstairs to get a glass. Instead, she removed the top, turned it up, and drank straight from the bottle.

Charlotte realized she'd fallen asleep because Curtina was in her bedroom waking her up.

"Mom?"

"What is it?"

"Did you talk to Dad about the sleepover?"

Charlotte sighed loudly. "Curtina, please tell me you didn't wake me up for that."

"Well, did you?"

"No, I decided it was best to wait until Friday. That way I'll have time to come up with a good reason why he should let you go and miss church."

"Maybe you should talk to him about it tonight."

"No, just trust me. Friday is better."

"Well, I also want to start going to the mall with my friends on Saturday afternoons. Not just some Saturdays but every Saturday."

Charlotte sat up, frowning. "I don't know who you've been talking to, but that'll never happen. And you also need to accept the fact that you can't do every single thing you want to do."

Curtina squinted her eyes. "Then why do you get to do whatever you want?"

Charlotte was growing tired of Curtina's mouth. "First of all, I don't do everything I want, and secondly, if I did, I'd be doing it because I'm a grown woman."

"You mean like how you drink because you're grown? Because I can tell you've already been drinking today. Your eyes even look funny."

"I haven't been drinking anything." Charlotte spat. She couldn't stand the way Curtina was using her secret to try to control her.

"I think you have," Curtina said, taunting her.

"I told you I haven't."

"But you were yesterday. I saw you with my own eyes. And anyway, I'm hungry."

"Then order a pizza, because I'm not cooking."

"I don't want pizza. I want Mexican."

"That would be fine except El Molcajete doesn't deliver, and I don't feel like going out."

"Why? Because you've been drinking?"

Charlotte was only two seconds from snatching Curtina back to her senses. But instead, she breathed in and out a couple of times to calm her frustration. "Why can't you just eat pizza, and we can get Mexican tomorrow?"

"I want Mexican today, and I want it from El Molcajete," she basically demanded and left the room.

Charlotte could barely believe what had just happened, and she definitely didn't want to drive under the influence. But then again, she had taken a nap, and she felt completely sober. Plus, the Mexican restaurant wasn't more than three or four miles away at the most. So to keep Curtina quiet, she would go get her the food she wanted. It was either that or once again risk having her blab things to Curtis that Charlotte didn't want him knowing about.

Chapter 26

It had been twenty-four hours since Curtis had watched Trina record messages for Amber and Eric, but he was just as heartbroken as if she had done so today. Now he was sitting in Jason and Trina's family room again, waiting for Denise to help Trina finish getting dressed and ready to record a video for Jason. Curtis knew speaking to Amber and Eric had been hard, and he couldn't imagine how saying her good-byes to Jason would be any different. Still, Curtis was glad she'd asked him to help her with this whole process. All he was doing was setting up her phone and starting and stopping the video, but Trina had been right about this giving them a chance to do something together—one of the last things they would ever be able to do as brother and sister.

Curtis picked up his cell to see if he had any important emails, but most of the messages weren't very urgent. Then he thought about Curtina and how glad he was to see that she wasn't texting boys, talking about sex, or visiting web sites that displayed the wrong kind of photos. With the way she'd been acting, he'd half expected to learn that she was, so he'd been monitoring everything she did daily. Actually, she seemed a lot happier, and although she'd recently told him how much she missed her biological mom, she appeared to be on much better terms with Charlotte. Just yesterday, she'd come downstairs to have breakfast before Curtis, and when he'd gotten home last night, Curtina had come to their bedroom and hugged both of them good night. It had been such a long time since she'd done that, Curtis couldn't remember when she had. So maybe this was a sign of change and proof that better days were ahead.

"Hey," Trina said, slowly walking into the family room, her arm held by Denise, and Curtis could tell she was much more tired than she'd been yesterday. She still looked good for being as sick as she was, though.

"Hey, good morning."

"My plan was to be dressed and ready before you got here, but when I woke up I didn't feel well. It might have something to do with the fact that Amber and Eric were here until midnight."

"That was definitely pretty late."

Trina sat down and Denise left the room. "We were watching Eddie Murphy movies."

"Which ones?"

"*Trading Places, Coming to America*, and *Harlem Nights*."

"Three of his best."

"Yes, and I haven't laughed like that in a long time. And for six hours straight."

"The kids must have come right after I left."

"They did. They got here around five thirty."

Curtis usually tried to stay until Jason got home, but yesterday he'd gotten off a little early. So Curtis had left at five.

"Well, I think I'm situated," Trina said, smoothing back the sides of her hair.

"Ready to roll?"

"Yep, I think so."

"Okay," Curtis said, reaching over and turning on the recorder.

"My dearest Jason. The best man I know. The love of my life. Well, I guess I should start by saying that not in my wildest imagination did I ever think I'd be leaving you a message like this one. Not at fifty-seven years old, anyway. Because I don't think anyone expects that they will say good-bye to the people they love at such a young age. And isn't it funny how when we were married nearly thirty-five years ago, we thought *fifty* was old, let alone fifty-seven? Yet now I don't personally consider anyone to be old until they're ninety," Trina said, laughing, and Curtis agreed with her. "But here we are, and all I can think about is how in love I've been with you for so many years. We married not long after graduating college, had Amber two years later, and then Eric came along. We've been through so much, but even during the toughest of times, we stood by each other, supported each other, and encouraged each other. We are husband and wife, but we are also best friends, and that has been the biggest blessing of all. I used to wonder why our marriage worked so well, but now I know the reason. It's because we don't just love each other, and we're not just *in* love with each other, but we also like each other. And that makes so much of a difference when you're married. Even more so when you've been married for more than three decades.

"I have also spent these last few months thinking about the way we met, how you treated me like a queen the whole time we were dating and then took Mom to dinner to ask for my hand in marriage. And you wouldn't let me go with you," Trina said, laughing. "I still remember wondering what in the world you could possibly have wanted to talk to her about, because not once had you and I had a real conversation about getting married. As a matter of fact, we'd only been dating for six months. But as it turned out, you proposed, and we were married six months later...and Jason...I want you to know that marrying you was, by far, the best decision I ever made. My childhood wasn't good, and to better describe it, it was a nightmare. But then you came along and showed me a whole different way of living. You showed me how to love and how to be loved, and as much as I loved my mom, Curtis and I never saw that in our home. So my first real example of a great marriage was when I met your parents. They laughed and talked the same way I did with my girlfriends, and I'd never witnessed anything like that before. And then if that weren't enough, they've always loved and treated me like a daughter. Even now when your mom calls me, she rarely uses my name and always refers to me as 'daughter.' And I so appreciate that. I'm very grateful to have been blessed with a second set of parents.

"Then there are the two beautiful children we brought into this world. To me, when we got married, our lives were already great, but when Amber and Eric came along, it made our entire world complete. We couldn't have asked or prayed for better children, and I'm glad that they are the kind of loving, compassionate children who will be there for their father. They love the absolute ground that you walk on, and you have been the perfect example of what a father should be. You are a strong, true man of God, you exemplify great integrity, and you're always willing to do whatever you have to for your family. So while my hope was to be able to celebrate another thirty-five years of marriage with you," she said, pausing and swallowing tears, "I'll now have to settle for quite a bit less. But Jason, my dear, my joy, my love...know that I love you with all my heart and from the very bottom of my soul. You have certainly given me the best years of my life, and I am forever grateful to you for that. I will also be with you from now on. Maybe not here on earth, but I will be with you in every other way possible. And finally, thank you for contacting my dear brother. Thank you for calling him and inviting him to our home, because these last three weeks allowed Curtis and I to make things right. It allowed us an opportunity to spend brotherly-sisterly time together, something we never would have been able to do had you not taken matters into your hands. So thank you, my dear. Thank you for just being you, and I will love you always."

Curtis turned off the recording, and tears streamed down Trina's face. She cried with her body heaving, and Curtis sat next to her, holding her again, the same as yesterday. He didn't say anything, but soon he cried just as hard as she did—as though she had already left them.

Chapter 27

*I*t had been a long time since Charlotte had manipu-
lated Curtis into doing something he didn't want to
do. But earlier this morning, she'd done exactly that.
She hadn't known whether he would go along with what she
was suggesting, but she'd finally convinced him to let
Curtina go to Taylor's sleepover *and* miss church tomorrow
morning. She'd had to make a sacrifice herself, though, in
the process, because in return, she'd told him that she
wanted to go with him today to see Trina. Curtis had seemed
pretty shocked, but he'd also been happier than she'd seen
him in a while. Especially when she'd told him that with
everything they'd gone through lately, including her father's
heart attack, she wanted them to spend some time together
with just the two of them; which was the reason they were
dropping off Curtina now at eleven a.m.

Curtis backed out of Taylor's driveway and headed down
the street. "It's so good to see the change in Curtina. She
seems more like herself."

If only Curtis knew the reason, was all Charlotte could

think. "It really is, and that's why I thought it might be nice to let her go to Taylor's right away this morning and stay until tomorrow afternoon. She's really trying," she said, knowing that this couldn't be further from the truth, and that Curtina was only pretending to have changed for the better so she could get what she wanted. If only Charlotte had set that alarm system and had heard her come back into the house last Sunday, Curtina never would've caught her drinking.

"I agree, and she's still not texting anything out of the ordinary, which is good. She did tell Taylor and Lauren on a group text, though, that she can't wait until she's sixteen so we can buy her a brand-new car. That way, she'll finally be able to drive and go anywhere she wants. Of course, Taylor and Lauren just loved that whole idea."

"I'm sure they did, and I guess none of them know that we'll still be monitoring everything Curtina does."

"Exactly, until she leaves for college."

"And what about her Internet browsing?" Charlotte asked.

"She visits a lot of department store web sites. And I do mean a lot of them. But I guess she has that honestly."

Charlotte turned and looked at Curtis over the top of her sunglasses, smiling. "Is that a hint?"

"Take it any way you want," he said, laughing.

"Yeah, right. Although you do have to admit, I don't shop nearly the way I used to."

"I agree, and why is that?"

"I don't know. I just don't feel the need to do that anymore," she said, wishing she had the courage to tell him that she no longer cared about trying to impress people at church or anywhere else. If only she could tell him her true feelings about being first lady. But for some reason, she still couldn't.

"Times change and so do people, and that's a good thing," he said.

"It is.

"But you know what else?"

"What's that?"

Curtis looked at her and then back at the road. "I'm really glad you wanted to go see Trina. I know you don't understand why I'm making all these trips back and forth to Chicago, but baby, she's getting weaker all the time. I noticed it a lot this week when she was recording those videos."

"I'm so sorry, and I'm glad I'll be able to see her today."

They drove another minute or so in silence, and then Curtis said, "And on a lighter note, since you thought we needed some alone time, I hope you'll still be feeling that way tonight."

Charlotte shook her head, and they both laughed. "You kill me, but we'll have to see what we can do about that."

Curtis eyed her up and down with a smirk on his face, and Charlotte hit his arm. She loved, loved, loved Curtis, and it was the reason she had to stop drinking before he found out. Before Curtina told everything. Because sadly enough, she'd done something this morning that she hadn't done since she'd started back drinking. She'd snuck into the guest bedroom while Curtis had been showering, taken a few sips of vodka, and then rushed downstairs to make a quick cup of coffee in the Keurig. A few days ago, she'd been searching online and had discovered that coffee, like onions and garlic, eliminated the smell of liquor. So by the time Curtis had come downstairs in his robe to have a cup himself, she'd just been finishing hers and had gone back up to their bedroom to get dressed. Then, when he'd returned upstairs as well, she'd gone downstairs again to make a second cup of coffee, which must have worked, because Curtis hadn't noticed that she'd been drinking.

When they arrived at Jason and Trina's, Jason let them in, and now the four of them were sitting around laughing and talking.

"Curtis, remember that time you stood up on one of the picnic tables at the park? You told me and some of the other kids to sit on the grass so you could deliver your message. And the thing is this, you were only ten."

They all laughed.

"Yeah, I remember very well, and I also remember all the Amens you guys gave me."

"I know," Trina said. "We were playing church, but in all seriousness, I knew you weren't joking. I always thought you would end up being a minister."

"Really?"

"I did. So when I heard all those years ago that you'd moved back to the Chicago area and had become pastor of Faith Missionary, I wasn't surprised. And neither was Mom."

"I received my calling very early, even though I tried to ignore it for as long as I could."

Jason agreed. "I think that tends to happen to most of us.

When we're kids we usually know what feels natural to us, but sometimes it takes years before we pay close attention to our passion and the purpose God has for our lives. When I was a teenager, I knew I loved drawing more than anything else, but it never occurred to me that I would become an architect for large commercial buildings."

"That's very true," Trina said, "because I was the same way. It took me years to realize I wanted to be a counselor for single mothers and rape victims. Mom wasn't a single mother, but it always felt like she was, and that feeling never left me. So I finally went back to school in my forties to get a master's in counseling."

"That's awesome," Charlotte said, thinking back to when she was twenty-five and recently married to Curtis. She'd held a position at a law firm as a paralegal, and while she hadn't thought it then, one of the firm's wealthiest clients had told her that she would make a great attorney. At the time, though, Charlotte had only been interested in Curtis doing all he could to make as much money as possible. She hadn't considered that there might come a day when she wished she'd done more with her life. Because even as first lady of a church, she was beginning to think there was a lot more she could be doing for women outside of it as well as for those who were members.

They all chatted and discussed old times, and finally Jason stood up. "So, Curtis, man, I need to make a run to a couple of stores to get a few things. You can ride along if you want."

"I will," he said, scooting his body to the edge of the chair.

"Can I get you ladies something to drink or eat before we leave?" Jason asked.

"I'll have some mango tea, if you don't mind," Trina said.

"And I'll have some coffee if it's not too much of a bother," Charlotte said.

"Wow," Curtis said. "Another cup of coffee? And not only that, you want one in the afternoon? Next thing you know, you'll be bouncing off the walls in here."

Everyone laughed.

"I mean, I know you love coffee, but you rarely drink any after noontime," Curtis continued.

He didn't know that she'd actually had two cups of coffee this morning and that this would be her third, otherwise he might question her more. "I don't know, I guess I just have a taste for it. Plus, I didn't sleep well last night."

"I guess," he said, and he and Jason went into the kitchen.

Then, after they brought Trina and Charlotte their beverages, they left the house.

Now Charlotte sat on the sofa with Trina, picking up her coffee from the glass table.

Trina sipped some of her tea, set it on the table, and slightly turned her body toward her sister-in-law. Then she grabbed her hand. "Charlotte, thank you."

Charlotte smiled at her. "For what?"

"Because I know how much Curtis loves you, your children, and your grandson. He loves all of you more than life itself. And I know my illness has really interrupted your lives. I know that all my phone calls to Curtis and his visits here to Chicago have been a lot. But I hope you can tolerate all of this just a little while longer, because what I want is to leave here knowing that Curtis and I have spent as much time together as we possibly could."

Charlotte squeezed Trina's hand, and then slid over and hugged her. Soon they were both crying, and Charlotte felt like the worst person in the world. Here she'd had the cruel audacity to be angry at Curtis because of all the time he was spending away from her and mad at Trina for calling so often. When all Trina and Curtis had wanted was to enjoy what little time they had left with each other. They'd had their whole childhood taken away from them and both their parents were deceased, so all they had now from that part of their family was each other. That was it. And worse, when Trina was gone, Curtis wouldn't even have her.

Now Charlotte cried harder than Trina—for the terrible loss Curtis would have to endure and also because of how selfish she'd been about everything. But from here on out, she would encourage Curtis to go see Trina anytime he wanted, day or night or even in the wee hours of the morning. Whatever it took, Charlotte would support Curtis completely.

Chapter 28

C urtis locked his hands against his abdomen and gazed out his office window. He'd driven to the church around eight this morning, and now he couldn't help thinking again about the great weekend and Monday he'd had. He, of course, always enjoyed spending time with Charlotte, but to be able to laugh and talk with her, Trina, and Jason all at once, well, that had been the best. Then, when Curtis and Jason had returned from the store, Amber and Eric had arrived, and Curtis was thankful for the close relationship he was building with his niece and nephew. For the first time in years, he knew what it was like to connect with extended family, and it felt good.

Then, after they'd left Jason and Trina's, they'd stopped by his in-laws' for a couple of hours, and he'd been glad to see how well Joe was doing. He acted as though he hadn't been sick, which was a blessing, and he and Curtis had laughed about everything imaginable.

So, yes, it had been one of the best weekends Curtis had had in a long time, and the fact that he and Charlotte had made love like two newlyweds when they'd gotten home had only added to his happiness. He still couldn't understand why Charlotte had missed church two days ago, though, but because she'd seemed noticeably tired on Sunday morning, he hadn't questioned it. Actually, she'd lounged around the house most of yesterday, too, so maybe she just needed some rest.

Many more thoughts crossed Curtis's mind, but most of them fell on Trina. Her time seemed more and more limited, and Curtis could tell she was losing weight and her appetite. Then, when he and Jason had gone to Sam's, Jason had told him that Trina was now making calls to everyone she cared about—family, friends, and even acquaintances she hadn't spoken to in a while—and she was constantly reminding him of the things she wanted to have at her funeral. Jason had shared all he could just before breaking into tears, and as Curtis sat in his office thinking about it now, tears fell from his own eyes.

Curtis sat in silence for a few more minutes and then turned around and picked up the book Trina had given him before he'd left her house last Tuesday. When he'd taken a look at it, he'd asked her what it was, but all she'd done was look at him and say, "Read chapter ten."

Curtis turned to that chapter, which was entitled "Forgiving a Deceased Loved One." He read the first two pages, and it was the following passage that caught his attention: "If you're angry at a deceased loved one who hurt you, you're still allowing that person to hurt you spiritually, mentally, and emotionally. It also means that you still haven't forgiven them, and until you do, your painful memories will haunt you for the rest of your life. Even if you walk around smiling as though all is well and announcing to the world that you've forgiven every *living* person who has hurt or betrayed you, if you don't forgive your deceased parent, child, or other family member, you will never be free. You will always struggle internally, and you'll be disobeying God's Word."

Curtis knew what he'd read was true, because as a pastor, he'd counseled many of his members and given them similar advice. But somehow, he just hadn't been able to forgive his father or his mother. For some reason, he didn't think they deserved it, and he wasn't sure he would ever be able to change his feelings about that.

Curtis read more of the chapter until his phone rang.

"Hi, Miss Lana."

"Hi, Pastor. I have Curtina's school on the line. It's her English teacher calling."

"Please put her through, and thank you."

Curtis waited for Miss Lana to connect the call and wondered what his daughter had done now."

"I have Ms. Anderson for you, Pastor."

"Thank you. How can I help you, Ms. Anderson?"

"Hello, Pastor. I'm really sorry to bother you, but when your wife didn't answer I decided to call you instead. I won't be here this afternoon, so if she calls me back there's a chance I'll miss speaking to her."

"It's no problem at all, and I'm glad you contacted me."

"Well, unfortunately, Curtina hasn't turned in her last two assignments, and when I asked her about them, she wouldn't respond. She simply stared at me like I hadn't said a word."

"I am so sorry to hear that, Ms. Anderson. And as you know, Curtina was also recently suspended, so we're not sure what's going on with her."

"I don't know, either, because when school started last August, she was one of my best students. She was also very outgoing and polite."

"She was the same way here at home, but now, not so much."

"Well, I know you and Mrs. Black have been requesting progress reports from a couple of her other teachers, so I wanted to let you know."

"Yes, I really appreciate it. Also, can you tell me what the assignments are? Because I'll be having a talk with her as soon as I get home."

"The one from last week was a one-page paper about any topic of her choice, and the paper I assigned last night was very simple. All she needed to write was a paragraph relating to something she'd read about in yesterday's newspaper. But she didn't turn that in today, either."

"This is so uncalled for," Curtis said.

"I agree, and please let me know if there is something I can do on my end. She's a very intelligent young lady, but for some reason, she's not doing her homework."

"Does she have new homework for tonight?"

"Yes, she needs to read the first two chapters of *To Kill a Mockingbird*. More if she wants, but I at least want the class to read two chapters per night."

"Sounds good, and again, I'll talk to her this evening."

"Thank you, Pastor Black, and please take care."

"You too."

Curtis was beyond angry and disappointed. What was wrong with Curtina? Didn't she know how blessed she was to not only have the opportunity to learn but also to attend a private school? She just didn't know how good she had it, and if she didn't get it together, her chances of getting into a good college would be next to none.

Curtis sat steaming, but then he thought about his own school years and how tough they had been. Not because he wasn't smart or struggled in school, but because he'd spent most of junior high and high school being teased by other kids.

"Hey, welfare boy," Johnny Mason yelled as he and three of his flunkies trailed closely behind Curtis. They were all headed to Casper Junior High School, and Curtis couldn't wait to get there and hurry inside.

"And look at those Goodwill tennis shoes he has on," Wilbur Jones said, laughing loudly.

The others laughed, too, but Curtis did what he always did: ignored them.

"And look how dirty they are," Timothy Lewis announced. "They used to be white, but now they're brown . . . like a pile of dog doo-doo!"

Curtis quickly turned and looked at them to see how much they were gaining on him. He wanted to cry when he saw all four boys laughing so hard that they had to lean against each other to keep from falling.

"Didn't your mom get her welfare check this month?" Donald Voss wanted to know. "Couldn't she at least buy you another pair of shoes from the Goodwill? Or maybe the Salvation Army?"

"How could she do that?" Johnny Mason said. "She probably had to use her check to buy his drunk daddy some whiskey."

"Oh yeah, that's right," Timothy Lewis added, "because my mom says Thomas Black is a worthless alcoholic."

"Well, I heard from my mom that he beats ol' Curtis, too," Donald Voss blurted out.

"Yep," Wilbur Jones said. "I heard the same thing, and remember that time he had that knot on his head, and he told everybody he fell down a whole flight of stairs?"

"Yep," Johnny Mason said, "and then we found out that the dump he lives in doesn't even have a second level. And outside, it only has three steps leading up to the front door."

Curtis's eyes filled with tears, and he stepped up his pace.

Donald Voss laughed. "Yep, he was just lying because he didn't want us to know his drunk daddy was beating that behind."

"Exactly, and that's probably why he keeps that big head of his buried in those books all the time," Wilbur Jones exclaimed. "If he doesn't get all A's, his drunk daddy will probably beat that behind some more."

Tears streamed down Curtis's face, and he walked even faster.

"Wait up, welfare boy," Johnny Mason yelled after him.

"Yeah, wait up, doo-doo shoes," Timothy Lewis said.

When Curtis couldn't take it anymore, he finally ran as fast as he could the rest of the way. He hated having to deal with Johnny and his crew, and he couldn't wait until the school year was over. He knew he would have to see them again next year in high school, but if he was lucky, something bad would happen to all four of them. Or at the very least, they'd be kicked out of school and sent to juvenile—where they rightfully belonged.

Curtis snapped back from his past and realized his face was wet. His painful childhood was still affecting him, and he wondered if he would ever move beyond it. He also wondered again if Curtina knew how good she had it. But even if she didn't, he was going to set her straight when he got home. Once and for all.

Chapter 29

Curtis walked into the house, shut the door harder than usual, and yelled for his daughter. "Curtina, get down here, now." He waited only a few seconds, and when he didn't hear any walking upstairs, he yelled louder than the first time. "Curtina!"

Finally she made her way into the kitchen, looking afraid and guilty.

Charlotte walked in behind her. "What's going on?"

"Why don't you ask your daughter?"

"Curtina, what is your dad talking about?"

"I don't know."

Curtis frowned. "I got a call from your English teacher," he said, and then looked at Charlotte. "She tried to call you, but you didn't answer."

"Oh, I don't know how I missed that. I'll have to check my voice mail."

"Well, your daughter here hasn't turned in two of her assignments. Even though she knows that we've talked to her about her grades."

"I'm only missing one assignment, not two," Curtina said.

"So are you calling your teacher a liar?"

"No, but she's not telling the truth, either."

Curtis folded his arms. "Okay, wait a minute. Are you try-ing to be funny?"

"No."

"Well, I'll tell you what. Both of those papers had better be turned in by tomorrow morning. You also have a read-ing assignment for tonight, so be prepared to tell me anything I ask you about the first two chapters in *To Kill a Mockingbird*."

Curtina's eyes widened, and she was obviously shocked that her teacher had also told him about her homework for this evening.

"And another thing," Curtis said. "Go upstairs, get your phone, and bring it back down here."

Curtina huffed loudly. "Why?"

"Because I said so, and because you don't appreciate special privileges. Now go get it."

Curtina looked at Charlotte with begging eyes. "Mom, please talk to Daddy."

"I will, but just go get your phone and bring it downstairs for now."

Curtina left the kitchen.

"What was that all about?" Curtis asked Charlotte.

"Well, she's been doing so well, maybe we can give her one more chance. But only if she turns in all three assign-ments tomorrow."

"But as it is, she's been suspended, and she's doing terribly in her classes. So I think we've given her all the chances she needs."

"I know, but with the exception of today, she's really been trying to do better."

"I agree, but I don't like this getting-calls-from-the-school thing."

"I don't either, and if she messes up again, then we will take her phone for good."

"I'll think about it," he said, but only because he did want to keep an eye on what Curtina was texting about.

Curtina came back into the kitchen and gave Curtis her phone, but she looked at Charlotte while she was doing it. "Mom, did you talk to him?"

"I did."

Curtis laughed, but he certainly didn't think anything was funny. "So you're going to talk about me in third person like I'm not even standing here? Who is *him*?"

"I'm sorry, Daddy, but please don't take my phone. I'll turn in my homework from now on. I promise."

"We'll see," he said, "and I suggest you get upstairs so you can get to work."

Curtina looked at both her parents with pitiful eyes, but that had stopped working on Curtis a long time ago. So when she realized that her father still wasn't giving her phone back to her, she left again.

"This can't continue," he told Charlotte, "and if she doesn't get better, she might be the first of our children to be sent away to a boarding school. A few years back, one of the elders at the church sent his daughter to a school for all girls, and I think it was faith-based, too."

"You don't think it's come to that, do you?" Charlotte asked.

"Maybe."

"You're really serious?"

"I am. I'll do whatever I have to if it means getting her the discipline and education she needs."

Charlotte walked around the island, and Curtis could tell she didn't like the sound of what he was saying. But he also wondered why she was placing a K-cup in the Keurig machine and filling the reservoir with water at five p.m., when normally she never drank coffee after noon. He'd brought this same point to her attention on Saturday, so he couldn't understand what the sudden change was about. But then it dawned on him. Was Charlotte drinking again? Was that the reason she had missed church three weeks in a row and was no longer complaining about the amount of time he was spending with Trina? Did she now *want* him to go to Chicago so she would be free to drink as much as she wanted? And was that the reason she'd missed the phone call from Curtina's English teacher? Had she been out at some restaurant drinking? Curtis sure hoped not, because he didn't need these kinds of problems right now. He had enough to worry about already. His sister and his daughter especially. So there was absolutely no room for alcohol issues. None whatsoever.

Chapter 30

Curtis had driven over to Trina's a little earlier than usual, but it was mostly because he'd needed to think. He'd also tossed and turned all last night, worrying about Curtina and hoping Charlotte wasn't drinking again. At one point, he'd thought about asking Charlotte, but if it turned out that he was accusing her of something she wasn't doing, he knew it would mean trouble. Charlotte would become angry and defensive, and one thing would lead to another. And he didn't want that. So instead of hanging around the house, he'd gotten up at three, worked out on the treadmill, showered, and slipped on a sweater and a pair of jeans. He'd left the house by six, and while he'd half expected Charlotte to ask him why he was leaving so early, she hadn't. This also made him think that she was glad he'd be gone for the day, but on the other hand, she did now completely support his visits to Chicago to see his sister. So maybe he was just being paranoid.

Trina tried positioning herself in bed so that she wasn't lying so far back, and Curtis added two more pillows to help her. For the past couple of weeks, she'd been getting up and spending most of her time in the family room, but today she'd wanted to stay in her pajamas—today, she not only looked weak, she was exhausted, and the circles around her eyes were much darker. Curtis had only missed three days of seeing her, yet her health seemed to have turned for the worse in that short period of time. Her blood pressure was dropping, and her bladder wasn't producing much output, which meant her organs were slowly shutting down. So much so that Denise had advised Jason that it might not be long before Trina would need hospice services. Curtis hadn't wanted to hear that kind of news and neither had Jason, but Jason had still decided that today would be his last day of work for a while. He was even planning to get off earlier than usual.

"So what did you think of the chapter I asked you to read?" Trina asked.

"I thought it was good."

"Then have you considered going to Dad's grave site to forgive him?"

"I don't know. Maybe. But I'd need to come to terms with quite a few more things before I do."

"Like what?" she said, covering her mouth and coughing.

"Well, for one thing, why didn't Mom protect me from Dad? Why didn't she take us out of that madness? And why did Dad take all of his anger out on me? Why was I the only one who got beaten? Why didn't he beat Mom? Because most men who beat their children always beat their wives and girlfriends."

Trina stared at him. "I know why. And the only reason I've debated telling you is because I've been so afraid it would hurt you even more and make you angrier than you already are."

Curtis couldn't imagine what was so bad that Trina didn't want to tell him, but he wanted to know what it was. He *needed* to know what it was. "Just go ahead and tell me. It'll be fine."

Trina sighed. "Remember when Daddy used to say to Mom all the time that she'd better be glad he didn't believe in hitting women or she'd be a dead woman?"

"I remember every word."

"Yeah, well, truth is, Uncle Bradley *made* Daddy not believe in hitting women."

Curtis scrunched his forehead. "How?"

"Before you were born, even while Mom was carrying you, Daddy would beat her, and then when I was born and you were two years old, he beat her so badly that she had to be rushed to the hospital. Both her eyes were swollen shut, and she had bruises all over her body. And that's when Uncle Bradley and one of his friends came to the house and beat Daddy nearly to death. They left him for dead, and he ended up being in the hospital for a lot longer than Mom. He was there for three weeks."

"And Mom told you all of this?"

Trina coughed again a couple of times. "Yes. She wanted me to know what life was really like for her, and then she apologized for bringing you and me into a violent situation we didn't ask for."

"Gosh, I hate that she had to go through that. And now I'm even sorrier for not seeing her for so many years. There's still something I don't understand, though."

"What's that?"

"Why he stopped beating her."

"He stopped because Uncle Bradley told him that if he ever saw another bruise, cut, or anything on Mom ever again, he would kill him. He would shoot him dead and then turn himself in to the police."

"Yeah, but Thomas Black was crazy. So it's hard for me to believe he just up and stopped abusing Mom simply because someone threatened him."

"Well, according to Mom, he did. He was really afraid of Uncle Bradley, but Mom also said that she believed it was more about Daddy's ego, too. By saying that he didn't believe in hitting women, that made him feel like it was his decision not to hit Mom instead of it being because he was afraid of his brother-in-law. Daddy would never have wanted to be seen as a coward. Not when he was so used to being a bully who controlled everybody. And to be honest, I think Daddy was bipolar. And then by the time we were older, his illness had gotten much worse, which made him more violent than he'd ever been."

Curtis wasn't sure he believed that theory. "Mmm, I don't know about that."

"You said yourself he was crazy, but I think he had real mental issues, because Mom told me that right after Uncle Bradley and his friend beat him up, he tried to change. He even went to see a doctor and started taking medicine. And it was the only time he treated her like he loved her. But after a few months, he told her that he didn't like the way those 'crazy pills' made him feel, and he threw them out. And, of course, all the drinking started up again. But then instead of beating Mom, he took his frustrations out on her in a whole other way."

"How?"

"He raped her whenever he felt like it. And she let him, because she didn't want us to know about it. She never screamed or did anything. She just let him rape her for all those years."

Curtis felt as though he was having an out-of-body experience. "This is totally insane."

"I know, but at least it explains why Mom couldn't leave. She was terrified of Daddy, and she was also afraid that if Uncle Bradley ever found out that Daddy was beating you, he would kill him and end up in prison. So that's why she never wanted him to know. She said she went out of her way to keep everything hidden from Uncle Bradley."

Curtis stared at Trina but didn't respond to what she'd just told him.

"I know this is a lot to take in, but you're never going to be okay until you forgive Daddy," she told him. "And Mom, too, because I know as a parent, you still feel like she should have protected you before protecting Daddy or Uncle Bradley. But, Curtis, Mom had battered wife syndrome. I know that doesn't make up for what happened to you, but she did."

Curtis heard what his sister was saying, but he still didn't speak. The reason: He didn't have words, and he could barely believe what Trina had just shared with him. But what stood out more than anything else was the fact that his mom had been raped repeatedly by his father. The man had raped his own wife and thought nothing of it. He'd terrorized all of them, Curtis, Trina and their mother, and now after all these years, Curtis was still suffering the consequences. He was still hurting like a small child, and he wondered when he would finally get over it. When he would finally be able to leave his past where it belonged and focus on all the blessings God had given him as an adult. Although, sadly, as he looked at his sister, he was reminded of how ill she was and how when she died, he would find himself feeling more pain than he already was. His childhood trauma had been one thing, but losing his sister was the kind of devastating loss that he just wasn't ready for.

Chapter 31

For a while, Charlotte had thought Agnes would never leave. She'd long finished cleaning the house and had even prepared a nice salmon dinner for them to eat this evening, but she'd then hung around talking to Charlotte for more than an hour. Charlotte loved Agnes, but today, she'd wanted her to leave on time so she could go upstairs, pull her vodka out of the closet, and drink it in peace—which was exactly what she was doing now. But then her phone rang, and she hoped it wasn't the school calling. It rang again, so she took another swig of vodka, finally picked up her phone, and saw that it was Sonya Miller. She had a mind not to answer it, but as it was, she still hadn't spoken to Sonya about the church's twentieth anniversary. Worse, the day Charlotte's dad had gone into cardiac arrest, she'd told Sonya to call her on that upcoming Tuesday, but because Joe had been in the hospital, she hadn't been able to talk to her. That had been more than three weeks ago, and in all honesty, Charlotte hadn't thought any more about it. Although, come to think of it, Sonya and a few other women at the church had left her messages, checking to see how she was doing. But what they'd actually wanted to know was why she hadn't been to church. So she hadn't bothered returning any of their calls.

Charlotte set her bottle of vodka down and pressed the Send button on her cell phone. "Hello?"

"Hi, Sister Black. How are you?"

"I'm good. What about you?"

"I'm doing well, and how is your dad coming along?"

"He's doing great. He's recovering very quickly."

"I'm so glad to hear that."

"Thank you."

"We've missed seeing you at church."

"I know. But with my father being ill, I've spent quite a bit of time over in Chicago. And you know Curtis's sister is very ill, too."

"Yes, we've all been praying for her."

"We really appreciate that."

"Well, the other reason I'm calling is to see if we can talk more about our women's ministry and the church's anniversary next year."

Charlotte didn't want to have this conversation, but she also didn't want to be rude to Sonya. "I liked the four ideas you told me about last month."

"Okay, well, I'll start putting together a meeting agenda. That way we can discuss it in more detail on Saturday."

"What's happening on Saturday?"

"Our women's leadership meeting."

Charlotte doubted that she would be there, but she said, "Okay, then that sounds perfect."

"Well, I won't hold you any longer," Sonya said, "but it was good to hear your voice."

"Same here."

"See you on Saturday."

"Take care."

Charlotte set her phone on the nightstand and took another large gulp of liquor, then she glanced at her watch. Curtina would be out of school in a couple of hours, so it was probably best for her to take her bottle back to the guest bedroom. But as she walked past Curtina's room, she thought she heard a dinging sound. So she stopped to listen, but there was nothing. She waited a few seconds longer and then walked down to the guest bedroom, wrapped her bottle in the blanket, and headed back to her own room. However, as she passed Curtina's room a second time, she heard the same dinging sound again.

This time, she walked inside and realized that what she was hearing was some kind of phone notification. Either for text messaging, email, or some social media platform. It seemed to be coming from Curtina's closet, so Charlotte opened it and searched through a couple of shoe boxes. She didn't see anything, so she searched inside one of Curtina's storage containers on her top shelf. Then the dinging started up again, and now Charlotte could tell it was coming from the far right of the closet. So she reached through a few pieces of clothing until she found what she was looking for in one of Curtina's jean jackets. It was indeed a phone.

Charlotte wondered whose it was, because once Curtina had showed Curtis her finished homework assignments last night, Curtis had given her phone back to her. Plus, this device didn't look like her phone, anyway. It looked similar, but it wasn't the phone Charlotte had purchased for her. Had Curtina somehow bought another phone without her parents' knowledge?

Still, Charlotte took a chance and typed in the same passcode that Curtina used for the phone she and Curtis *did* know about. But it didn't work. She tried a couple of others, but when the phone still didn't open, she stopped trying before she reached the maximum number of attempts allowed. She then debated calling Curtis. But she knew if she did, Curtina would tell her father that Charlotte was drinking again, and she just couldn't chance that kind of disaster. So instead, she would wait and make Curtina give her the code when she got home.

Charlotte closed Curtina's closet and went back down the hallway, then she heard her own phone ringing again. It was the school, and Charlotte was almost afraid to answer it, because there was no telling what kind of trouble Curtina had gotten in. Why wouldn't she stop all this nonsense? Because if she didn't, Curtis would follow through on his idea about sending her to a school that could deal with her.

The phone rang again and again, and Charlotte finally answered it. "Hello?"

"Mrs. Black?" the school principal said.

"Yes?"

"This is Mr. Norton, and if possible, we need you to get here as soon as you can."

Charlotte panicked. "Oh no, is Curtina okay?"

"She is for now, but one of our security officers just caught her and another student having sex in the girls' bathroom."

Charlotte dropped down on her bed, speechless. Surely she hadn't heard Mr. Norton correctly. Either that, or she was simply dreaming and needed to wake up. She knew it had to be one or the other, because there was no way Curtina was having sex at school. There was no way she was having sex, period.

Chapter 32

Charlotte hurried through the main entrance of Mitchell Prep, signed in at the security desk, and walked down the atrium corridor to the administration office. Her stomach twirled round and round, and her heart raced at the same time. What a nightmare, and there was a part of Charlotte that kept hoping that Mr. Norton had made a mistake. Maybe the security officer had only thought he'd heard or seen them having sex.

Charlotte opened the door and went inside the principal's office, and his administrative assistant looked up from her computer.

"Good afternoon, Mrs. Black."

"Good afternoon," Charlotte said, wondering what this nice woman must be thinking about Curtina and all the trouble she continued to get into.

"Mr. Norton and Curtina are waiting in his office for you, so please go right in."

Charlotte breathed deeply, strode toward the door, and opened it.

Mr. Norton stood up, and while he normally walked around his desk to shake her hand, that wasn't the case today. "Mrs. Black, thank you for coming in so quickly."

"Of course," Charlotte said, now looking at Curtina, who had her head down, crying. "What are you crying for?"

Curtina looked up with her face soaking wet. "I'm so sorry, Mom. I'm so, so sorry."

Charlotte sat down next to her. "Sorry for what?"

"I'm just sorry. I'm really, really sorry."

"So is it true?" Charlotte asked her.

"Mom, I didn't mean it. I made a—"

Charlotte frowned and interrupted her. "Just stop it, Curtina. Because I don't want to hear any lies or excuses. You know better than to do something like this."

"But I didn't. I mean, I almost did, but I didn't do anything."

Now Mr. Norton took a seat. "Curtina, we know what you and Mark were doing."

"So what happened, exactly?" Charlotte asked him.

"Before the bell rang, Curtina's math teacher saw her walking past her class, but then Curtina never showed up. At first, her teacher had just thought she was maybe coming to class late, but when five minutes turned into ten and then fifteen, she called me from her classroom phone. That's when I called the security office, and one of the officers began searching for her. He searched two of the girls' restrooms, and lo and behold, he found Curtina and another student, Mark Stevens, locked away in one of the stalls, having sex. The security officer heard a lot of movement and other noises, and when he realized what was going on, he kneeled down and looked under the door. That's when he asked them what they were doing."

"We weren't doing anything," Curtina said, still crying.

"Curtina," Mr. Norton said calmly and cordially, "the officer saw both of your pants and underwear touching the floor."

Curtina looked surprised and didn't say anything else, and that's when Charlotte knew that the officer had caught them in the act. It was enough to make Charlotte sick to her stomach.

"Then, when they finally came out of the stall," Mr. Norton continued, "he ushered both of them here to my office."

"I am so very sorry for this, Mr. Norton. And I'm so embarrassed. So disappointed."

"I understand."

Charlotte looked at Curtina and got angrier by the second. "Apologize to Mr. Norton. Now."

"I'm sorry."

Mr. Norton nodded. "Your apology is accepted, but unfortunately, this time that won't be enough."

"What do you mean?" Charlotte asked."

"Mitchell Prep has a public lewdness and public indecency no-tolerance rule, so both students are being expelled."

Charlotte's stomach spun so forcibly, she grabbed hold of it. "Expelled?"

"Yes, I'm afraid so."

"And there's nothing that can be done?"

"No, unfortunately not, and we'll also need to have her clean out her locker this afternoon. One of our security officers and myself will escort both of you over to it, and we'll provide a box for you to pack everything in."

Charlotte tried to find words, but nothing logical came to mind. This whole ordeal was simply outrageous. But then she thought about something. Mitchell Prep was a K–12 institution. So what if the boy she'd been with was a junior or senior? Seventeen or eighteen? Because that would constitute statutory rape.

"Can you tell me how old this boy, Mark, is?"

"He's thirteen, just a year older than Curtina, so there won't be any charges filed against either of them. And thankfully, none of the other students had to witness any of this, or we'd have some real trouble on our hands. Some of the other parents would speak out and cause public outrage."

Charlotte still couldn't believe her twelve-year-old daughter had been caught having sex. At school. In the middle of the afternoon. In the girls' bathroom. At Mitchell Prep, one of the most prestigious Christian academies in the region.

"Do you have any questions?" Mr. Norton asked.

"No," Charlotte said, "I don't think so."

"What about you, Curtina?" he asked.

She shook her head no, with more tears streaming down her face.

Mr. Norton stood up. "Well, I'm sorry that this had to happen, but please know that we'll be wishing you all the very best wherever you end up enrolling. You're a highly intelligent young lady, so I hope you get things in order. I hope you find your way."

Charlotte got up and shook his hand. "Thank you for all you've tried to do for her here, and again, I'm very sorry."

Mr. Norton walked toward his door and opened it, but Curtina didn't move.

"Let's go," Charlotte said between gritted teeth. "Get up, so we can go clean out your locker."

Curtina finally stood and walked out into the administration reception area, but when some woman stormed in front of them in a huff, Charlotte, Curtina, and Mr. Norton stopped in their tracks.

"How dare you manipulate my son like this. I oughta press charges against you and your awful parents."

"Mrs. Stevens, please," Mr. Norton said. "If you'd like to come into my office, I would be glad to sit down and talk to you, but right here isn't the place."

"When I send my child to school every morning, I expect him to be protected from little heifers like this. My husband and I pay a lot of money for Mark to attend here, and this is the kind of treatment we get? What kind of madhouse are you all running?"

Charlotte pulled her handbag farther up on her shoulder. "Heifer? I know you didn't just call my daughter out of her name. Because I'm not going to stand for that."

Mrs. Stevens stepped closer to Charlotte. "Well, if you and your pastor husband were raising her the right way, she wouldn't be coming on to my son like some grown woman."

"You know what?" Charlotte said. "If I were you I would

pick my son up and leave before you're sorry. Before my husband and I file a lawsuit against you, your husband, and that mannish little boy of yours."

"You're the one who needs to be worried about a lawsuit," Mrs. Stevens said, and then turned to Mr. Norton. "Now, where is my son?"

"He's sitting in the vice principal's office. Just a couple of doors down."

Mrs. Stevens rolled her eyes at Curtina. "How sad. But it's not like you've had the greatest example of a mother to learn from, anyway, though," she said, eyeing Charlotte up and down, as though she were the tramp of the century.

Charlotte wanted to tell this woman about herself, but deep down, she knew why the woman had turned this whole Curtina-Mark thing on her, and she was ashamed. As Curtis's wife, so much of their business—the good, the bad, and the ugly—had been publicized nationwide. So no matter how many years had gone by that she'd been completely faithful to Curtis, it just went to show that most people would never forget her sins. Some would hold them against her for the rest of her life, and she only had herself to blame for that. Still, she couldn't help wondering if folks would be so cruel and unforgiving if she weren't the wife of a well-known pastor. Something told her that if she weren't, things would be a lot different. People wouldn't pay as close attention to what she was or wasn't doing, and she would give anything to have that kind of privacy. She would give everything she had to be normal.

Chapter 33

It was now four o'clock. Trina had slept for a couple of hours, woken up and then dozed off again for another hour. Curtis was still thinking about everything she'd told him this morning. His father had raped his mother, over and over. He'd violated her, day after day, month after month, and she'd taken years of abuse in silence.

But even knowing the truth and feeling deeply sorry for his mom, he still wished she'd found the strength to leave his father. To some degree, he understood why she was afraid to, but he also couldn't help the way he felt about it.

Trina smiled. "So you're still here, huh?"

"Yep, where else would I be?"

"You're a good brother."

"And you're an awesome sister."

Trina smiled again and then said, "I know I told you some very unsettling stuff about Mom and Dad this morning, but I wanted you to know the truth."

"No, I'm glad you did. It explained a number of things that I've always questioned, but I do still wish Mom had taken us away from Dad. I wish she'd thought more about you and me. Or if nothing else, I wish she'd stood up for us. Stood up for me at least one of those times when Daddy was beating me. There were days when I thought he would beat me to death."

"I know, and I'm sorry, but I wish you could somehow find a way to let that go."

"Me too, but I honestly don't know if I ever will."

Trina stared at him and then said, "My hope was that I would never have to tell you this, but now I think I should."

"Tell me what?"

Trina coughed harder than she had been.

"Are you okay?"

"Yes," she said, coughing again.

Curtis leaned forward in his chair. "Are you sure? Do you need some water?"

"No, I'm fine," she said, and finally settled down. "So here's the thing. Remember the day Daddy died?"

"I'll never forget it."

"Neither will I, but there's so much more to the story. A lot more than what we were originally told."

"Like what?"

"Well, I wanted to know why Mom stayed, too. Why she didn't have the courage to leave Daddy, so that you, her, and I could have a better life. But when she got sick, she finally told me everything. Daddy really did have liver disease because of all the drinking he'd done for so many years, but then he came down with pneumonia. So while they were in bed one night—the night he died—he'd reached over to his nightstand, picked up a roll of summer sausage that he'd brought into the bedroom from the kitchen, and started eating it with a few crackers. He was eating it while watching television, but his head must not have been propped up high enough, because Mom said the next thing she knew, he was eating and laughing at an episode of *Andy Griffith* but then started to choke. And for some reason, he couldn't get control of it. He was struggling to breathe and trying to cough up everything in his throat, but after a while, his breathing slowed and then it finally stopped altogether."

Curtis lowered his eyebrows. "Wow, I always thought he died of a heart attack with liver and lung complications."

"He did . . . but Mom also finally got the courage to stand up for herself and for us."

"How do you mean?"

"While he was choking, he reached out for her, but she just stared at him and never moved. She said she just sat in bed next to him, watching and thinking about all the times he'd raped her. All the times he'd beaten her little boy. All the times he'd made her little girl feel like she was a worthless animal who would never find a man who wanted her. She said she just watched him struggle in distress until he took his very last breath. Then she called 911."

Over the years, Curtis had come to realize how wrong it was to want anyone dead, but he remembered, as a teenager, being thrilled about his father's death. He'd felt free and more relieved than he ever had in his life, and he hadn't shed a single tear. Not the day his father had died, not the week the arrangements had been made, and not the day of his funeral. He hadn't cried about it a day since then, either. They'd lived such a dysfunctional life, and Curtis had just been glad to know that with his father gone, he would no longer have to live with a drunk who hated him.

"I guess I don't know what to say," Curtis finally said. "I mean, I had no idea."

"I know. Neither did I, but I just couldn't leave here without telling you."

The last part of her sentence broke Curtis's heart, but he didn't let on that her statement about leaving here had bothered him. "Why didn't you tell me this morning when you told me about Dad raping Mom?"

"Because I didn't want you to think badly of her. Mom was a good woman with a good heart, but I wasn't sure how you would feel about her letting him die. How you would take the idea of her not helping him when she certainly could have."

"I know it's not what God would expect any of us to do, but I do know that when a woman has battered wife syndrome—which I do believe now—you can't say what she will or won't do. I've always known about battered wife syndrome, and I've even studied it so that I can help some of the women at the church. But for some reason, I've never wanted to see that Mom fell into that same category. I guess it was just easier for me to wonder why she didn't leave. And easier to blame her for what happened to me."

"Sometimes it's hard to see things for what they really are when you're so close to them."

"Exactly."

Trina slowly closed her eyes, and Curtis thought about the one memory that was always at the forefront of his mind. Curtis had been seventeen, and it was the last time his father had beaten him. This day had also been only a few months before his father had died.

Thomas burst into Curtis's bedroom, holding a broom handle with both hands, and hit him across his body with all his might. It wasn't until then that Curtis had awakened. His father whacked him hard again, and Curtis bellowed out in pain and slid backward toward his raggedy wooden headboard.

"What did I do?" Curtis yelled.

"Didn't I tell you to take out that garbage?"

"I'm sorry, Dad. I had to study for my finals, and I fell asleep."

Thomas slammed the broom across Curtis's arm. "I don't care what you had to do. I *told* you to take out that garbage, and that's what I meant."

Curtis tried protecting his head. "Dad, please don't. I'll go take it out now."

"You're gonna do what I tell you, you hear me?" Thomas said, bashing Curtis across the side of his head.

"Owwwww!" Curtis shrieked and wept loudly. "I'm sorry, Dad. Please stop."

"I guess you think you're grown, but I'm about to let you know who the grown man is in *this* house," Thomas said, tossing the broom to the floor and lunging on top of Curtis. He punched Curtis in his head, face, and chest with both fists, over and over, and Curtis tried to push his father off him. But then Thomas dragged Curtis by his legs off the bed.

When Curtis's head hit the hardwood floor, he howled in pain. Then his vision blurred, and he quickly scooted away to the same corner he'd been taking cover in for four long years.

But as he gazed at his father, watching him trying to catch his breath and preparing to attack Curtis again, something came over him. It was a feeling he hadn't experienced before, but at that very moment, he knew his life would be changing.

And he got to his feet.

"Get back down on that floor," Thomas yelled. "And you stay down there until I tell you to get up."

Curtis stared him down. "No."

"What did you say?"

"I said no."

Thomas glared at him like he was crazy, and rushed toward Curtis, but Curtis shoved him backward and then pounded every part of his father's body that he could, one fist after the other. Thomas staggered to the side, but Curtis had no mercy on him.

"I told you to stop beating on me," Curtis yelled, and then grabbed his father by his collar and slammed his body across the room.

Thomas's body hit the wall and then slid down to the floor.

Curtis was so out of breath, he could barely stand up,

but then Trina and his mother came into the room, covering their mouths with their hands. Neither of them said anything, but it was then, as he looked at his father lying on the floor, moaning and bleeding, that he knew Thomas Black would never touch him again. He would never as much as raise a hand to Curtis, because Curtis was no longer a scared little boy. He was a seventeen-year-old young man who wasn't afraid of him. And if for some reason his father did try to beat him again...well...Curtis just hoped it never came to that, because he wouldn't, under any circumstances, ever allow it. He wouldn't take another beating from his father for as long as he lived.

Chapter 34

Charlotte walked inside the house, pulled the mysterious phone from her shoulder bag, and tossed it on the chair.

Curtina lagged in behind her, looking like a wounded animal.

"Sit down," Charlotte told her, and then sat across from her daughter.

"What's that?"

"You tell me. I found it in your closet."

"Mom, you went through my stuff? Why?"

"Where did you get this from?"

"I don't know."

Charlotte wasn't in the mood for games. "Look, either you tell me where you got this from, or I'm calling your dad right now to tell him what you did at school today. Then I'm telling him about this secret phone of yours."

Charlotte was going to tell Curtis everything anyway, but she needed to make Curtina believe that she wouldn't so she could get her to tell the truth about this phone.

"I saved most of my allowance every week until I had enough money to buy it."

"And what about the monthly charges? And how did you get it activated? And why haven't any statements come to the house?"

Curtina hesitated until she saw the impatient look on Charlotte's face. "I buy prepaid debit cards from the convenience store, and I pay the bill online. The statements only come to my email address."

"Did you buy the phone online, too?"

"Yes, and that's also how I activated it."

"But you have to be eighteen to have your own cell phone account."

Curtina looked away from her and didn't comment.

"Did you lie about your age?"

She still didn't respond, but now fake tears flowed down her face.

"Did you?" Charlotte said, raising her voice.

"Yes."

"Curtina? It's almost as if I don't even know who you are anymore. And when did you get this phone? And whose house was it delivered to?"

"Mom, why do you keep asking me all of these questions?"

"Because I want to know everything. Now answer me."

"I had it delivered to Mark's house last September. His older brother had the flu really bad that week, so he signed for it and gave it to Mark when Mark got home from school."

Charlotte narrowed her eyes. "You've had it for six months?"

Curtina stared at her with more fake crying.

"Well, if you've had it that long, then why did you always have a fit every time we took the phone that *we* bought for you? You would even constantly beg to have it back. And what about that Sunday in church when you told your grandpa that we took your phone? You had tears in your eyes, like you were devastated."

Curtina shrugged her shoulders.

"You know what? I'm going to ask you again. Why did you always get so angry when we took your other phone? And kept asking for it back?"

"So you would think I really needed it."

"I don't get what you mean."

"I knew that if you and Daddy thought I was desperate to get my phone back, you would never suspect that I had another phone I was using."

Charlotte wanted to laugh out loud, because this girl was way too much. She was only twelve years old, yet she'd plotted, schemed, and deceived Charlotte and Curtis like they were children. Charlotte also hadn't realized how much damage giving a child a fifty-dollar-a-week allowance could do. Plus, it wasn't like they usually monitored what she did with it. Mostly they'd just assumed she spent it on junk food, lip gloss, fingernail polish, young adult books, Frappuccinos, and other normal things that girls tended to want. "So let me get this straight. You were putting on an act? Deceiving us the whole time?"

"I'm sorry, Mom, and please, please, please don't tell Daddy."

"And what about this boy, Mark? Did he use a condom?"

"We didn't do anything."

"Stop lying, Curtina. That officer saw both you and that boy with your pants and underwear down. So you either tell me the truth or else. Did he use a condom or not?"

"Yes."

"Are you lying again?"

"No, Mom, I told him I didn't want to get pregnant, so he always used—"

Charlotte bugged her eyes. "Always? What do you mean 'always'? You've done this before?"

Curtina broke into tears yet again, but this time they seemed genuine.

Charlotte wanted to cry, too, but she couldn't show any signs of weakness. "What's the passcode?"

"Mom, please, don't go through my phone."

"Either you tell me that passcode or I'm calling your dad. Then I'm calling your sister and two brothers and your grandparents. And I'm telling them everything."

"But, Mom—"

"But Mom, nothing! Tell me the code. I mean it, Curtina."

Curtina still hesitated, but when she couldn't see a way out, she rattled off the numbers.

Charlotte typed them in and opened the phone.

"Mom, we were just playing around. That's all."

"Who was playing around?"

"Me and Mark when we were texting."

Charlotte opened the text messaging icon and scrolled pretty far up so that she could read the texts in chronological order. Still, the date that appeared was from yesterday, so Curtina and this Mark boy had to have been texting all evening. But when Charlotte read the first text, sent by her sneaky, lying daughter, she could barely contain herself.

Curtina: I want u 2 do 2 me wut that man just did in that video. U never go down on me, n Taylor's man goes down on her all the time.

Mark: That's not my thing. But I'll think about it.

Curtina: Wut is there 2 think about? I've been doin it 4 u for months.

Mark: That's different.

Curtina: How?

Mark: Just is.

Curtina: If Jeff can do it 4 Taylor so can u. He even did it Saturday nite when we snuck you guys in her house. He always does it.

Mark: I'm not Jeff. I like the real thing. We still doin it 2morow at school tho right?

Curtina: Are you gonna go down on me?

Mark: I already told you. I'll think about it.

Curtina: Maybe I should find me another man. lol

Mark: Maybe u should. lol

Curtina: That's not funny.

Mark: U know ur my woman. And only u.

Curtina: Then u betta start actin like it. We been doin' it ever since last year and I'm tired of doin it the same ole way. Maybe I shoulda never gave it up to u.

Mark: Yea, and u wouldn't be my woman either. I told u. I don't date women who think their stuff is too good to give up.

Mark: R u still there?

Curtina: My dad is callin me. Yellin his head off. I'll text u later.

Mark: I can't wait til after 6th hr 2morow. Ur goin 2 get it good.

Curtina: lol. I gotta go boy

Charlotte set the phone down and was too distraught to comment. But when she gathered her thoughts together, she looked at Curtina. "So you girls snuck boys into Taylor's home last weekend?"

"I told you, Mom, Mark and I were just playing around. Those messages aren't real."

Charlotte got up and grabbed Curtina by her arm. "Don't you lie to me . . . not even a little. You hear me?"

"Yes."

"Now answer me. Did you sneak those boys in or not?"

"Yes."

"And what video did you and this Mark boy watch? And where?"

"Online."

"You watched it together?"

"No, we watched it and then started texting again."

"And you've been having sex with this boy all this time and giving him oral sex, too, Curtina?"

This was the part that Charlotte couldn't get over. Her daughter was having both oral sex and sexual intercourse— at twelve years old.

"I'm sorry, and I won't do it again."

"You got that right," Charlotte said, scrolling through the phone to an earlier date.

Curtina hopped out of her chair. "Mom, give me my phone...or I'm telling Daddy that you've been drinking. And then I'm telling him that you've been drinking and driving me around, putting my life in danger. Because I know you've been drinking today. I can smell it."

After Mr. Norton had called Charlotte, she had left the house so quickly that she hadn't thought about drinking coffee, and apparently the gum she'd chewed hadn't worked very well.

"Give me my phone, Mom."

"Look, Curtina, I'm still your mother, so don't you ever try to threaten me like that again."

Curtina locked eyes with Charlotte. "You're only my stepmother. My *real* mother is dead...and I hate you."

Charlotte's mind must have been playing tricks on her. Or maybe she was hearing things. She had to be, because there was no way the girl she'd loved and raised as her own for the last ten years would ever speak to her this way. "What did you say?"

Curtina never as much as flinched and boldly stood her ground. "You're not my real mother, and I hate you."

Charlotte was furious, but she was also hurt beyond words. "Why would you say something like that?"

"Because you never wanted me to come live with you and Daddy in the first place. You hated everything about me, and you were cruel to me when I first moved in here."

"Who told you that?"

"One of the girls at church. Her mother told her everything. And her mother can't stand you."

Charlotte felt dazed and out of sorts. Like she was losing her mind.

But Curtina couldn't have cared less. "And she also told me how you slept around on Daddy and got pregnant with another man's baby. Some man named Aaron. So now I know the truth about your daughter, Marissa. The one who died. She wasn't even Daddy's real daughter, which means she wasn't my real sister. So I wish you guys would stop pretending like she was."

Charlotte's hands shook the way they sometimes did when she'd had too much caffeine, and all she could do was set the phone down and look at Curtina. She couldn't deny any of what she'd just said, and she was so sorry that Curtina had found out all of this from someone else—and at the church, no less.

"Curtina, I'm so sorry, honey. I'm really, really sorry."

"Well, don't be, because I don't need you. All you do is lie to Daddy all the time, anyway. And I hate that you're a drunk. You're drunk right now, and I'm so ashamed to call you my mom. I was so embarrassed when you came to pick me up, because I'll bet Mr. Norton smelled liquor on you, too."

Charlotte covered her face with both hands, but then grabbed her purse and Curtina's phone.

"Mom, give me my phone back," she said.

But there was no way Charlotte was leaving that phone in Curtina's possession, when all she would do is delete every single message. So she dropped it in her purse and left out the door. She seriously needed to get away and clear her head. And Father, forgive her, she needed a drink. She needed something now, so she got in her car and drove down the long driveway and into the street.

She drove for a couple of blocks, sniffling and wiping her face, and then it dawned on her that before she'd left home to go pick up Curtina from school, she'd taken another quick drink of vodka and dropped it in her handbag. She'd completely forgotten about it, so she pulled it out, drank a large gulp of it, and kept driving. She drove for miles until she turned a corner much too fast and lost control of her vehicle. She slammed on the brakes, but it was too late. She couldn't stop in time and plowed her car into a tall brick wall that surrounded a huge cemetery.

Chapter 35

Curtis had driven as fast as he could from Chicago, and now he hurried toward the automatic double doors of the emergency room and walked inside.

Curtina immediately rushed toward him, crying uncontrollably and hugging him around his waist. "Daddy, it's all my fault. I didn't mean it, I didn't mean it, I didn't mean it. I don't hate Mom, Daddy, and I don't want her to die."

Curtis had no idea what she was talking about, but whatever it was, he knew it wasn't good. "Honey, try and calm down. And why do you think this is your fault?"

"It just is, and I'm so sorry, Daddy. I really messed up this time. But I didn't mean it."

Curtis took her by both her arms. "Sweetheart, you're going to have to pull it together so I can go see what's going on with your mom."

Curtina still wailed loudly, but he wrapped his arm around her shoulders and led her over to where their friends and family were sitting and standing. Curtis spoke to everyone, and many of them got up and hugged him.

Alicia stood next to Curtis. "We're still waiting to hear something, Daddy. But they've had Charlotte in there for almost two hours."

"What happened?" Curtis asked.

Alicia's eyes turned sad, and everyone got quiet: Matthew, Stacey, Dillon, Porsha, Levi, Janine, Carl, Bethany, a few of the elders of the church, Sonya from the women's ministry, and a few other friends and members of the church.

"Tell me," Curtis said.

There were other families in the waiting area, so Alicia took him by his arm, and they walked back over near the entrance. "You see those policemen down the hallway?"

Curtis looked to the left and nodded.

"Well, they're waiting to talk to you."

"About what?"

"Charlotte."

"What about her?"

"Daddy, try not to get mad. Please."

"Just tell me. What is it?"

"They think she was driving under the influence."

Curtis's heart beat faster. "Please don't tell me she was drinking."

"They asked Matt, Dillon, and me if we thought she might have been, but we told them no."

"I really hope she wasn't."

"I do, too. And I hope she's going to be okay."

"Was Curtina in the car with her?"

"No."

"Then why is she so upset and saying it's all her fault?"

"I don't know, Daddy. She told me the same thing, but when I asked her why, she just hugged me and started crying again."

"Who brought her to the hospital?"

"Once we all got here, we wondered where she was, so I called her and then went to pick her up from home."

"Something bad must have happened, but right now, I'm just going to focus on what the doctors have to say about Charlotte," Curtis said, and saw the two police officers coming toward them.

"Pastor Black," the older one said, "I'm Officer Dean, and we're sorry to have to bother you right now, but can we have a word?"

"Sure," he said, walking with them back in the direction they'd come from.

The other officer, who looked to be no more than twenty-five, said, "I'm Officer Conroy, and we're really sorry about your wife's accident."

"Thank you. I appreciate that."

"We just wanted to ask you a few questions," Officer Dean said.

"Okay."

"Were you aware that your wife was drinking and driving?"

"No, not at all. I wasn't aware that she was drinking, period."

"Well, when we searched her vehicle, we found a bottle of vodka with a broken seal. It was lying on the floor of the passenger side, but wasn't completely empty."

Curtis was hurt, angry, and embarrassed. "I guess I don't know what to say."

"I understand," Officer Dean said. "We don't know if she drank some of the vodka today or another day. We're waiting on her blood alcohol results now, but even if she wasn't drinking, we'll still have to charge her with an open container violation."

Curtis sighed deeply.

"And if it turns out that her blood alcohol level exceeds the maximum, she'll be charged with reckless driving and a DUI. My hope is that this won't be the case. But we still needed to inform you about what we know so far."

"Thank you for telling me."

Officer Dean pulled out a card with his name and number on it and gave it to Curtis. "If you think of anything at all or if we can be of help in some kind of way, please don't hesitate to give me a call."

"I will."

"And again," Officer Conroy said, "we're very sorry about your wife's accident."

"Thank you."

The officers walked away, but all Curtis could do was think about the fact that he hadn't followed up on his suspicions. He so regretted not confronting Charlotte to see if she was drinking again, and now she'd had a terrible accident. He also had a feeling that her blood alcohol results were going to return sky high, and that she would be arrested on all three of the charges the officer had mentioned.

Before walking back toward the family waiting area, Curtis pulled out his phone and called his in-laws. When Alicia had called him about Charlotte, he'd jumped in his car, heading back to Mitchell, but he'd also contacted Joe and Noreen to let them know what was going on. He'd then promised to call them with an update.

"Curtis, how is she?" Noreen asked right away.

"We still don't know anything."

"After all this time?"

"Yes, but I'm sure she's going to be fine, and I prayed all the way here."

"Well, we're praying as well, but now I hate that we didn't ride back with you."

"I know you want to be here, but I also think you did the right thing by staying. Joe doesn't need to be here, getting himself all worked up, and as soon as I find out anything, I'll call you."

"Please take care of our baby, Curtis. But I know you will."

"Yes, and please try not to worry."

"We love you."

"I love you, too."

Curtis slipped his phone into his jeans, but when he looked up, he saw a doctor walking toward the waiting area.

"I'm looking for the Black family."

Curtis moved closer to the doctor. "I'm Pastor Black, Charlotte's husband."

The man shook Curtis's hand. "I'm Dr. Tisdale."

"It's nice to meet you."

"If you want to come with me, I'll give you an update on your wife. Your children are welcome to come also."

Alicia, Dillon, and Matthew stood and walked over, but Curtina stayed seated.

Curtis looked at her. "Honey, are you coming?"

She shook her head, and Curtis wondered again what had happened between Curtina and her mother. Curtis could tell she was afraid, but what he couldn't understand was why she thought her mother's accident was all her fault. And why she'd told Charlotte that she hated her.

When they entered the conference room and took their seats, Dr. Tisdale spoke.

"I'm sure you're wondering why it took us so long to come talk to you, but for a while, we had a very hard time getting your wife's bleeding under control. She has some pretty deep lacerations, and she lost a lot of blood. She also kept going in and out because of low blood pressure. But we finally got everything under control."

Curtis had never felt so relieved. "So she's going to be okay?"

"Yes, for the most part."

"Praise God," Curtis said.

"She's not completely out of the woods, though," Dr. Tisdale continued, "because in addition to her lacerations, she has a concussion and two fractured ribs."

"Oh my," Alicia said.

Matthew sat back in his chair. "Gosh."

"Will she need to stay in the hospital long?" Dillon asked.

"No, but we are going to keep her overnight. Then, if all looks okay tomorrow, she'll be released."

"That's good to hear," Curtis said.

"You'll also be able to see her very soon, but do you have any other questions?" Dr. Tisdale asked.

Curtis dreaded bringing up the alcohol issue, but he had a feeling that this was the reason they'd had a tough time with her bleeding. "Did she have alcohol in her system?"

"She did. And it was after we received her blood alcohol results that we understood why her blood was so thin. And why it wasn't clotting properly."

Curtis wasn't surprised, and neither of his children looked too shocked, either. They all knew Charlotte's history with drinking. Curtis had told her a long time ago that she was an alcoholic who needed inpatient treatment. But when she'd gone years without drinking anything, he'd thought maybe she would be okay. Now he knew that she still needed professional help. Curtis wouldn't try to force her to do something she didn't want to do, though—not this time. So all he could hope was that her injuries and DUI-related charges would be enough to wake her up. Curtis loved Charlotte with all his heart, and he wanted to be there for her, but only if she surrendered. He couldn't ride this vicious cycle with her again. Not when life was way too short to be miserable. So bottom line, he wasn't willing to compete with alcohol. Not on any day he could think of. Not ever.

Chapter 36

C harlotte lay in her bed with tears rolling down both sides of her face. She hadn't been in her room for more than twenty minutes, but as two of her nurses worked to get her settled in, she couldn't stop thinking about what she'd done. She'd almost killed herself. And she could've killed someone else in the process. All because she'd started drinking again. She'd known how things had turned out in the past whenever she'd thought she could drink socially and keep things under control, but for some reason, she'd honestly believed she could do it this time. Other people certainly did, so why couldn't she? Why did she have to have a problem with alcohol? But then, even if she didn't, Curtis still wouldn't be okay with her drinking socially. He'd been through so much with his father that he just couldn't stomach being around anyone who drank. He'd been this way the entire time she'd known him, and she didn't blame him. But Charlotte liked alcohol and the way it made her feel. She loved how it eliminated all her problems, even if just for a while.

But after today, none of that mattered anymore, and she

was done. She would finally get the help that Curtis had insisted she needed years ago.

"Are you having any pain?" one of her nurses asked.

"Just a little. I'm more sore than anything else, though, and it hurts to cough or turn over."

"That's because of your broken ribs, and sometimes it feels worse when you're lying down. But here's your button for pain medication. The dosage and frequency is controlled, so just push it when you need it."

Charlotte looked to the side of her to see where it was located. "Thank you."

The other nurse checked her IV and made sure her blood pressure and pulse readings were registering correctly. "We should be able to leave you alone for a while, but you have a lot of people here to see you."

"I'm sure," Charlotte said, and both nurses laughed with her.

"Your husband has already made it clear, though, that only he and your children will be coming in to see you tonight. And only for a few minutes."

"Sounds good. I can't wait to see them."

When the nurses left, Charlotte thought about Curtina and everything she'd said to her. It was hard to fathom what it must have been like for Curtina to learn that there had been a time when Charlotte hadn't liked her or wanted her. And that Charlotte had conceived a baby with another man. Curtis and Charlotte had worked hard to make sure Curtina never heard about either scenario, yet some woman in the church had told her own daughter and the daughter had told Curtina. Charlotte knew it wasn't the girl's fault, but she still hated that Curtina had heard so much painful information from a stranger. It wasn't fair, and now Charlotte wondered if hearing that Charlotte had once been mean to her was the reason she'd suddenly begun acting out.

Charlotte saw the door to her room opening and smiled when Curtina rushed in. Curtis walked in behind her.

"Mom, are you okay? Daddy said you were, but that I couldn't hug you because you have broken ribs. I'm so sorry about all the terrible things I said."

Charlotte grabbed her daughter's hand. "I'm sorry, too. I'm sorry you had to hear the things you heard and for feeling the way I felt when you came to live with us."

"It's okay, Mom. You will always be my real mom, and I only said that you weren't because I was so hurt and angry. But I didn't mean it, though. You have to believe me."

"I do believe you, and we're going to get through this. We'll work everything out."

"I won't ever try to hurt you again, Mom, and I love you so, so much."

"I love you, too, sweetie. More than you'll ever be able to understand, and you will always be my baby."

"And I'm sorry about what happened at school today," Curtina said, casting her eyes at her father. "But I haven't told Daddy about it yet. Mom, he's going to be so mad."

"Mad about what?" Curtis asked.

Curtina quickly looked at him but didn't respond.

Charlotte didn't want to tell her daughter how right she was. Because Curtis was, in fact, going to be outraged when he learned that his twelve-year-old daughter was having sex.

But in time, Curtis would get over it. He would forgive his daughter, and life would go on. What Charlotte worried about more was whether Curtina was telling the truth about that boy using condoms, because the last thing she wanted was for Curtina to be pregnant or for her to have some deadly disease. So even though Charlotte wouldn't be able to get around as easily for a while, she would ask Alicia to take Curtina to the doctor for a full examination. Curtis could certainly take her as well, but Charlotte wanted a woman to be with her.

"Okay, young lady," Curtis said, "why don't you let me talk to your mom for a few minutes before your brothers and your sister come in."

Curtina kissed Charlotte on her forehead. "I love you, Mom, and I hope you have a good night."

"You too, and I love you back."

When Curtina left, Curtis leaned over and kissed Charlotte on her lips. "How are you feeling?"

"As well as can be expected."

"Yeah, I guess so."

"I know you're angry," she said.

"Yeah, but I'm more disappointed than anything else."

"I know, and I'm sorry. But I'm finally going to do something about it. While I'm healing up from this accident, we can even look for a treatment facility together. Then I'll go admit myself as soon as I'm better."

Curtis looked at her as though he wasn't sure he believed her.

"I know you're probably skeptical, and rightfully so, but I mean it this time. I know I could be dead or I could've killed an innocent bystander, and I'll always have to live with

277

knowing that. Dr. Tisdale also told me that if they hadn't gotten my bleeding to stop I could have bled to death."

"Exactly. So when did you start back drinking?"

"Four weeks ago. I went to a restaurant in Schaumburg the day after we first went to see Trina. I had some wine, and then I bought more from a liquor store, but it wasn't long before I wanted something stronger. That's when I bought vodka and brandy."

Curtis folded his arms and shook his head. "I'm really at a loss for words. I mean, why, Charlotte? Why after all this time? And how many more relapses are you going to have?"

"If I can help it, none. I know I have a problem now. I've always had a problem, but it wasn't until today that I realized it and knew how serious it was."

At first Curtis just stared at her. Then, he leaned his shoulder against the wall with his arms still folded. "I so want to believe that you're going to get help this time, but right now, it's hard for me to believe anything you're saying. You and I have been through so much. For nearly two decades, we've experienced everything imaginable. For years, it was either me doing something to hurt you or you doing something to hurt me. It's been a constant and very vicious cycle . . . but baby, I'm tired. I love you, I always have, and I always will. And as a pastor, I certainly know how important the sanctity of marriage is, and that we agreed to stay married for better or worse. But something has to change. Life is way too short to be miserable and way too precious to keep struggling through the same painful drama. I've always known that. But with my sister being so ill, I'm that much more aware of it."

"I know, baby, and I'm sorry. I don't want to keep saying that, because I know my words don't mean very much to you, right now, but I really am. I promise you with all that I have, that I'm going to get help. I'll do whatever it takes. For me, you, and the rest of our family. It's time I deal with all my issues. The drinking, my unhappiness...everything."

Curtis lowered his eyebrows. "What are you unhappy about?"

"Being first lady. But I don't want to talk about that until I'm better physically. If it's okay with you, I just want to work on one thing at a time."

"It's fine, but I hope you're serious about getting professional help. I hope you're not just saying what you think I want to hear, because I won't be letting up this time. I won't pretend that today didn't happen and simply move on business as usual."

"I hear you, and I don't blame you for feeling the way you do. But baby, I've never been more serious about anything."

"There's something else, too, though," he said.

"What's that?"

"Your blood alcohol level was over the legal limit, so you're going to be arrested on three charges."

Charlotte was so ashamed and hurt. She'd known there was a chance of this happening, but hearing it made her feel much worse. And as much as she'd decided that she didn't care what people thought of her, she wasn't looking forward to having anyone see her photo displayed on the Mitchell Mugshots web site. But she'd also brought every bit of this on herself and had to face consequences.

"Oh, and I called your mom and dad to let them know you're in your room, but I told them I would call them back so you could talk to them. Before I do, though, what was Curtina talking about? What happened between the two of you earlier today, and why was she saying I was going to be mad at her?"

"It's a long story, so why don't we talk about it tomorrow?"

"If you say so, but it sounds pretty serious to me. Did something else happen at school?"

"Like I said, it's a long story."

For whatever reason, Curtis stopped pressing her about Curtina, and she was glad. Then, as he prepared to dial her parents, his phone rang.

It was his brother-in-law calling.

"Hello?" Curtis answered. "...Yes, she's doing well. She has a concussion and two broken ribs, but the doctor says she'll be fine...Yes, they're keeping her overnight...When?" Curtis said, and Charlotte saw his face turn sad. "As soon as Charlotte is released and I can get her home and settled, I'll head that way. But please call me if you need me before then...Okay, Jason, you take care and I'm praying for your strength...I'll see you soon."

Curtis ended the call and looked at Charlotte.

"What's wrong?" she asked.

"Trina isn't doing well, so hospice will be starting tomorrow. Jason had already decided to make today his last day of work, and she was very weak when I left this afternoon. She's declined a lot in just the last four days, so I have a feeling it won't be long now. It's just a matter of time before my baby sister leaves here and makes her transition."

Chapter 37

*C*urtis and Charlotte exited the highway and turned down the main street leading to his sister's house. As planned, Charlotte had been released from the hospital two days ago, so Curtis had driven over to see Trina that same afternoon and again yesterday. He'd felt bad about leaving Charlotte behind, partly because she was still recovering from her accident and partly because they'd had to report downtown so she could turn herself in. The police had booked her, fingerprinted her, and taken her mug shot, but thankfully Curtis had been able to bond her out right away. She'd already decided to plead guilty, pay the $2,500 fine, and accept the one-year license suspension she knew the judge was going to punish her with. So, needless to say, while she'd accepted her unfortunate fate, she'd been very depressed about it.

But nonetheless, she'd still insisted that Curtis go spend as much time with his sister as possible. There had also been a few moments when Curtis had prayed that Charlotte wouldn't start drinking again, but so far, she seemed serious about being in recovery, and she and Alicia had already begun researching treatment centers, both in and out of state. Then, even though Charlotte and Dillon had never been very close, he'd come to see her and had brought her a copy of *Alcoholics Anonymous*, the primary book that was used to help recovering alcoholics. Dillon had also given Charlotte a schedule of local meetings, which he attended at least four times per week.

So, for the most part, all was well with Charlotte, and even though she still had pain and soreness because of her fractured ribs, what she'd discovered was that sleeping in a recliner at night versus lying down in bed was helping her heal a lot faster.

Curtis turned the corner and looked at Charlotte. "Baby, how's your pain?"

"It's actually pretty good. Sometimes when you hit a bump it hurts a little, but it's not as bad as I thought it would be. Still, I wasn't going to miss coming to see Trina today. So I'll be fine."

"I'm really glad you were able to come," he said, and then looked through his rearview mirror at Curtina. Curtis focused his attention back on the road, but just thinking about those text messages Charlotte had shown him made him cringe all over again. He'd known Curtina was acting too grown and unruly for her own good, but not once had he thought she was having sexual intercourse. To tell the truth, when Charlotte had told him about it, he'd almost wanted to call her a liar, even though he'd known she would never lie about something this serious. She would also never lie on their youngest daughter, and as it had turned out, it was Curtina who had been the one lying every time she opened her mouth. Then, on top of that, she'd been having sex right inside her school and had gotten expelled. His twelve-year-old-daughter. It was still very hard for Curtis to comprehend, but this had all helped make his decision to send her to a Christian boarding school a whole lot easier. Even Charlotte now thought it was the best thing they could do for her, and while Curtina wasn't happy about going, she also wasn't dead set against it.

Curtis turned onto the street that his sister and brother-in-law lived on, but as he drove closer to their house, tears rolled down his face. Ever since leaving Trina last night, he'd tried to keep it together, but now harsh reality had hit him. There were cars everywhere, including those that belonged to all three of his adult children. Yesterday morning, Trina had told him that she wanted her family to spend the entire day together, and he was glad everyone had honored her request.

Charlotte touched Curtis's arm. "Are you okay?"

"I'm good. Just having a moment is all."

Curtis pulled into the driveway and was glad there was still space available, so Charlotte wouldn't have to walk so far. When they got out, Curtina carried her mom's purse and Curtis helped her up to the door. Then Curtina rang the doorbell.

Eric opened it and smiled. "Hey, Uncle Curtis, hey, Aunt Charlotte, hey, little cousin."

They all hugged Eric and went into the family room.

Everyone was gathered around Trina's hospital bed, the one the hospice organization had delivered on Thursday. Trina smiled when she saw them, but it broke Curtis's heart to see how fatigued she looked and how pale her skin had become.

"You know you shouldn't have come all this way," Trina told Charlotte. "You should be home resting and taking care of yourself."

Curtis noticed how weak and raspy his sister's voice was. Tomorrow would mark five weeks since they'd first come to see her, and her condition had deteriorated very quickly.

"I'll be fine," Charlotte said, stepping closer to the bed and grabbing hold of Trina's hand, "and I'm so sorry I can't hug you. But even though you're sitting up, it still might hurt if I try to lean too far forward."

"No worries at all. I'm just glad you're here," Trina said, looking at Curtis. "Hey, brother."

"Hey, sis," he said, hugging her for a few seconds longer than normal.

"So did you get any sleep last night? You left here pretty late."

"Just a little. But I'm okay."

Curtis glanced around the room, watching his children, their spouses, his grandson, Porsha, Jason, his niece and nephew, and Jason's parents, who Curtis had had the pleasure of meeting yesterday. Charlotte was across the room chatting with them now, and they were such wonderful people.

Over the next couple of hours, everyone laughed and talked and ate some of the food that Amber had ordered in from one of the gourmet delis in the area. Curtis had expected

Trina to sleep through most of their visit, the way she'd done when he'd come to see her yesterday, but she was wide awake and chatting with anyone who came to her bedside. He especially paid attention to the way she smiled when she was talking to all four of his children and his grandson. Then he saw her beckoning for Denise and telling her something.

"Can I have your attention, everyone?" Denise said.

Everyone got quiet and looked at her.

"Miss Trina wants me to take some photos of the entire family gathered around her bed, so if you'll all come on over, I'll take a few of them."

Everyone made their way over to the bed and got in position, but then Trina said, "Where's MJ?"

He stuck his head around his dad. "I'm right here, Auntie Trina."

"Well, can you come here for a minute?"

MJ slid around a couple of other people and stood at the side of the bed. "Yes, Auntie Trina?"

Trina smiled at him, and then asked Jason to let down the rail of the bed. "Come sit with me."

MJ climbed in next to her, and Trina locked her arm inside his. "I just wanted to have a photo with my only great-nephew. You're the only great-nephew I have right now, and I'm the only great-aunt *you'll* ever have.

MJ looked at her. "Is that because my Paw-Paw doesn't have any other brothers or sisters except you, and my Nana doesn't have any brothers or sisters at all?"

"That's right, so you and I have a very special relationship. We'll always have one."

"Even when you're gone?" MJ wanted to know.

"Even when I'm gone, and you know why?"

"Why?"

"Because I'll be right here," she said, pointing to his heart.

"Then can I get a photo with just you and me? I mean after your nurse takes the photo of all of us?"

"Yes, that's a good idea," Trina told him, and then looked at Curtina. "And I also want to get a separate photo with you, too, sweetie, okay? Because you're the youngest of my first-generation nieces and nephews."

Curtina smiled and nodded.

Everyone looked on in tears, and now Curtis wished that MJ and Curtina had gotten a chance to spend some real time with Trina. He wished all of his children had.

"And I certainly need to get a photo with my beautiful niece who's carrying my precious great-niece or -nephew," Trina said, smiling.

Curtis wondered what she was talking about, but then Alicia walked closer to her father and held his hand. "Levi and I just found out yesterday, Daddy. And since we knew everyone was coming to see Aunt Trina today, we decided to announce it here. But then, when I told Aunt Trina about it a couple of hours ago, she asked us if she could be the one to tell you. And, of course, Levi and I were so honored and happy about that."

Curtis hugged his daughter and didn't want to let her go. Then he hugged his son-in-law, but he still didn't say anything to either of them. He wanted to, but he was too full inside—both with the sheer joy of knowing that he was having another grandchild and with deep sadness because of what was happening to his sister.

"God knew you would need some happy news today," Trina told Curtis, "and it just doesn't get any better than this."

When each person moved back into photo position, Denise told everyone to smile, and she pressed the camera icon on Trina's phone multiple times. Next, she took several photos of Trina and MJ by themselves, along with many others with various groups of people.

After another hour passed, Trina summoned each of them all back to her bedside again, and they all assembled closely together.

"I just want you all to know how happy and grateful I am to have all of you here today. It has given me such great joy, and I love you all so very much."

"We love you, too," everyone said.

"My illness has been a tough cross to bear, but I also know that it hasn't been easy for any of you, either. Then, last night, my sweet, beautiful daughter looked at me and said, 'Mom, why did you have to get sick? Why did you have to get cancer?' So just in case some of you are wondering the same things, this is what I told her: 'Look at what Jesus had to go through. All the turmoil, pain, and suffering He had to endure. And while He certainly didn't deserve it, it was still His destiny.' So as Christians, we all have to go through something, too. But it will never be as painful as what He experienced. Then my sweet, handsome son asked me why God was taking me at such a young age. He wanted to know why I wasn't going to live to be seventy the way the Bible says. He was referring to Psalm ninety, verse ten. But my response to him was 'Even Jesus passed away when He was in his thirties.' So, what I believe is that right when we're conceived, God already knows which day will be our last. He knows when we've completely fulfilled the purpose He has for each of us. And while I know it's not easy to accept losing the people we love—because to this day, I still miss my mother more than anything—passing away is still a necessary part of life. It's the one thing that none of us can bypass. That's the reason it's so important to love everyone and to treat others as well as you can. It's important to enjoy every single day of your life and to enjoy your family and friends as much as possible," she said, smiling and slowly making eye contact with every single person in the room. "This is the reason I wanted all of you to come here today. This is what I knew would make me happy, and it has. I've also gotten a chance to spend hours alone this week with Jason, each of my children, and my mother-in-law and father-in-law, and yesterday I got an opportunity to spend time with just Curtis and me," she said, smiling and reaching her hand out to him.

Curtis held her hand and sat on the edge of her bed, facing her.

"My dear, dear, brother. You and I went through a lot as children, and regardless of how many years we didn't see each other or talk to each other, I still loved you. I was angry at you, too, but deep down, you were still my big brother and the only brother I had. You were always in the back of my mind, and I used to wonder if we would ever become close again. And if we did, I wondered how it would happen. I never even told Jason my feelings about that," she said, looking at her husband, "but I still wondered. And look at the plan God had for us. He brought us back together when I needed you most. He turned something bad into something very good, because you and I are closer now than any sister or brother could ever hope to be. Jason, Amber, and Eric have given me the absolute best years of my life, but you have given me the best last five weeks of my life, and I so thank God for you. It took a long time for us to get here, but better late than never, right?"

Tears flowed down Curtis's face, and he squeezed Trina's hand, not wanting to let it go.

"And, even with how happy I am to have had this time with you," Trina continued, "there's still one more thing I need for you to do. I need you to go visit Mom and Dad's grave sites. Remember chapter ten in that book I gave you to read?"

Curtis nodded with tears flowing more heavily.

"Well, doing what that chapter talks about is my last request of you. Do it for you, Curtis. Do it so you can be free."

"I will," he said, hugging her. "I promise."

Trina went on with the rest of what she had to say. "Do it so that you and I can be an example to the world that forgiveness is possible for everyone. Even if a person hasn't spoken to their brother or sister for decades. Even if their father abused them and their mother didn't protect them. There's still an opportunity to forgive, live a good life, and be at peace when your time on earth is over. And that's what I want for you, my dear brother. More than anything. That's what I want for all of you," she said, scanning the room again as everyone hugged the person next to them. "I just want my family to be happy and at peace like me. Because when it's all said and done, love, happiness, and peace are the only things that truly matter."

Curtis held his sister, and then after everyone else hugged and kissed her again, she closed her eyes...and twenty minutes later, she was gone and finally resting in heaven.

Epilogue

One Year Later

The day had finally arrived. Deliverance Outreach was celebrating its twentieth anniversary, and Charlotte and Curtis had never felt so appreciated. Every seat was taken, and this wasn't even the main celebratory service, which would commence this evening. Of course, feeling appreciated by members of the church had always been the norm for Curtis, but for years, Charlotte hadn't believed that most of the members cared whether she existed or not—that is, except for when they wanted or needed her to do something for them. There were some who did show Charlotte a great amount of love and respect, but to her, they'd been few and far between. Yes, she'd done plenty of shameful things over the years, to her marriage and in other ways, too, but she'd still felt as though the majority of the members paid very little attention to how she felt and had mostly kept their minds focused on what she was doing wrong—or they kept their focus on Curtis. It was very clear that they loved, loved, loved their pastor, but when it came to their pastor's wife, Charlotte had sometimes been treated no differently than an accessory.

But today, Charlotte did feel that the entire congregation not only loved and cared about her, but they also valued her as Curtis's wife. And she knew some of that had to do with the fact that right after she'd left for the alcohol rehabilitation facility in Texas, he'd shared with them how miserable she'd been serving as their first lady. He'd also told them that once she returned from rehab, she wouldn't be back at church for a while, but that when she did return, a number of changes would need to be made. Janine had told her how shocked everyone had seemed, both about her being admitted to rehab and about Curtis basically telling the congregation that he would now expect his wife to be treated a lot better than she had been.

There had been many different rehab facilities to choose from, but once she and Curtis had settled on which boarding school they were sending Curtina to, she'd decided to search for something nearby. Which had worked out wonderfully, because even though she and Curtina could only see each other on set visitation days, it made life a lot easier when Curtis flew to Texas to see both of them. All had turned out well, because Charlotte had learned a lot during her sixty-day program, and just a few days ago, she'd celebrated her one-year sobriety date. She went to AA meetings regularly, and she was in the process of starting a weekly women's AA meeting at the church. Deliverance Outreach already had an addictions program, but Charlotte had decided that it was time they created something specifically for women. Dillon was going to create something just for men, too, and for the first time since he and Charlotte had met, they were happily working on something together as stepson and stepmother. Or as Curtis now liked to refer to them, as "bonus son and bonus mom."

Then there was Curtina. At first, she'd been very homesick at boarding school, and rightfully so, but as time had gone by, she'd begun to love her new home and the girls she went to school with. Then, after about three months, Curtis and Charlotte had noticed a major change in her attitude and her outlook on life. She'd become much more patient, kind, and unselfish, and after six months, they almost hadn't recognized her overall conversation. She'd certainly been learning a lot educationally, but she'd also learned a massive amount of common sense and adopted some amazing Christian values. As a pastor's daughter, she'd been born and raised to love God, and she knew the Bible well, but the boarding school had taken every bit of that to a whole other level. They'd taught her and shown her why she needed to consult God about every single decision she made, versus just talking to Him when she wanted or needed something. Curtis and Charlotte had tried teaching her that same philosophy for years, but somehow, she hadn't taken it as seriously until enrolling at the boarding school.

She also no longer focused on texting all the time or trying to act older than she was, and thank God, she hadn't gotten pregnant or ended up with some sort of STD. That whole sex-in-the-school-bathroom incident had happened a whole year ago, but Charlotte would never forget it. Curtis would never forget it, either, and there were still times when he would look at Charlotte and say, "Can you believe our daughter got caught having sex at twelve years old inside a school restroom?" He didn't hold it against Curtina, but he was still stunned and hurt that it had happened. Now, though, Charlotte and Curtis were very proud of her, and once she finished eighth grade in a couple of months, she would be home for good. She would then enroll at a new Christian academy there in Mitchell for high school and begin preparing for college.

Charlotte walked up to the glass podium at the front of the church and pulled the microphone from its holder. "Good morning, everyone."

"Good morning," they all said.

"I'm not going to take up too much of your time, but I just want to say thank you. Thank you for all the love and support you have shown our family over this last year, but especially for the love and support you have shown me individually. I know I haven't been here since the day my dad went into cardiac arrest, but I have so appreciated all the cards, flowers, and Edible Arrangements deliveries you sent me over this last twelve months—*especially* the Edible Arrangements, because sometimes I ate whole boxes and never gave Curtis a chance to eat one single piece," she said, and everyone laughed. "But in all seriousness, I really did need your support more than you could possibly imagine, and the good news is that, through it all, I learned so much about myself, and I've made a lot of positive changes. I know Curtis shared with all of you a year ago that, as first lady of this church, I was very unhappy. As a matter of fact, not even he was aware of how unhappy I was all that time, because I'd never told him. Partly because I know how much this ministry means to him, and partly because I wasn't sure he or anyone else would understand why I felt the way I did. I wasn't even sure my children, my parents, or my best friend, Janine, would fully understand, either, so I stayed silent about it. I walked around for years with a huge smile on my face, pretending that I couldn't be happier. I wore nice clothing so I could look great on the outside, when on the inside I was nearly dying—the only time I was truly happy was when I was at home or doing things that had absolutely nothing to do with the church.

"Still, when I did finally tell my husband everything last year, he heard me and asked all of you to be mindful of it. You didn't have to do that, of course, but you did, and I will always be grateful for that. But today, he's asked me to openly share some of the reasons why I felt the way I did, and while I wasn't sure that our church's twentieth anniversary was the appropriate time to do it, my husband and *your* pastor," she said, and the congregation laughed again, "told me it was the perfect time to reflect on the last twenty years and to be as transparent as possible. What he wants is for us to be open and honest, so that we can journey into the next twenty years all on the same page.

"But before I do share a few examples with you, I also want to say that during my time at the rehab facility, I did do a lot of praying and soul-searching, and what I ultimately had to realize was that none of us can find internal happiness through others. For years, I spent my life either depending on Curtis to make me happy or depending on worldly possessions to do it. I also came here to church every Sunday, hoping that I could impress all of you in every way I could. I know that none of you asked me to do that, but what you didn't know was that there were many times when certain members would walk past me without speaking—and they'd do it right as they were on their way to speak to my husband. Sometimes he'd only be standing a couple of feet away from me. And there were also times when I felt as though I was carrying the weight of the world, even when I was too tired to leave our home. But I did it anyway, because if I said no to certain people I then had to worry about what would be said behind my back. I'd even gotten to a place where I was actually *afraid* to say no to anyone who attended Deliverance. Then there were times when I felt as though no matter what I did, it was never enough. And on other occasions, when I sometimes made certain decisions relating to the women's ministry that some women didn't like, I would see negative comments about it on Facebook or Twitter. So, yes, in case you're wondering, there was a time when I would search my name and anything connected to Curtis or Deliverance Outreach through search engines on social media. And I have to tell you...I saw things I never would have imagined people would say about me. People who smiled when they saw me in person or who referred to me as their first lady whenever they thought it might benefit them with someone I knew well in the community. Then, as much as I hate to bring it up, my husband asked me not to leave this part out, either. There were some women who went out of their way to throw themselves at Curtis, and they didn't try to hide it from me. Some didn't try to hide it from anyone, and that was always very hurtful. I'm certainly not going to stand here and claim to have been an angel all my life when it comes to my marriage, but I'm just sharing with you how this kind of thing sometimes made me feel. Women in the church going after their pastor should be unheard of, and my prayer is that I won't have to experience anything like that again. My prayer, too, is that none of the other married women who attend Deliverance will have to experience that with their husbands, either.

"And finally, I just want to say how much taking a twelve-month sabbatical from the church really helped me. It made a difference for me on so many levels, and I'm a better person because of it. I did things for me and my family, and I was able to focus on so much of what I never seemed to have time for in the past. And please don't get me wrong. I love all of you, and I am honored to be your first lady, but as a woman, wife, mother, and grandmother, I needed some time away from the church. I didn't lose my faith, I didn't stop reading and studying my Bible, and I didn't stop worshiping and praising God. I just needed some personal time, and to be honest, had I not gotten that time, I'm not sure I would have finally found the courage to take care of my alcohol addiction. Taking time away gave me time to think and realize what was important. It allowed me to get my priorities in order. So as of June, I'll now be taking what I call a first-lady sabbatical every summer. I'll be taking off June, July, and August, and yes, *your* pastor has given me the okay to do this," she said, and there was more laugher. "I also want to end with saying how truly grateful I am to all of you for supporting Deliverance Outreach and for supporting my husband for two amazing decades. If it weren't for all of you, we wouldn't be able to help thousands of people all year long, every single year, the way we do. So, from the bottom of my heart, thank you again, and again, and again. I love you all."

As Charlotte took her seat, everyone stood and applauded, and she felt better than she had in the twenty years since she and Curtis had founded Deliverance Outreach. Not because she was first lady, but because she finally felt free to be all God had created her to be. For so many years, she'd been focusing on the wrong things and worried about what everyone else thought she should be doing, but now she was focused on the purpose God had for her life—the life he had spared that afternoon she'd crashed into the brick wall surrounding a cemetery. To this day, she still believed that He'd used that cemetery as a way to warn her. He'd made her see the road of destruction she'd been quickly tumbling down. So even though she would continue to serve as first lady of the church, she would also help other women who were working hard to stay sober in any way she could. Then, once she built a strong community of alcoholic women in recovery, they could begin helping women who had never entered a treatment facility or gone to an AA meeting. There was so much Charlotte could do to support them, and her vision was great. And with God she knew she could see that vision come to pass. She knew this, because with Him, anything was possible, and she would forever believe that. She would trust Him and depend on Him until she took her last breath.

As the choir sang, Curtis looked down the front row at all his family members, including Jason, Eric, and Amber, and he thanked God for all that He'd blessed him with. He thought about not just the last year or the last twenty years of his life, but all sixty of them. Yes, he'd actually turned sixty years old this past January, and it was sort of hard for him to believe. Not to mention, he and Charlotte sometimes still laughed about the fact that even though she was fifteen years younger than him, their age difference had served them well. They'd gone through a lot during their twenty years of marriage—well, quite a bit *more* than a lot—but they were true soul mates who were meant to be together. This was one of the reasons Curtis couldn't understand why he hadn't noticed how unhappy Charlotte had been. What he'd learned was that she'd *never* fully been happy in her role as first lady, and that she'd basically only gone along with it because she hadn't thought anyone would understand. She hadn't felt comfortable enough to tell him—her own husband—and this was the part that bothered him most. She'd certainly *wanted* to tell him, but at the same time, she hadn't wanted to ruin things for him. Not when she'd known that ministry was his calling from God, and that being pastor of the most well-known church in the region came with a lot of responsibilities. Hence her decision to keep quiet and just accept being in a role that many women coveted and saw as a blessing.

But this was also the reason Curtis had begun having conversations with all of his pastor friends nationwide, asking them if their wives were happy. Were they being treated with the utmost respect by all members of their congregations? Were they being asked to do more than they could mentally or emotionally handle? Were they afraid to say no to unreasonable requests? Were they afraid to make their true feelings and opinions known because they feared awful backlash? Were they spending so much time in church, focusing on their husbands' calling, that they'd lost themselves in the process? Did they even know what their own callings were? Was anyone, including their pastor husbands, even asking them about it? Were they walking around with huge smiles on their faces, dressed in the best clothing that money could buy—as Charlotte had pointed out—even though they couldn't be more miserable?

Curtis had asked question after question, and sadly, many of the pastors he'd spoken to—those who led megachurches and those who had less than a hundred members—hadn't even considered any of the above. Some of them had even decided that once God called a man into ministry, and even more so when that man became a pastor, his wife had an obligation to make *his* calling her priority. Curtis did think a pastor's wife needed to support his ministry the same as she would support her husband with any calling He might have on his life, but he didn't believe that a wife should give up everything she might want to do herself. His feeling was that even when a man and woman married and became one, each person still had their own individual callings from God to fulfill. He also had to admit that, until now, he hadn't known what Charlotte's was exactly, either. She hadn't talked about any passions she had, but today he knew her calling was to help women who were finally sober as well as those who weren't. Her purpose was to share her own testimony with them, letting them know what a mistake it was to walk around unhappy year after year, and then use alcohol as a way to mask their pain.

But then, thanks to his dear sister, Trina, God rest her soul, he'd learned the same thing about himself. He hadn't known just how much his childhood had still been affecting him or how deeply he'd buried every violent memory, but Trina had helped him realize it. In only five short weeks, she'd forced him to relive his past and deal with it. She'd advised him to forgive his parents so he could move beyond all of it. Still, no matter what she'd said, he'd been hesitant— even on the day she'd died and had made this her one last request of him. But then, as he'd stood at her home with the rest of his family, watching her slowly slipping away, he'd known he couldn't continue on the way he had been—and that it was time to visit his parents' grave sites.

He hadn't known when exactly he would do it, but when they'd left Trina's homegoing service and ridden in the processional over to the cemetery, he'd learned that Jason and Trina had purchased their burial plot right next to Curtis's mom and dad; which reminded him that until the very end, his mom hadn't fully hated her evil husband. She'd still chosen to take her final rest side by side with him. Curtis still couldn't say he'd understood that back then, but today he understood it well. Today he knew exactly how powerful forgiveness truly was, because once everyone had left the graveside part of Trina's service and gone back to their cars, he'd forgiven both of his parents. He'd spoken his words out loud to them in tears, and for the first time in his life, he'd felt free—just as Trina had told him he would. He'd also learned something else in the process: For everything bad, something good always comes out of it. A year ago, Curtis couldn't have imagined how any good could evolve from his sister's illness, but it had been that very illness that had brought them back together—and brought about his willingness to forgive the parents he should have forgiven a long time ago.

But he didn't just have his own example, because there was Charlotte's accident and DUI arrest, too. It would be easy to believe that absolutely no good could possibly come from that, too, yet those scenarios were the very reason Charlotte's eyes were now wide open about her alcoholism. It was the reason she now knew her God-given purpose and was helping other women just like her.

So yes, for everything bad, something good always came out of it. For every bad choice that any human being might make, there was always an opportunity for them to correct it. There was always a chance for anyone to change for the better. It was something Curtis knew all too well because his entire family was proof of it. And yes, in most cases, they had taken a very long time to turn things around, but what mattered was the fact that they had. What mattered was that they were finally living their lives according to God's Word. The Black family wasn't perfect, and never would be, but they now genuinely tried to do the right thing, and they treated others the way they wanted to be treated. They lived by the golden rule. This certainly hadn't always been the case—*But better late than never*, Curtis thought, and smiled. By all means, being late was better than losing your eternal soul, and this made Curtis smile even more.

Acknowledgments

What a journey this has been, writing twenty-seven books, including fifteen titles in my Reverend Curtis Black Series. There are certainly many people I need to thank, but first and foremost, I humbly thank my Lord and Savior Jesus Christ for the unconditional love, mercy, grace, and favor You have bestowed on my life since the day I was born. Without You, absolutely nothing would be possible, and I am eternally grateful to You.

Then, to my dear husband, Will. Words simply cannot express how much I love you and how grateful I am to have you as the love of my life. More than anything, before I met you, what I longed for and prayed for was to find a man who loved me as much as I love him, and you have certainly been that man since the very beginning. You have also supported my writing career in countless ways, and you have stood by me and encouraged me on every level...even when there were times when I didn't always believe in myself. These last twenty-seven years—and how interesting that I finished writing my twenty-seventh book during the same year we celebrated our twenty-seventh anniversary—but these last twenty-seven years of being married to you have made such an amazing difference in my life, and I thank God for you and our marriage. I love you with all my heart and soul, now and always.

To the best mom ever, Arletha Tennin Stapleton, and to the best grandparents ever, Clifton Tennin, Sr., and Mary Tennin—after all these years, I still miss all three of you so tremendously. There are days when I still shed many tears because of that. But, nonetheless, I am forever grateful to each of you for loving me, supporting me, and teaching me to love and honor God, no matter what. You made such a significant and heartwarming difference in my life, and I will love you always.

To my dear brothers: Willie Stapleton, Jr., (and dear sister-in-law, April) and Michael Stapleton (and dear sister-in-law, Marilyn). To my stepson, daughter-in-law, and grandsons: Trenod Vines-Roby, LaTasha Vines, Alex Lamont Knight, and Trenod Vines, Jr. To my brothers-in-law and sisters-in-law: Gloria Roby, Ronald Roby, Terry and Karen Roby, Robert and Tammy Roby, and James Roby (who is gone but will never be forgotten). To all my nieces and nephews: Michael Jamaal Young, Malik Stapleton, My'Shyle Young, My'Kyle Young, Shelia Farris, William Stapleton, Nakya Arletha Stapleton, Kiera Holliman, Nyketa Roby, Lamontrose Love, Krissalyn Love, Bianca Roby, Shamica Newkirk, Greg Newkirk, Brittany Roby, Demario Sorrells, Talia Brown, Amaya Love, Kristen Love, Malachi Love, Kasondra McConnell, Kaprisha Ballard, Kiara Bullard, and

Acknowledgments

Ronald Roby, Jr. (who is also gone but will never be forgotten). To my aunts and uncles: Ben Tennin, Fannie Haley, Ada Tennin, Mary Lou Beasley, Charlie Beasley, Vernell Tennin, Ollie Tennin, Marie Tennin, Shirley Jean Gary, Ed Gary, Ruby Gary, Lehman Gary, Thressia Gary, Rosie Norman, and Isaac Gary. To all my cousins and other family members (all of you!): Tennins, Ballards, Lawsons, Stapletons, Beasleys, Haleys, Greens, Robys, Garys, Shannons, and Normans—family is everything, and I am so beyond blessed to have each of you in my life. I love you all so very much.

To my dear cousin, sister, and fellow author, Patricia Haley-Glass (and Jeffrey and Taj); my two dear best friends, who are like sisters, Kelli Tunson Bullard (and Brian) and Lori Whitaker Thurman (and Ulysses); my dear cousin and friend, Janell Green; my dear friends and fellow authors, Trisha R. Thomas, Trice Hickman, Marissa Monteilh, and Cheryl Polote-Williamson; to my dear friends and book club members, Lori Whitaker Thurman, Regina Taylor, Cathrine Watkins, Valerie Hanserd, Cookie Givens, Mattie Holden, Emily Sanders—I love you all so very much, and I thank God for you.

To Pastor K. Edward Copeland, Mrs. Starla Copeland, and our entire New Zion Missionary Baptist Church family; to my wonderful spiritual mom and family: Dr. Betty Price, Apostle Frederick K.C. Price, Angela Evans, Cheryl Price, Stephanie Buchanan, Pastor Fred Price, Jr., Angel Price, and the entire Crenshaw Christian Center family—thank you all for everything, and I love you dearly.

Acknowledgments

To my awesome publishing attorney, Ken Norwick. To everyone at my amazing publishing house, Hachette Book Group (Grand Central Publishing): Beth de Guzman, Linda Duggins, Genevieve Kim, Elizabeth Connor, Stephanie Sirabian, Kallie Shimek, the entire sales, publicity, marketing, and production teams, and everyone else at Grand Central Publishing. To my freelance team: Pam Walker-Williams, Ella Curry, and Sharvette Mitchell. To every independent bookseller, major bookseller, and other retailers who sell my work; to every newspaper, radio station, TV station, magazine, online web site, and blog that promotes my work; and to every book club that continually chooses my work as your monthly selection. Thanks a million to each and every one of you for all that you've done for me for so many years. Your support of me and my work has made a huge difference in my life, and I so very much appreciate it. xoxo

With all my love and many blessings to you always,

Kimberla Lawson Roby

Email: kim@kimroby.com
Facebook.com/kimberlalawsonroby
Twitter.com/KimberlaLRoby
Instagram.com/kimberlalawsonroby
Periscope.com/kimberlalawsonroby